Praise for *Ne̶*

WINN̶ OF T̶ ̶ ̶ ̶ ̶ ̶ ̶ ̶ ̶
L̶O̶N̶ ̶ ̶ ̶ ̶ ̶ ̶ ̶ ̶ ̶ ̶ ̶ ̶ ̶
̶ ̶ ̶OOD READ AWARD̶

'Lisa Cutts is the real thing; a novelist who knows the police inside out but who can also create complex, multi-layered plots full of interesting characters. I look forward to reading more of her books.'   Elly Griffiths

'*Never Forget* does what crime fiction has never managed to do before – to take the reader directly to the fast-beating heart of a police investigation. Lisa Cutts has a unique voice, one that resonates with the knowledge of years of police work – and in DC Nina Foster she has created a character so genuine and honest that she feels like your best friend. This is a complex, chilling and brilliantly clever debut that keeps you guessing to the final, thrilling sentence.'   Elizabeth Haynes

'An impressive debut.'   *Euro Crime*

'Lisa Cutts delivers a good story that stays true to the way that it really happens. Very pacy: short chapters and rapid changes of scene keep you on your toes. It is a book you'll read again – you might know the name of the villain, but you'll read for the pleasure of seeing how it was all done.'   *Bookbag*

'It is wonderful to find a new series with an interesting and realistic protagonist, a well-written story and a complex and well-executed mystery. I'm going to keep an eye out for future Nina Foster mysteries. If this debut is anything to go by, the wo̶ ̶ ̶ ̶ ̶ ̶ ̶ ̶ ̶ ̶ ̶ ̶ ̶ ̶ ̶author richer.'

̶ Than a Reading Journal

To read an extract from Never Forget,
turn to p.330

REMEMBER, REMEMBER

LISA CUTTS

Myriad Editions

Published in 2014 by

Myriad Editions
59 Lansdowne Place
Brighton BN3 1FL

www.myriadeditions.com

1 3 5 7 9 10 8 6 4 2

A CIP catalogue record for this book is available
from the British Library.

ISBN: 978-1-908434-39-5

Printed and bound in Sweden
by ScandBook AB

For my dad

For many things, but including
the Metropolitan Police stories,
the fruit and veg and Borough Market stories,
the 1960s London bus routes, cafés and
pie and mash stories,
and the Dave Brown stories...

Chilhampton Chronicle

20 June 1964

Seven killed in train crossing disaster

At 9.35am yesterday, an express train hit a lorry on the automatic crossing at Wickerstead Valley. The coastbound Chilhampton Express train had travelled from London, running at 70 miles per hour, carrying some 200 passengers and weighing over 400 tons.

The lorry driver, Malcom Bring, was unhurt in the crash, telling police he had been lost and the lorry had stalled on the level crossing. Unaware of the imminent arrival of the train, he had left his lorry and attempted to use the telephone in the half-barrier apparatus to warn the signalman of the lorry's location.

Mr Bring was alerted to the train's approach by the 24-second warning.

Five passengers and two railway workers were killed and 34 people injured in the derailment.

1

Bill stood in the kitchen doorway, tiredness showing on his face. He leaned against the frame.

Instinctively, I moved towards him with my arms out. I needed a hug.

He stepped back into the hallway away from me.

'What's wrong?' I said.

'Nina, I'd rather you didn't kiss me. I've just got back from a shooting. The bloke's stomach was all over the tarmac. I've got blood on my shirt.'

I scrutinised the front of his police uniform, paying particular attention to the collar. Some wives and girlfriends might check for lipstick; I looked for entrails.

'A shooting? That's unusual. There's something on the side of your face, just by your right ear. I hope it's not body tissue. I was about to have a bagel,' I said, wandering back towards the toaster. 'Do you want one?'

'No, thanks. I'm off to have a shower and then go to bed; I'm shattered. Tell you all about it tonight, but right now I need sleep. They only let me leave 'cos I'm at court this afternoon. What time's Wingsy picking you up?'

As I set about making myself some breakfast, I replied over my shoulder, 'About eight-thirty. They said there's no rush but I'm keen to get back to normal.'

'Well, have a good day, Nin. I'll call you when I get up.' He blew me a kiss. I hoped he'd washed his hands.

I listened to Bill trudge upstairs to wash the night shift's trauma from his skin before catching a few hours' sleep. I'd never been able to adjust to nights. My whole body clock rebelled against it. One of the reasons a police officer's life expectancy was so low, I supposed. I thought about calling up the stairs to tell him not to put the bloodstained black T-shirt in with the white wash, but thought better of it: he'd managed well enough for all those years on his own, before I came to stay a few months ago.

The half-hour before Wingsy was due to arrive was filled with thoughts of how I was going to find my first day back at work and how people were going to treat me. My emotions were mixed: I'd been very well looked after by both official work colleagues and friends offering unlimited support, but I was worried about going back to the police station. The Serious Crime Directorate's Murder Investigation team, with which I had been working before my time off, had made no move to get me back. I couldn't blame them. I was more trouble than I was worth.

The arrival of the postman snapped me back to full attention. Most of the post was bills and mailshots, but a postcard of two dragons on a bridge caught my attention. I smiled as I turned it over and read the back. Stan had taken the trouble to write to me. The postcard didn't say much, just the usual about the weather being great, how I'd love the cheap wine and the cruise was very pleasant. My old friend was currently in Ljubljana, clearly enjoying his retirement. But the places were beginning to merge into one. I thought that Slovenia was a landlocked country so I wasn't sure how he'd got there on a cruise, but I wasn't going to overthink it. I had enough on my mind.

Catching sight of myself in Bill's hallway mirror, I saw myself frowning. Something about the postcard bothered me. Stan had sent it to me at Bill's home address.

He'd known I'd still be here. He'd set off on his cruise two weeks ago, and clearly didn't think that I might be back in my own house by now. Bill's place was in a quieter area than my own, and that wasn't the only reason I'd been taking refuge here: I didn't fancy being at home at the moment. But I couldn't stay here forever. Perhaps it was time to regrow my backbone and face being alone again.

I gathered up my coat and bag and took a seat by the bay window, waiting for Wingsy to arrive. After months of staying at home, or, more precisely, at Bill's home, watching daytime television, trying to work out if 'I gave birth to my brother's lover' really could be true, I was ready to get cracking. Just listening to the wailing and moaning of those prepared to air their dirty linen in public was making me stupider by the day. I needed to be back earning a living, dealing in person with the types of people I'd been watching on TV.

It wasn't long before Wingsy's Honda turned into the cul-de-sac. I watched him turn one large circle in the road, the sunshine flashing across his balding head. I smiled to myself. By the time he'd stopped the car at the top of the driveway I was leaving the house, handbag over my shoulder, coat over my arm and a large grin on my face.

'What are you looking so chuffed about?' Wingsy asked as I got into the car.

I leaned across and kissed him on the cheek. 'I'm glad to be here.'

'Make sure you don't overdo it. I take it Bill's been looking after you?' He glanced across at me as I put my seatbelt on.

'Course he has. He's just finished a night shift and gone to bed. He had a bit of someone's stomach on his shirt from a shooting last night.'

'It's good to see that after six months of you two being together the romance is still very much alive. What are you doing for Christmas, a pantomime of *Death in Custody Through the Ages*?'

'Just drive the car, Baldy.'

'Nin, it's great to have you back.'

I winked at him, and we went to work.

2

'Nina, welcome back,' said Ian Hammond. 'We're glad to see you here. Do take it easy for the next couple of days... but can you read through this file?' Detective Inspector Hammond picked up a buff-coloured file about four inches thick and slid it across to me.

He adjusted his cuffs for the second time in two minutes. That was going to get on my nerves, but perhaps I needed to warm to him.

'What's it about, sir?' I asked, mustering as much interest as I could on my first day back.

'Well, as you already know, you're going to be working with the Cold Case team. They come under the Serious Crime Directorate where you were working before your time off, but it's only a temporary arrangement. The idea is to allow you to settle back in after your – er – incident.' He smiled an empty smile and gave me a sympathetic head-tilt. I'd got used to them over the last few months, ever since someone had entered my house and tried to kill me.

'Since I was stabbed,' I said, watching him wince at my words, 'I've gone from resting to wanting to get back to work. I am really pleased to be working with the Cold Case team. I only hope I'm up to it.'

He nodded, happier to discuss the topic now that it no longer made him feel uncomfortable. 'You can go along in a minute to meet the rest of the team, but I think you know most of them anyway. The file we want you to work on relates to a train crash in 1964.' He tapped the front of the worn cover. The light caught his shiny cufflinks. A dandy DI, how quaint. 'It's being reviewed because it's fifty years since it happened and information has come to light that makes it look as though it may not have been a terrible accident after all. It may have been murder. Seven people died that day, and scores more were injured. There's a reason that you're being put to work on this and not anything else, but I'll let your sergeant tell you about that when you go along to your new office. Once he's got you up to speed, you're to read the file and review it for any lines of enquiry.' He hesitated for a second, before adding, 'You won't be handling the new information. Your role will be mostly office-bound.' Another smile attacked his mouth.

We'll see about that, I thought.

As DI Dandy had said, I knew most of the Cold Case team. By fantastic luck, Harry Powell was to be my detective sergeant again. He had been some time ago, when dinosaurs roamed the land. My not so good luck was that the team's other DS was Kim Cotton. We'd met when I'd had my stay on the Murder Squad. I thought that she was a great big miserable individual. Wingsy had moved over to the Cold Case team too. And yes, he might have put in a good word for me. It was what friends did for each other. At least I had him and, even luckier, Kim was currently on annual leave.

Once I'd left my new DI, I made my way back to the tiny office that catered for eight of us. It coped fine for most of the week, but on Wednesdays the shifts meant that the whole office was on duty at the same time. This forced some of us to sit on chairs in the corridor. Hardly the stuff of Jack Bauer's dreams, but never mind. The superintendent had recently returned from a three-month exchange visit to Australia to see if they had any crime, and I was to be wheeled out into the corridor once a week. Life wasn't fair, but if you couldn't take a joke you shouldn't have joined.

Approaching the office door, I slowed down: the hefty file I'd been given was in danger of slipping out of my hands. I didn't want to be chasing the best part of fifty years of paperwork along the corridor, so I paused to tuck the sheets back into the buff file. As I did so, I heard Harry say, 'I've known Nina a long time and I know she'll do it if we ask. But I don't think we should be putting her in that situation.'

I took a breath and pushed the door open with the file. 'What's that, Harry?'

He was sitting motionless in the centre of the room, the others at the banks of desks around the walls and windows of the crowded crevice. Harry had been centre stage with, no doubt, all eyes on him. They were now all on me. Me and my fifty-year-old file.

Fair play to Harry, he didn't falter. He didn't even blush, and that was no mean feat for a man with a head of red hair and pale, freckled skin to match. He held my gaze while I heard a couple of others rustling paperwork and the only person in the room I didn't know picked up a phone that I was sure hadn't been ringing and said, 'Hello, DC Sullivan speaking. How can I help you?'

I'd been warned about Jim Sullivan by Wingsy. Slimy creature, he'd said.

'Nin, I was just saying,' said Harry, getting up and pushing a chair towards me, 'that you're likely to say yes to the challenge even though it's a really bad idea and the DI said you're to be office-bound for at least the next few days.'

I said nothing.

He perched on the edge of the desk in front of Sullivan, blocking my view of him. It didn't bother me or him: he carried on his fake call. Harry twisted to his left and hit the loudspeaker button. The sound of the dialling tone came across loud and clear.

'You're such a tosser, Jim. Make yourself useful, put the kettle on,' said Harry.

Harsh but fair. Jim nipped through the open office door to the sound of sniggers.

'As I was saying,' said Harry, 'you don't have to give me an answer now and you can say no, but we've had a request from Pensworth prison via Winstanley solicitors for you to do a prison visit and speak to burglar and drug addict Joe Bring.'

I hadn't expected my DS to mention Joe's name. None of the problems over the last few months had been Joe's fault – quite the opposite. He'd saved my life, tackled a serial killer and, for his trouble, got arrested for attempting to burgle my home when the police officers he'd summoned to my door had arrived. Nevertheless, it gave me a jolt. I hated feeling as though people were avoiding talking about my stabbing, but then I wasn't always prepared for it when they did. No pleasing some people, was there?

I liked to think that I sat, impassive, taking in the information. It probably didn't happen that way. Harry seemed to take my silence as a cue for him to continue. Chattering and laughing from two of the typists walking past the doorway on their way to a break filled the room. Harry leaned to his right and, so small was the room, he pushed the door shut without getting up.

'Jim clearly lives in a barn,' he commented. 'Nina, Joe asked for you. He wants to talk about the train crash in '64. He has some information but will only talk to you.

We've told the solicitors that Bring can't demand who visits him – '

'I'll do it,' I said. I'd had about ten seconds to weigh up whether I wanted to see Joe, assess how I'd feel about it and wonder why he wanted to see me. 'Any idea what he wants to tell me?'

'Yeah,' said Harry, leaning back, and crossing his arms across his rugby player's chest, just above his rugby drinker's beer belly. 'And we're gonna need a statement.'

'Don't we always?' I answered, tapping my foot.

'Definitely in this case, since Joe wants to tell us how seven people were murdered that day.'

3

Whatever anyone's political views and affiliations, I always told them that, whoever was in government, they would never stop the endless stream of documentation needing to be completed by police officers. To visit a prison required paperwork, and quite rightly so. Those inside had committed crimes and were serving custodial sentences. The governor of the prison had the last say. If they wanted paperwork, paperwork they would have.

I wrote a letter of explanation to get me into the prison. It was a fairly short request on my part – it was, after all, Joe who had asked to see me. I gave my name, rank, force number and the date and time I wanted to see him. Even getting the visit authorised by DI Dandy was relatively painless.

The quickest I could set up my meeting with Joe was Wednesday. It was to be me and Joe. No solicitor, no one else. That suited me. I wanted to thank him but didn't really want to do so in front of another police officer. Even Wingsy being there would have felt strange, and I trusted him implicitly.

The rest of the morning went by without much of great interest happening. I took a dislike to Jim Sullivan such as I'd never experienced at work before, except for when dealing with a prisoner. He was a despicable specimen. I made an effort to tolerate him which I knew would turn into avoidance. That would be difficult with eight DCs crammed into one room and a passing DS thrown in for good measure.

I took myself off to lunch in the canteen with a sense of dread. The food was always awful, and overpriced, and the staff's lethargy sapped your energy to the point of making you feel too tired to lift the burnt offerings to your mouth. Still, any port in a storm. I was hungry and couldn't face the walk into town today. When I got back to the office afterwards, Harry, Jim and Wingsy were switching off terminals and gathering their stuff to leave the office.

'Where are you off to, fellas?' I asked.

'Been a shooting the other side of town,' Harry said. 'Victim isn't looking so good. Main CID office is short so, until the Murder Investigation team get here from Headquarters, we're off to fill the gap.'

'That must be the same one Bill went to last night. They took their time sending you to it. Need me to come?' I found myself asking this without really thinking it through. A terrible habit of mine. As soon as I'd said the words, I wondered if I was being a bit rash.

Harry lifted his hand to scratch at an already stubbly chin. While he pondered my question, I marvelled at the speed of his advancing facial hair. He'd been clean-shaven that morning on my arrival in the office. Halfway through the day and he already had five o'clock shadow.

'Best not, Nin. You're supposed to be taking it easy. I'll give you a call later. We've been on duty four hours. It happened ten hours ago. Don't know why they couldn't get their fingers out of their arses and sort this out earlier.' He started walking away to catch up with Wingsy and Jim, then called back in my direction, 'Take a job car home tonight. I doubt Wingsy is going to be back to run you home.'

I didn't even need to appear disappointed, as he was no longer looking at me but talking into his mobile phone. I made out the words, 'On our way, Ian.'

I went into the office, shut the door and logged on to a computer to check my email. I cast an eye over the 'Question the Boss' section on the intranet, where staff were able to ask practical and procedural questions of the force's chief constable. I was in the office on my own; a shooting meant that no one else would be coming back before I went home. I felt exhausted and couldn't really settle.

Motivation was missing from my day. I made an effort, albeit a small one, to get started on the buff file to prepare for my meeting with Joe Bring in two days' time, but I was in the wrong frame of mind. Tomorrow was bound to be better. I wanted my shift to end so that I could go home to Bill and find out how Crown Court had gone. I'd also be finding out about the shooting that had got itself into the weave of his uniform and sent my new office scurrying off to the area's latest major incident.

4

In the car, I put my handbag behind the driver's seat, telling myself that it gave me more room in the front. But I couldn't recall one single time I had checked the back seat or boot of my car since I'd been living with Bill. I didn't know what horrified me more – that I'd been so careless, or that I'd come to rely on someone else so much.

I drove the borrowed Astra out of the car park, feeling unhappy with myself. Something felt wrong. It had taken me several months of hiding at Bill's house to realise it. Perhaps it was going back to work that had jolted me awake, stopped me being such a pathetic individual, but I shook off my hesitation and decided to go to my own home.

The route I took was a familiar one but one I hadn't done either alone or in the dusk for some time. There weren't many other vehicles on the road and within fifteen minutes of leaving Riverstone police station I found myself outside my house. As I sat outside, steeling myself to go in, my phone rang. It was Bill.

'Hi, lovely,' he said. 'Where are you?'

'Just left work,' I said. Well, it was true. 'I won't be long.'

'OK,' he said. 'Fancy going out tonight? Thought we could try the new Thai place in Riverstone.'

Nothing was less appealing right at that minute. 'That sounds great,' I lied. He'd just finished five night duties.

I'd languished in his home. It was the least I could do. 'I'll be there in ten.'

I hung up and rested my forehead on the steering wheel, breathing slowly until I had the energy to turn the key in the ignition. 'Bloody hell,' I said to no one in particular, before driving back towards my boyfriend's home.

As I pulled up at Bill's house, I felt a surge of pleasure at being back here. That annoyed me too. I was getting far too comfortable *chez* Bill. It wouldn't do.

I got to the front door just as Bill opened it.

'Hi,' he said, reaching out to touch the side of my face. 'You look tired.'

Listen, you thoughtful bastard... I wanted to say, but realised how unreasonable this made me. I smiled, moving my face to nestle into the gesture.

'I didn't really think my idea through about going out,' he said, moving back to let me inside the hallway. 'It's your first day back at work and you're bound to want to stay in tonight. How about a takeaway?'

'I could do with a drink,' I said, kicking my shoes off. I was turning away so that he wouldn't see how annoyed I was with him. Now he was trying to say I was weak and couldn't handle being stabbed and going back to work! Coat, shoes and bag deposited, I went scouting for Rioja. As I picked up the bottle, my eyes halted on a white cardboard box sitting on the counter, the words 'DC Nina Foster' handwritten in black marker on the side.

'Pierre Rainer dropped that round about a minute after I called you,' said Bill, seeing me eye it.

'I know what this is,' I said, grinning at him. I put my hand out to open the box.

Bill put one of his hands on top of mine.

'Don't you think it's a bit much?' he said, glaring at the delivery.

I shook my head. 'No, I don't,' I said. 'This isn't a celebration of a crime, it's a memento for a job well done – an offender caught and charged.'

Bill removed his hand with a sigh. I teased the lid open and removed a crystal wine glass engraved with the words 'Operation Guard 2013 DC Nina Foster'. Underneath was an engraving of a knife. Bill left the kitchen as I poured a healthy glug of red wine into my new glass and savoured every sip.

5

Most of the next morning was dominated by getting the borrowed Astra back to work and going for a hospital check-up at Wickerstead Valley hospital. Bill offered to come with me but I knew that he didn't really want to spend his only day off hanging around the hospital. He'd be doing enough of that once he was back on duty.

Finding a parking space was tricky, but the beauty of having no money was that I drove the kind of car I was happy to park in the tightest of spaces and not worry about other drivers scratching the paintwork. Having found a space about two inches bigger than my old BMW, I made my way to the entrance, passing several marked police vehicles in the Accident and Emergency bay. I'd heard on the news that the victim of the previous day's shooting was still alive. Little about the investigation had reached me through the nick, as I'd been knocking back Rioja at home by the time Wingsy and the others had got back to the office. Bill hadn't had much to add: he hadn't been the first on the scene, so had ended up helping with first aid until paramedics arrived, and then with scene preservation – which involved standing by the cordon. I'd got up to speed from the local media, which was usually accurate, if scant on detail.

Going over to the hospital map, I located the department I wanted and headed to the lifts. Getting out on the first floor, I turned left when I should have turned right. A familiar face was coming towards me from the antenatal unit: Belinda Cook. I'd met her carrying out enquiries on Operation Guard last year. She'd sworn a lot on our previous meeting. I regretted not taking the correct turn.

Her face softened as she saw me. This was a good sign.

'Nina,' Belinda said. 'It is Nina, isn't it?' She put her hand out as if to take my arm but then seemed to think better of it as she dropped it back to her side.

'Hello, Belinda,' I said. 'How are you?'

'Really good. Just had my first scan. The next six months are bound to fly by.' She was smiling the whole time she spoke.

'Well, that's great,' I said, while wondering if it was possible to tactfully ask someone you've only been associated with because their boyfriend was a murder suspect whether that same boyfriend was the father of their unborn child. On the other hand, half an hour on daytime television was looking likely for Belinda. I decided I couldn't be tactful, so chose to say nothing.

'Good to see you, Nina,' she said, heading towards the lifts. 'And good luck with your baby,' she added, glancing down at my stomach.

Now I was depressed. Several months of eating, drinking and sitting on the sofa, not to mention being knifed in the stomach, and Belinda thought I was pregnant. Chance would be a fine thing. With heavy heart – and apparently stomach – I stomped off in the direction of my appointment.

Forty-five minutes later, I made my way back out of the hospital, curiosity taking me past A&E in case there was anyone in there I knew from work. I saw two uniform PCs I vaguely recognised, talking to the receptionist, and two firearms officers I didn't know going to wherever the shooting victim was being kept. I presumed that they were the shift change.

As I was about to give up on finding anything out, Wingsy came out of the triage nurse's office, followed by a very attractive nurse. For a minute or two I watched him flirting with her. When it got to the stage where I felt embarrassed for him, I walked over to them. She smiled, perfect white teeth dazzling me. Wingsy looked guilty. A streak of red ran to the tips of his oversized ears.

'Nina,' said Wingsy. 'Forgot you were up here this morning. How did it go?'

I glanced from Wingsy to the nurse and back again. He was shifting his weight from one foot to the other.

Feeling that he'd suffered enough discomfort, I said, 'It went fine. Do you have a couple of minutes when you're finished here?' I gestured towards the car park with my head.

'Sure,' he replied to me before turning his attention back to the nurse. 'Thank you for your time, Elspeth. You have my number if there's anything else I can help you with.'

We walked through the automatic glass doors back into fresh air. The crispness of the day pinched me after being inside in the stale hospital air.

'Does your mate Elspeth know that you're a happily married baldy?' I asked as we made our way out of earshot of the patients in wheelchairs smoking cigarettes outside the entrance.

'You're so funny,' said Wingsy, as we parted ways to walk either side of a man attached to a drip trying to roll tobacco into a cigarette paper with his free hand. To get his voice to carry across the gap between us, Wingsy increased his volume. 'Does Bill know that you were going to ask the doctor at your appointment this morning if it's safe for you and him to have sex yet?'

The man on the drip looked startled at this remark. Some of his tobacco drifted to the floor from his Rizla. As he looked up from his task, I saw how jaundiced he was.

'That's the last time I confide in you, Wingnut.' We were now clear of the smokers and I was back by his side. 'What's the story up here at the hospital, then?'

'It's a bit of a strange one,' said Wingsy, leading me by the elbow into a more remote part of the car park. He made a cursory sweep of the area to make sure no one was about, checking the parked cars too. Satisfied that we couldn't be overheard, he leaned towards me and said, 'Very unlikely to have been a robbery, and, besides, nothing seems to have been taken. The victim's alive, but he's been unconscious since someone called 999 and the paramedics arrived on the scene. We know a bit about him. He's not long been released from prison for a serious domestic incident, apparently. I don't know much else at the moment, until I do a bit of digging later. We'd missed the briefing by the time we got called out today. Someone's clearly displeased with him, 'cos he was shot a number of times. Whoever dialled three nines did it from an unregistered mobile phone. The interesting thing is, though, that one of the shots was heard by the operator.'

'So whoever made the call was very close to the scene at the time of the shooting.'

6

Having been prodded and poked at the hospital, I didn't feel like hanging around with Wingsy. I hadn't even asked him the victim's name. I was tired and not back on track yet. I went back to Riverstone police station and spent much of the remainder of the day reading through the Cold Case file.

I had to admit, I was bored. My mind kept going back to what Wingsy had said about the anonymous caller still being present when the shots were fired. Why would you call the police but not wait around, unless you were in some way involved?

Curiosity won at the end of the day. The file I was supposed to be reading was older than me and not doing much to set my world on fire. I looked up the original log of the call to the police for the previous day's shooting but could find very little. A man who didn't give his name said that someone had been shot twice and was lying outside Screwfix on the industrial estate off London Road, Kilnchester. The operator then typed on the log that a gunshot was heard before the caller cleared the line. The operator tried to call the number back but the phone was switched off. I read from the log, 'Firearms officers arrived at the scene – an area search for the male caller was negative.' They did, however, find an unconscious man bleeding from chest and leg injuries.

I knew that I should be concentrating on the railway accident from 1964, especially as I was due to see Joe Bring the following day and he was going to tell me all about it. I turned my attention back to the paperwork in front of me.

The rest of Cold Case who weren't called in to help on the shooting were at Crown Court for a rape trial, for an offence in 2002. A woman had been attacked walking home from her friend's house just past midnight after she missed her last bus. That part of the team's working day had begun in the office and before I'd left for the hospital I'd eavesdropped on their run-down of the previous day's evidence. Several months ago, about the time I was working on my first murder enquiry, Barry Oakes, rapist and waste of a skin, decided that the time was right for him to punch his wife in the face. He was arrested, and his DNA taken and loaded into the database. We then had a match against our unsolved crime from 2002. Not to mention a rape victim who could stop peering at every man she met and wondering if it was him.

It would appear that the defendant was a low-life lying bastard and the jury were openly sneering at everything he said. It was to be expected: we had his DNA. It might have taken twelve years, but we'd never stopped looking.

I wasn't concentrating on the train crash. The words weren't sinking in. I found myself reading about how the lorry that had caused the train to derail had been one used for carrying fruit and vegetables and marvelling at how, in 1964, no one would have heard of internet shopping. Back then, my Great-Aunt Lou's head would have exploded if someone had told her that one day she would be able to tap on a keyboard and a van would deliver whatever groceries she wanted, straight to her door.

Interrupting my daydream, the door burst open, revealing a white-faced Jim, red-faced Harry, and Wingsy, whose expression I couldn't fathom.

Harry kicked the door shut. The force of the kick caused it to ricochet against the frame, catching Wingsy's arm. He rubbed the back of his upper arm. 'It's lucky the door hit me and not him, Harry,' he said, closing the door again with a little more restraint. 'If it had been this grass here, you'd be getting nicked for assault.'

'Fucking pack it in, you two,' said Harry, cheeks still red. Then, lowering his voice to a rumble and pointing at Wingsy, he said, 'You, John, I expected better from.' The use of his first name rather than his nickname was a sign that this was serious. He turned his attention to Jim. I watched Harry's facial muscles contract and his mouth tighten as if he was about to yell something abusive at him. The three-second pause led me to believe that he was holding himself back for some reason. Wingsy was looking like the guilty party. I hoped it was something funny.

All Harry could manage to say to Jim was, 'I'll speak to you in a minute. Go and put the kettle on while I speak to this tosser.'

Jim skulked out of the room. For the first time, Wingsy and Harry turned to acknowledge me.

'Do I dare ask?' I risked.

'It would seem that Jim left his terminal logged on yesterday before we all went out to the shooting,' said Harry. 'Wingnut here accessed the "Question the Boss" forum on Jim's log-in and asked the chief constable if he was any good in a fight.'

I laughed really loud at that. Wingsy was keeping his eyes on the ground but I saw a smile on Harry's face. 'I'm your sergeant, so don't think for one minute that I'm taking this lightly. Chief Inspector Halliday's going to be speaking to you about your behaviour, too.' The smile was gone by the time he said this part.

'Hang on, though, Harry,' I said. He looked at me. 'What about Jim – he may have had no choice but to grass Wingsy up, but he shouldn't have left his terminal unlocked either.'

'She's got a point, Harry,' said Wingsy. 'What about him?'

'Just be grateful it's me dealing with you and that Kim Cotton's on leave for a couple of weeks,' said Harry, before finding a free computer to log on to.

I went back to my file, flicking through the crash scene photos and wondering what had happened to all the fruit and veg.

7

On Wednesday morning I got to Pensworth prison early to see Joe. I queued up with the families and friends of loved ones locked up in prison, along with the legal representatives. It was easy to tell them apart: the legal reps tended to have bags and files of paperwork and weren't standing around in groups looking as if their world had come to an end.

Inside the entrance for visitors, I walked over to the prison officer behind the glass partition. I dropped my acceptance letter approving my visit, along with my warrant card, into the box below the counter.

'Do you have a mobile phone or any recording equipment?' he asked through the glass, bending slightly to get closer to the slotted part for speaking through.

'No,' I said, automatically also stooping slightly even though I was on a level with it. I'd left my mobile phones in the car; it made life easier.

'Go on through the doors when they open,' he said, checking my ID. He pushed the paperwork back to me and I went over to the doors where three other people were waiting.

Having gone through the security procedures, and been searched by a female prison officer, then beckoned forward by another officer, I was led to a desk where a third officer took my photograph. I had to admit, I wasn't expecting that. On none of the prison visits I'd made before had I ever had my picture taken.

I was pointed across the hall, which was full of purple easy chairs and low tables, giving it the appearance of a low-budget coffee house but without the appealing smell of freshly ground coffee. Oh, yes, and it had bars at the windows. Along the far wall, stretching the length of the room, were cubicles. Each one had a window and half-glass door. All but one were empty.

I made my way to number six as instructed, and waited. Several minutes later, I spotted Joe Bring as he sauntered towards me, hands tucked inside the Viagra-blue bib he was wearing over his grey sweatshirt and joggers. He looked as though he'd put on a few pounds since I'd last seen him, but he was still gangly.

He reached the door of the cubicle, stopping short of entering. The prison officer behind him kept a discreet distance to ensure that Joe made it to the correct room.

'Hello, miss,' said Joe.

'Hello, Joe,' I said, standing up. I'd been about to shake his hand when I realised that he'd removed it from resting inside his bib and it was now rummaging inside the front of his joggers. I waved instead. It seemed very inappropriate to wave when only a two-foot-wide table separated us, but it was the sensible thing to do.

I heard a chortle from the prison officer, who said, 'Well, I'll leave you two to it, then. Shout if you need anything.' He made to shut the door, forcing Joe to move inside the room with me. We both watched as the officer noisily sealed us in and went back to escort the next waiting visitor to an inmate.

Joe and I sat down at the same time on the black plastic chairs. 'How have you been, Joe?' I began.

'I'm good, thanks, miss. You?'

'You don't have to keep calling me "miss" now,' I said. 'We're alone.'

Joe grinned at me. His teeth were terrible. Drugs did that to you. On a positive note, he smelt a lot better than he used to.

Many times, I'd practised what I'd say to Joe when I saw him next. I'd gone over in my mind how I would tell him I was grateful that he'd saved my life, but, truth be told, now I had the opportunity I was struggling to find the words. I wriggled in my plastic chair, the fabric of my blouse threatening to stick to my back.

'Thank you, Joe. You saved my life.' As I said the words, I realised how trite they sounded.

Joe shrugged and flashed his barcode grin at me again. 'S'right, Nina. You turned a blind eye to me living in your shed and didn't even call the Old Bill when I let myself in and put your telly on...'

He broke off as I started to laugh. I hadn't been aware he'd been living in my shed until he'd got arrested by the patrol officers responding to his 999 call, and until now I had never been too certain it was Joe who'd entered my house in the weeks leading up to me being attacked. The smell that lingered had certainly suggested he'd been there, but I had always been reluctant to point the finger of blame at him, particularly since his presence meant he'd been there to save me when a serial killer decided to make me his next victim.

Whether it was my burst of laughter or Joe's revelation that cleared the air, it didn't matter, as we both let our shoulders drop and got to the matter I'd driven forty miles to discuss.

'What did you want to see me about?' I asked.

Joe scratched his pointy, stubbly chin with the hand that had been around his genitals. He paused to sniff his fingers. I forced myself to remember that this man had saved my life.

'The Wickerstead Valley train crash in '64,' he said, frown line creasing his brow. 'I saw on the news that the police are appealing for new information as it's now fifty years since it happened. My dad, the fucking idiot, was the lorry driver that caused it. He left his lorry on the crossing. But it was no accident: he deliberately derailed the train. He killed them people.'

'How do you know this?'

'He told me a couple of years back. He's dead now, the useless twat. Some dad he was. Know how I got hooked on heroin?'

I raised my eyebrows at Joe's miserable face.

'I was fourteen when he first injected me. Didn't stand a fucking chance, did I? Everyone's supposed to want better for their kids than they had themselves. He fucked up his life and mine with it.' He looked down at his hands, now in his lap but mercifully outside his pants. 'He started on puff when I was a kid, then he upped his game to cocaine before moving on to heroin. He told me a few years back that he'd derailed the train on purpose. Said it caused him so much grief that he turned to drugs. He could still hear the screech of the train and the thud when it hit the lorry.'

At this point, Joe paused, I thought somewhat dramatically given that what he'd said so far wasn't of much use. His dead dad had left his lorry on a crossing, derailing a train nearly fifty years ago. Quite what I was supposed to do with this information was escaping me right now.

'Did he say why he did it?' I asked Joe, wondering how much access to drugs he had inside.

'No, he didn't, but he knew a bloke called Leonard Rumbly. Used to be a small-time villain. Fancied himself a bit. He owned several of the local bookies. My old man, the fuckwit, was a gambler. He couldn't resist a bet – on the horses, dogs, boxing… anything that was legal and a few fights that weren't. The dozy prick owed a fortune. Apart from being so far in the cack, up to his neck in debt, it was illegal in them days to run up credit for gambling. The thing my dad told me was that Rumbly had him by his nuts.'

'Go on,' I said.

He leant across the table, eyes flitting in the direction of the glass panel in the door before saying, 'Rumbly was always up to stuff. The Wickerstead train had three footballers on their way to a match. One drug- and booze-filled night my old man started talking about how much Rumbly would gain from delaying the train to get the match cancelled or at the very least postponed. You much of a football fan?'

'No, Joe, I'm not.'

'You wanna take a look at what was going on in the 1960s around the beautiful game. Very interesting stuff.'

Joe slung himself back in his plastic chair before pushing himself off from the edge of the table so he was leaning back on the two rear legs. He kicked his feet out in front of him as he rested back against the wall. He was looking pleased with himself but I failed to see why. He clearly thought that this was the big reveal, but I wasn't getting it.

'Thanks, Joe,' I said, falling short of sounding over-whelmed. 'You going to put that in a statement?'

There was that barcode grin again. 'Not yet, Nina. You've got to promise to do something for me. My son's fourteen next week.'

He paused to let the information sink in. I thought he might be expecting me to make him a cake or take him to the zoo or whatever you did with fourteen-year-old boys whose fathers were in prison for burglary. Again.

'You've got to look after my boy.'

As he said this, he pitched himself forward, the metal-studded ends of the chair legs clanking on the hard floor.

'I don't mean like going and babysitting him. You're still the Enemy at the end of the day. You'll have to work out how to do it on the quiet.'

Clearly someone was serving up in prison and Joe was scoring better gear here than he ever had on the outside. Why would I keep an eye on his son and heir for shaky information on a train collision fifty years ago?

'You're wondering why you should do this?' said the perceptive Joe.

I rubbed my eyes, sighed and said, 'That's one way of putting it. Exactly why would I look after your boy?'

'Luke,' he said, 'his name's Luke. And you gotta be subtle,' said the world's worst burglar. To date, Joe had left his DNA at sixteen crime scenes. Sometimes he left his fingerprints instead. His current stretch was looking like a couple of years. But still I liked him.

'And why should I subtly look after Luke?' I asked, growing weary of this conversation.

'Because one of his older mates, Daryl, has just died of a heroin overdose and I don't want him going the same way as his mate – or me.' As he said these words, Joe seemed to grow taller in his chair and look less like a colossal moron. Some sort of parental responsibility seeped through his pores and gave him a purpose in life. The kid was probably doomed anyway with genes from the Bring family; I'd met the mother and she wasn't much better. Still, if you couldn't help the masses, why not try to help an individual?

'And besides,' continued Joe, 'Rumbly's still alive and he's branched out. He's gone from gambling to drugs now. It's where Luke's dead mate got his gear. It's a family business mainly run now by Rumbly's son, Andy, and grandson, Niall, but it's Leonard who's behind it. Though from what I hear it's not all happy families. The son has had some sort of a fallout with Leonard over Niall, so I've heard in here. I'm only telling you this because I'm worried about Luke and can't do anything else to help him, from here.'

The information Joe had given me was a totally different matter from what I'd thought I was coming here for. I opened my notebook and began to write down everything Joe told me about his father Malcolm Bring and his son Luke, and everything he could tell me about Leonard Rumbly and his line. When he finished talking, I put down my pen, flexed my fingers and wondered what Harry Powell and DI Dandy were going to make of all this.

'Thing is, Joe...' I began, pausing to get my words right.

'Thing is, Nina,' interrupted Joe, 'you're about to tell me how this information won't get me a reduction on my sentence. I know that. I've got nowhere to go anyway. Missus kicked me out. That's why I was living in your shed. Luke thinks I'm a loser and he's quite right about that. In here – ' he gestured at the bars on the windows ' – they've got workshops and stuff. Fucking saddest thing of all is that I'm more use in here than out there. Know what I've being doing?'

He put his hands back inside the waistband of his joggers. My eyes were drawn to his groin.

'No, you saucy cow.' He grinned, flashing his manky molars at me. There weren't many other teeth still in his head. 'Not that. Not with three-man bang-up in my cell.

I'm sharing with Jingo George and Fat Frank. You know 'em?'

Sadly, I didn't. They sounded like just the kinds of losers Joe should share a cell with. I bet some deep and meaningful conversations went on in their snug room at night.

'I'm building bird boxes,' he said.

This I hadn't seen coming.

'You any idea how much the tree sparrow population has declined since the 1960s?' Without waiting for a reply, which was for the best, as I was struck dumb at this point, he gave me the answer. 'It's dropped by *ninety-seven* per cent. That's incredible. The RSPB – have you heard of them?'

I managed to utter, 'Uh huh.'

'Well, they're doing this project, see and they want us to build, like, fifty boxes for the southeast of England. They may get us to build more. See how it goes. It's well good, well good.'

The only birds I'd ever known Joe be familiar with were the chickens he tried to shoplift from the supermarket. He might have been tempted to branch out into turkeys, but his *modus operandi* was theft by gusset. Turkeys might have been that tiny bit trickier to fit down his joggers. Perhaps it was an urban thief's type of primitive birdwatching and he'd managed to move on to better things in prison. Here he was, getting animated at the thought of saving the tree sparrow. It was actually good to hear, if a little unexpected.

We said our goodbyes shortly after that and I made my way outside, via another strict security check, to where I'd parked the car. As I turned on the air-conditioning and waited for it to clear the windscreen, I took both my work mobile and my personal one out of the glove compartment.

I had missed calls on both. Making a decision whether to listen to personal messages first or work ones, I threw my job one up in the air a couple of times before going for the one in my hand.

The first missed call was from Wingsy. His message simply said, 'Nin, think you need to call me. It's your mate Annie Hudson. I'm with her now.'

Annie wasn't exactly a friend but a battered wife I'd met years ago, couldn't quite let go of and visited from time to time. Very little rattled Annie, apart from the time her husband had held an iron to her face and tried to strangle her. If she needed my help, then my help she would get.

Swapping phones to hear the other message, I listened to Annie shouting as she demanded to know 'why the fucking useless police haven't had the fucking decency to tell me that not only have they released Patrick from prison so he can come and finish me off but he's been shot and has been in hospital under armed guard for two fucking days?'

Annie wasn't the only one who would have liked to know that. Patrick Hudson had dislocated my shoulder and knocked my head against several household surfaces the last time we'd met. I was hoping he'd regain consciousness so he could feel the pain of dying.

8

My usual routine, when I visited Annie every couple of weeks, was to pull up around the corner in my old BMW so that her neighbours weren't aware the police were at her door. But there was no hiding the police being in her house on this occasion. A marked police car was across her driveway with a uniformed occupant, and an unmarked police Škoda parked behind that. What made it perfectly clear that it was a police car was a large sign in the window on the dashboard that told anyone passing by to call DC John Wing if it needed to be moved.

As I walked up to the front door, it opened and Wingsy came out. He rolled his eyes at me and said, 'Annie wants to see you.'

Annie's face appeared behind him. Her bottom lip trembled and her eyes moistened. Just when I thought she might crack, she shouted, 'About fucking time, young lady. Where have you been?'

I knew it was bravado but I didn't let on. Why would I? This was Annie.

She turned and stomped back to her living room. I followed her, giving Wingsy's shoulder a quick squeeze as I passed him in the hallway. He was tense. I didn't usually make a habit of touching my colleagues – unless I was having sex with them, and that definitely wasn't the case as far as Wingsy was concerned.

Following Annie into her living room, I noticed it had been wallpapered since I was last here. It didn't seem the right time to mention it. I stood waiting for the barrage that was to come, and I couldn't really say I blamed her. I was angry that no one had told me that Patrick Hudson was out of prison. I was also annoyed with myself for not asking Wingsy the name of the shooting victim when we'd spoken at the hospital. I could have helped Annie avoid facing more distress in her life.

A uniform PC sat in one of Annie's armchairs. He was perched on the edge, stab-proof vest almost touching him under the chin, he was so far forward on the seat. He looked uncomfortable in every way. He was also vaguely familiar. I'd seen him at the station from time to time but didn't know his name.

'Hello. You must be Nina,' he said, standing up to face me. 'Annie's been asking when you'd get here. I'll leave you to it. I'll be outside. Thanks, Annie.' He left the room, talking into his Airwave radio, giving the control room an update that DC Foster was now on the premises.

Annie stood at the window with her back to me, arms crossed. As she turned, the sunlight hit the side of her face with the iron burn upon it. The burn her ex-husband had inflicted on her the night he'd tried to kill her and beat the living daylights out of me. My injuries were only physical, and had been caused doing the job I'd chosen to do. Hers were caused by being married to a violent bully. There were no better words to describe someone who inflicted physical and mental injury on the person they were supposed to love. It could only be called cowardly, and these types of people were oxygen thieves.

He was now a cowardly oxygen thief with several bullet holes in him.

'Did you know about this?' snapped Annie.

'No,' I said. This appeared to take the wind out of her sails. I heard Wingsy enter the room behind me. 'You should have been told. I should have been told.'

Wingsy had drawn level with me by this stage, and out of the corner of my eye I saw the movement of his head turning in my direction.

'Your husband didn't do me too many favours either,' I said, in tones as even as I could manage.

'Yeah, I always forget that you got a kicking that night as well as me,' said Annie.

I turned away from her to look at Wingsy, who was making minuscule head-shaking gestures at me. I think it was dawning on Wingsy that both victims of the last two violent convictions listed on Patrick Hudson's Police National Computer printout were standing in the room with him.

Wingsy then broke the silence. 'One of our detective inspectors is on his way to see you, Annie. His name's Clint Stirling and he's going to explain a couple of things to you. The thing is, you live in the Metropolitan Police area. They were the original force who arrested your husband and put him inside. They will want to speak to you, but for now we're here, and we'll deal with anything you need. Patrick was in prison in our county. He was also shot in our county.' Wingsy pointed his forefinger back and forth between me and him to demonstrate who he was talking about. I hoped I'd remember later to tell him how stupid it made him look.

Annie was still standing close to the window. Past her, I could see that a tall man in a black suit was talking to the two uniform officers outside. I recognised DI Clint Stirling. I liked him. He was both a good man and a good officer. Everything DI Dandy wasn't, Clint was. We'd gone on a couple of dates years ago. It had been a disaster.

'That's the DI now,' I said to Annie, mainly to explain why she'd caught me gazing out of the window in her hour of need. 'I'll go and let him in.'

I opened the door, saying, 'Hi, Clint,' as I did so.

'Alright, Nin?' he said, shutting the door behind him and following me back to the living room.

I said, 'Sir, this is Annie Hudson, an old friend of mine.'

I heard her tut and say, 'Let's not go that far, Nina.' Normally I would have responded by telling her that she was quite old, but I mumbled that I was going to make the tea and left them to it.

Wingsy followed me out into the kitchen. 'Cups are in that cupboard above your head, mate,' I said, pointing to the wall unit. I filled the kettle, but as I turned to plug it back in I noticed that he hadn't moved but was staring at me. 'What?' I said, mid-turn towards the fridge.

'Exactly what is it with you, duchess, and people having it in for you?' he asked.

'I'm a police officer, Wings. In case you haven't noticed, we're not always that popular. Take the rough with the smooth and all that. I don't think – '

'Stop changing the subject.'

I dropped my voice and got closer to my friend. 'The stuff that happened with Annie and her pig of a husband was years ago. I had a bit of personal grief going on too at the time. I left the Met and transferred. It was for reasons of necessity but I'm glad I did. I was in uniform then so I moved on. I never regretted it. I've never let go of Annie, though. She's not quite as tough as she makes out.'

Wingsy rubbed his hands over his face before turning to reach up into the cupboard for the cups. Over his shoulder he asked, 'What kind of personal grief? Not someone else trying to kill you?'

'Don't be ridiculous,' I said moving to get the milk. 'All the grief in my life's well behind me.'

Fortunately he couldn't see the worried expression on my face from behind the fridge door.

9

We took the tea back into Annie's living room to find her sitting on the sofa while Clint explained to her that an attempted murder investigation was under way.

Putting the tray down in front of Annie, I deliberately rattled the cups to make her look at what I'd put before her. In the cupboard, I'd found a packet of Belgian-chocolate-covered cookies. On my visits, I brought her expensive brand goodies from time to time and she always delighted in giving me the cheapest biscuits she could get her hands on. I watched her face as she pursed her lips at the open packet.

'Fucking cheek,' she said.

'I beg your pardon, Annie?' said Clint.

'Not you, Cliff,' she said. 'I was talking to her.'

'It's Clint actually,' said Clint.

'Whatever, love,' said Annie, picking up her tea. 'What I want to know is what happens to me now. And stop talking to me about fucking risk assessments. I couldn't give a bollock. Am I going to get shot?'

'Boss,' I said, sitting next to Annie, 'can I try to explain what's going to happen and what we know so far?' He nodded. 'OK,' I said, 'you should have been warned that Patrick was coming out of prison. As should I.'

I locked on to Clint's eyes but he held my stare. It didn't seem that I'd be getting an apology any time soon.

'As far as Patrick is concerned, he's in hospital with armed police officers guarding him twenty-four hours a day. The attempt on his life is being investigated by a team of detectives from Headquarters. Part of that investigation involves speaking to Patrick's family members, including you as his ex-wife, and also – and I know you don't want to hear about risk assessments – but also assessing if there is any threat to your life. What DI Stirling was saying when I came in is that, as you haven't seen Patrick in eight years – you've had nothing to do with him – any risk to you is minimal.'

I heard Clint clearing his throat. 'Thank you, Nina. That's correct. But we're still going to fit a panic alarm in your home,' he said, looking at Annie. 'Also, the local firearms sergeant is on his way to carry out a strategy plan in the very unlikely event that we need to respond to an emergency of any kind. I'm leaving John here to take a statement from you. Nina, it may be best if you go back to the station.'

He stood up, shook hands with Annie and made towards the door. I followed him to be sure that there was nothing else he hadn't wanted to say in front of Annie. But all he said was, 'Thought they'd put you on Cold Case with a fifty-year-old train crash to keep you out of trouble, Nin? I see it didn't work. You need to get back and see Ian Hammond, give him an update.' He flashed me a smile and was gone through the front door.

Back in the living room, Annie was trying to put the cookies back in the packet. Wingsy looked up at me from the armchair as I came back into the room. 'Are you leaving or staying?' he asked me.

'The DI's right,' I said. 'I shouldn't really be here while you take Annie's statement. The night Patrick got nicked involved me too. It would be inappropriate if I stayed while you asked her questions. The chances are that at some time someone will take a statement from me too. I may even need to be ruled out as a suspect.' At least Bill could vouch for my being at home a couple of hours after the shooting, if it came to it. That, and I wouldn't know where to get a gun, how to load it or how to aim straight. I'd had a bottle of Chianti that night, too, so my aim would have been right off. I'd have blown his head off whether I meant to or not.

'Listen, Annie, I'm gonna shoot...' I trailed off, aware of what I had said, fluttered my hands at her, and finished, 'Oh, you know what I mean.'

'It's a wonder you hold down a job, girl,' she said, getting up to give me a hug.

'Give me a call when Wingsy's done if you want me to come back over,' I said, knowing full well she wouldn't.

Annie followed me out to the front door. As she stretched across to unlatch the door, she pressed her face up close to my ear and said, 'You shag that Clyde bloke?'

'It's Clint, Annie. And no, I didn't.'

10

Two missed calls from Bill prompted me to call him back on my way to the car.

'Hello, darling. You OK?' he said.

'Hi, honey,' I said, glad to hear his voice. 'In case you haven't guessed, I'm running a bit late. I'm nipping to work and I'll call you when I'm leaving.'

'OK,' he said. 'I'm making Moroccan chicken. Nina?'

The pause was me wondering what Moroccan chicken was when it was at home. 'Oh, great, I love Moroccan chicken.'

'You've had it before, then?'

Now I was in trouble. I wasn't used to coming home to someone who cared. This was going to be harder work than I'd first thought.

'Yeah, in Morocco.'

'I didn't know you'd been to Morocco.'

Stone the crows. I was going to have to stop lying.

'Got to go, darling, got another call coming through,' I lied, before hanging up.

My drive back to Riverstone gave me time to think about what I wanted to say to DI Hammond. If he gave me the chance to work on the shooting of Patrick Hudson I would jump at it, but I knew he would never do that. He was going to tell me that someone would talk to me in the morning about my earlier dealings with Hudson, they would want it in writing to eliminate me from their enquiries into where I was when he was being shot, and I was to go back to my train crash from 1964. It wasn't that I wasn't interested in the deaths of so many people, but after fifty years I wasn't so sure I'd get to the bottom of it. And a recent shooting had more urgency to it: I could feel myself being swept up in the drama.

I made a quick stop at the Cold Case office and said a brief hello to Jemma Russell and Micky Gowens, another two DCs who had just returned from Crown Court after a further day with the 2002 rapist Barry Oakes. Micky was an incredibly ugly man who always seemed to have really beautiful girlfriends. I'd never got the bottom of it, and suspected that he used escorts. It might have been his charm, but I thought it was more likely to be his Mastercard.

Having left them laughing about Oakes's evidence and how obnoxious the jury clearly thought he was, I went off to find my dapper DI. He was in his office drinking tea, a box of Earl Grey in front of him.

I rapped on the open door. 'Hi, boss. You wanted to speak to me?'

'Hello, Nina. How are you getting on in Cold Case?'

'Very well, thanks. They're a good bunch. I've been to see Joe Bring in prison. I can tell you about that, but I think you wanted to speak to me about Annie Hudson and her ex?'

He flicked the teabag into the bin and pointed across his desk at me with his spoon. He then pointed it at the vacant chair in front of him. Clearly, asking me to take a seat was too difficult.

I obliged.

'Yes,' he said, wiping the drip from the end of the spoon on a tissue, 'I know that you were in the Met at

44

the time and suffered some injuries; that's why it's better that you don't get involved in the investigation into the attempted murder of Patrick Hudson. HQ are sending a team tomorrow to take it over. The chances are they'll take it back to Headquarters with them and run it from their own Incident Room. No need for you to get involved or attend their briefings.'

I got the message loud and clear. I got up to go. 'While I think of it, sir, I've not yet taken a statement from Joe Bring but, in summary, he says his father was put up to it by a bloke called Leonard Rumbly. Bring senior had some gambling debts and in order to cancel them Rumbly got him to delay the train, which resulted in it being derailed. Rumbly and his family are now the local heroin suppliers. I'll put in a report to Intel before I go off.'

I got the impression that Hammond wasn't really listening to me. It was the rummaging through the desk drawers and the lack of eye contact that aroused my suspicion. I went back to the office to finish typing my notes and Google Moroccan chicken.

Within the hour I was back at Bill's, my feet up on the sofa and a glass of Merlot on the table next to me. It hadn't escaped my notice that Bill had pushed an unengraved glass into my hand as I walked through the door. I pretended not to mind. I was going to have to get used to letting him have some small victories. Apparently it was one of the things that made a relationship work. It smacked more of giving in, to me.

'Dinner will be ten minutes,' he said, topping up my wine glass and kissing me. 'Oh, and here's your work phone. I heard it bleep from the stairs.'

I took the phone from him as he went back into the kitchen with the diminishing bottle of red, muttering something about mangetouts. I unlocked the phone and read the text message from Ian Hammond. It read, *Briefing tomorrow 9am re Patrick Hudson. You're needed. Speak to Clint Stirling if you have any problems with this.*

I couldn't fathom what would cause Hammond or Clint to have such a sudden change of heart. They'd been determined to keep me away from Patrick Hudson's shooting investigation, and now they'd told me to be at a briefing. As I pondered whether I'd been sent the message in error as part of a group text, my phone started to ring. It was Wingsy.

'Hi, mate,' I said. 'How was Annie when you left her?'

'Yeah, she's OK, duchess. But you certainly know how to throw the cat among the pigeons, don't you?'

'Does this have something to do with being invited to the briefing in the morning?' I asked.

'Yes, it does. It was your report about seeing Joe Bring in prison and the Intel report you put in. We've done some checking on who Patrick Hudson was inside with. Before he got released from Mill End prison, he'd been sharing a cell with none other than Niall Rumbly.'

'Bloody hell. The grandson of the man who was behind the 1964 Chilhampton Express crash?'

Things had just got a whole lot more interesting, and I was being invited to join in.

11

At eight am on the dot, I walked into the Cold Case office and said my hellos to Jemma and Micky, who were about to head off to Crown Court. Today was the day for the jury to be sent out to consider their verdict for Barry Oakes. By the sound of it, he was going to prison.

Out of the corner of my eye, I saw Jemma put her suit jacket on and heard her say to Micky, 'Wait a minute, Mick, I want to say hello to Mark if he's here yet. He was coming over from Headquarters.'

I looked up at her. She caught me staring. 'Mark?' I asked, partly because I'd worked with Mark Russell on a previous operation and partly because the penny had dropped that Jemma's surname was also Russell.

'Yes,' she replied, one arm in her jacket, the other flapping around behind her. 'Mark's my husband. We got married last year.'

'Congratulations,' I said, 'I was a bit slow on that one. I don't think I've said anything negative about my time on Major Crime. I'd love to go back there one day.'

Jemma smiled as she buttoned up her jacket. 'I wouldn't have passed it on if you had, Nin.'

Micky's oversized, acne-scarred face appeared from behind his computer screen. He gave an unattractive chortle and said, 'My silence would need to be bought, though.'

'Micky,' said Jemma, 'Nina lives with Bill Harrison. Why would she look twice at a rubber-faced bastard like you?'

'I'm naturally charming,' said Micky.

'Yeah, but she's right, Mick,' I said.

As he gathered his own jacket and rucksack, Micky winked at me with his good eye and said, 'I love it when they play hard to get.'

I'd missed these kinds of conversations. They made the grief and stress tolerable.

As Jemma and Micky headed past me to the door, Micky said, 'See, I made her laugh. That's what women look for in a man – a good sense of humour.'

From the corridor, I heard Jemma say, 'Have you been reading my *Cosmo* again? "That's what women look for in a man"? Trust me on this: no matter how funny you are, if a woman can't stand you touching her, winning Stand-Up Comedian of the Year won't get her into bed.'

I spent the time I had left before the briefing looking through the various databases I had access to, for information I could gather on Patrick Hudson and the Rumbly family. Apart from Hudson's PNC record, which hadn't changed since he'd been locked up for an attempted murder and assault on police – and I knew more than most about those offences – our force's databases held little on him. There wasn't much to say about a man who had been serving a lengthy custodial sentence, except his release date. I found that on the Prison Intelligence Database. At the very least, Annie should have been warned. I'd be asking on her behalf.

The Rumblys were a different tale. I started with Niall. He was thirty-three years old and his record showed that he'd been in prison three times. He was currently serving a sentence in Mill End prison. He at least had a rock-solid alibi for Hudson's shooting. Before I had a chance to look up Leonard Rumbly, and aware of the time slipping away before the briefing started, I locked the computer, made myself a cup of tea and got ready to leave. Wingsy rushed through the door just as I was about to set off for the conference room. I left him shouting about the traffic being a nightmare and there being nowhere to park because the car park was full of Murder Squad vehicles from Serious Crime.

I felt a bit jittery about seeing some of the team again. The last time I'd seen some of them I'd been in hospital, out of it on all sorts of drugs. I didn't even recall some of them visiting me, but whenever I woke up there was a card, note or present from someone new.

Outside the conference room door, holding my notebook in the crook of my arm, my mug of builder's tea clamped in my hand, I took a deep breath and pushed the door open. For a second I stood in the doorway, casting an eye over those in the room. A few looked up from around the table that could easily seat forty people. It was half-full.

'Nina,' said Pierre Rainer, a DC I had worked with on Operation Guard, 'you're looking well.' He got up from the far side of the table to weave around the others, who were making no attempt to get out of his way as they swapped notes and last-minute details. Pierre reached me and hugged me. 'Hear you've been getting involved again,' he said into my ear as we embraced.

'You know me,' I said, pulling away but leaving my free hand on his arm, 'I can't help it. And thanks for dropping my wine glass round.'

I followed him back around the table to sit next to him, making my way past Mark Russell and saying hi to him and a few others I knew. Wingsy bowled through the door seconds ahead of DI Clint Stirling and a woman in a striped navy suit.

A hush fell upon the room. The woman accompanying Clint smiled as she looked around at us, and took a seat at the top of the table. Clint sat on her right. I allowed myself a smile at the thought of him being her right-hand man. Wingsy was sitting opposite me and, as I scanned the room, he scowled at me. He probably wondered why I was smiling. I decided that after the meeting I would tell him it was because his flies were undone.

'Welcome, everyone,' said the woman. 'Thank you for coming to the first full briefing of Operation Magpie. Yeah, I do know that they're a bad omen but that's what we got when we rang the control room.' Operation names were given alphabetically, but more than one was always allocated for each letter of the alphabet. It made me wonder how many other operations there had been since I'd been on Operation Guard last year. There had to have been a lot of shootings, stabbings, rapes and kidnaps to go from multiple Gs to Ms.

'Most of us know each other,' she continued, 'but if we can go around the room and everyone give their name, rank and where they work, that will be a useful start.' She paused and then said, 'I'm Janice Freeman, the Serious Crime Directorate DCI. I'm the senior investigating officer for Op Magpie but I'm grateful for any help the local borough commander has been able to provide as, in addition to the shooting, we're running a number of investigations unrelated to this incident, including two rapes, a stabbing and a murder. I've run out of staff again.'

A quick glance around the room at those assembled told me that Janice Freeman was not a woman to be easily hoodwinked, and I doubted much got past her. I thought that we'd probably get on, but I'd see how things went.

Clint then took his cue to introduce himself as the area on-call DI, then each member of the enquiry team assembled in the room took their turn to say their part. As my own got closer and closer, I weighed up whether I should tell everyone that I'd been on the receiving end of a good hiding from our victim. A lot of those in the room probably knew anyway. I decided to play it down.

'I'm Detective Constable Nina Foster. I've recently joined the area's Cold Case team. I have previously had dealings with Patrick Hudson when he was arrested for the attempted murder of his wife, Annie, and for assault on police.' I was looking directly at Janice Freeman as I said these words, but noticed that Clint was leaning on his elbows, staring directly at me. I cast my eyes straight down when I finished talking.

Soon we got down to the business of who might have shot Patrick Hudson. Officers and investigators threw in all the information that had been amassed about him and his movements since he'd been released from prison three days before. In that short space of time, he seemed to have been nowhere but a local pub, a corner shop for a few essentials and to see his probation officer. His mobile phone was still at the hostel where he had been staying, and there had been no movement that day in his very paltry bank account. Patrick Hudson had, for his seventy-two hours of freedom, lived a seemingly rehabilitated life. Until, that was, he was shot.

'Mark,' said DCI Freeman, 'you've made the most recent contact with the hospital. What did they have to say?'

Mark cleared his throat and glanced down at one of a number of pieces of paper he had laid out in front of him. 'The hospital ward has changed the code word again, by the way,' he said, looking back up at those in the room. 'If you want to make contact with them, come and see me for it or check on HOLMES. They won't give you the time of day without it. The sister there is one scary woman.' He glanced back down at his notes. 'OK, our victim is still critical. The hospital staff have been as helpful as they can, but we're some way off being able to speak to him, even if he does wake up – and they don't think that's likely. The scary sister, Ellen Trimble, told me I can talk to the staff there, but she wouldn't give any estimates on when or if we can talk to Hudson. He's had no visitors apart from police officers.

'Patrick Hudson's gunshot injuries are two entry wounds to his back, one entry wound to the left of his torso, one entry wound to the right of his torso, one entry wound on his right thigh and one entry wound to his right lower arm plus one exit wound at this point. Oh, and the strain on his heart is still a worry for the hospital.'

It wasn't a worry to me. I hoped the bastard would die. I lost myself momentarily, thinking how the only violent encounter I'd had with him meant my shoulder still ached in cold weather, and then I realised I hadn't been paying attention. Sarah Mitchell, the DC from Prison Intelligence, was giving the run-down on the information they'd managed to cobble together about Hudson's time inside, especially that spent in HMP Mill End with Niall Rumbly.

'Patrick Hudson and Niall Rumbly were sharing a cell for two months prior to Hudson's release. Rumbly was given six months for an assault on a doorman at the Roundabout nightclub. He's serving three months after pleading guilty to an unprovoked attack and by all accounts keeps his head down and is to be released in a couple of weeks' time. The prison has no record of any altercations between them. They seemed to get on, or certainly had no problems that were brought to the prison officers' attention.'

'Hudson have any visitors in the last twelve months of his stretch?' asked Clint.

'Only one,' said Sarah. 'His eldest son, Richard.'

Not that I hadn't been paying attention, but this was like a slap around the face. Annie's two boys, Richard and Lewis, had disowned their father the day he tried to kill their mother.

Sarah ran her finger along the lines of her notes to ensure she was looking at the correct line before reading out, '28th March. That was the day Richard visited his father.'

'Right, OK. Thanks, Sarah,' said the SIO. 'We'll sort out who sees him after the briefing. If you've nothing else about Mill End prison, I think that will bring us nicely on to Pensworth prison. Nina?'

All eyes were on me now. I didn't need to look down at my notes; I knew what I was going to say. The conversation with Joe Bring was etched on my mind. Even the testicle-fondling part.

'Due to a Cold Case investigation into a train crash in 1964, I went to see Joe Bring about some information. His father was the lorry driver whose truck caused the accident. Joe told me that his father, now deceased, might have caused the collision on purpose. Joe's dad had a mounting gambling debt and the person he owed it to was Leonard Rumbly.'

I paused at this point and went tactical.

'Joe's son's friend died of a heroin overdose recently. Joe is desperate to stop his own son going the same way and wants to assist in any way he can to prosecute Rumbly, as he thinks he's behind the area's heroin supply.'

'How reliable is Bring?' asked Freeman.

'Strangely enough, ma'am, I've never known him lie. He's just about the worst shoplifter and thief, but he always admits whatever he's done when he's caught. And he gets caught. A lot.'

A couple of the others around the room nodded in agreement. Seemed as if Joe had been dealt with by a fair few of us.

'Right, in that case I want whatever you can get me on every member of the Rumbly family,' said the DCI. 'We'll start with Leonard, although he's no doubt getting on a bit now. I want a full intelligence profile on every one of them and an officer assigned to each of them. Sounds like this will be our first priority. We need to establish drugs links. People do not get shot numerous times for a bit of personal gear. My guess – and that's all it is as the moment – is that Patrick Hudson got involved in something that was way bigger than he was used to, and the risk of shooting him and leaving him for dead was lower than the risk of leaving him alive to talk.'

12

By the time the briefing was finished I was glad to get out. It had been the longest I'd sat still for ages. I was a fidget at the best of times, but, following months off work, sitting in an uncomfortable chair for an hour and a half was excruciating. Having said my bit, I fully expected to be sent back to the confines of Cold Case and for that to be the end of it.

As I reached the door, however, Clint called me back to the table. He and Janice Freeman both regarded me with neutral faces. I stood mutely in front of them, waiting for them to speak. Clint pushed out a chair in my direction. Why couldn't anyone simply ask me to sit down?

Taking a seat, I waited until the noise behind me died down and the room emptied. It was going to be one of those conversations.

'Nina...' began Clint, touching his left earlobe. From our terrible dates years earlier, I knew he did this when he was nervous. 'DI Ian Hammond has told me that you're to be left on Cold Case to help out with the '64 train accident.' He took a sharp intake of breath. 'The thing is...'

He looked to Freeman for help. She left him to it.

'Joe Bring will talk to you,' Clint continued. 'Has he got a thing about you?'

'No,' I said. 'I've been on some pretty shit dates in my life, but never with the likes of Joe.'

That seemed to take the smug look off his face.

Freeman said, 'Nina, we'd like you to work with us for a short while. You'd be mostly office-bound, but the rest of Serious Crime who've worked with you before hold you in high regard. What you'd be doing would be the Cold Case side of things, but focusing on where they cross over into our investigation, with some office research and paperwork looking into the Rumblys. It wouldn't have anything to do directly with Patrick Hudson. Anything you're not happy to be dealing with, we would take from you. What do you think?'

'Why not?' I said. It wasn't as if I had any option. Apart from feeling pleased that I'd been asked to join the team, I was a police officer. I did what I was told. Sometimes I was told what to do by brilliant leaders and supervisors who inspired; sometimes it was by total dickheads.

I had made my mind up that Janice fell into the former category.

13

I finished speaking to the DCI and Clint and went to look for Wingsy. Failing to find him, I phoned him.

'Alright, duchess,' he said. 'I'll see you in the car park. We're back on house-to-house for the shooting for the rest of the day.'

I made my way to the yard, preparing myself. So much for being office-bound for a few days. I enjoyed house-to-house, to be honest. Although it did mean knocking on doors and asking the same questions over and over, of everyone within a set parameter around a crime scene that was decided by the senior investigating officer, it meant that you got to meet normal members of the public. All too often, in police enquiries, officers met either criminals or victims. Both could be equally difficult. But with something like a shooting people usually wanted to help, and it meant taking time to chat to the public and reassure those living near by.

By the time I found him, Wingsy had the rest of our day planned out. I didn't mind. I was in one of those moods where I needed to be told what to do. It didn't necessarily mean I was going to do it; I just couldn't make a decision for myself.

He'd found us a car to use. Vehicles were a bit thin on the ground at the best of times in a police station, but with a Category A shooting – no immediate suspects and no one in custody – they were particularly difficult to come by. We met in the yard and proceeded to clear out the empty wrappers, drinks bottles and receipts before driving to the nearest petrol station to fill up the car's empty diesel tank. Glancing at the log book, I saw that the last person to use it had been Jim Sullivan.

Wingsy saw me looking at the mileage book and leant over to examine the force number and name.

'I see Spunk Bubble can't even fill a car with fuel. He's such a chopper,' he said.

'I know, mate. Where to first?'

'There were a couple of houses where we got no reply when we went out yesterday and it needs completing as soon as. It may be a late one, 'cos if these are people who are at work or school we may need to be on duty much later than five pm.'

'That's OK,' I said. 'Bill's back on lates and I could do with the overtime.'

I sifted through the paperwork as Wingsy drove towards the crime scene. 'I'm a bit out of sorts now,' I said, trying to grasp what I was expected to do. 'Stuff with Annie has thrown me a bit. What are the house-to-house enquiry parameters?'

'Well,' said Wingsy, pulling up at the traffic lights on the town's ring road, 'the premises to be seen are over a large area but the main addresses are on the road in and out of the industrial estate. Oh, and the tower block behind it.'

'And let me guess,' I said with a sinking feeling, 'you and I have been given James Knoxley House?'

'You guessed it, sweetheart.' He grinned at me. 'Got your stab-proof?'

A couple of minutes later we pulled into one of the county's most run-down high-rise blocks. Fifteen storeys of concrete depression stood all alone against the skyline.

Saddest of all was that sprinkled around at ground level were old people's retirement bungalows. All were immaculate and the occupants never caused any grief to each other or anyone else. Their punishment for getting old was for someone to think it was a good idea to build fifteen floors of flats feet from their property and fill them with the kinds of people you'd cross the road to avoid. On a positive note, a lot of the old folk were deaf, so they couldn't hear the sound of breaking glass coming from their undesirable neighbours.

We parked away from the block, alongside two other unmarked police cars we recognised, and set off towards the entrance to the flats. It started to rain just as we reached the entry panel. The architect's idea had been that you buzzed the number corresponding to the flat you wanted and the occupant let you in – or declined to, if they didn't like the look of you. Fortunately for us in the downpour, the residents of James Knoxley House had taken time out of their day to smash the living daylights out of the security system and smear some very unpleasant substances across the buttons. Getting in was therefore just a case of pushing the door.

We climbed the stairs, the unmistakable stench of urine reaching our nostrils as we neared the landing. I was glad we hadn't taken the lift; heaven only knew what that smelt like. From the top of the first flight of stairs, I could hear a familiar voice. It was Jim Sullivan, talking to someone on the next floor up.

Wingsy and I needed to speak to someone on the first floor who hadn't been at home when the first house-to-house enquiries were carried out. We were making our way along the balcony to the flat when something about the tone of Jim's voice changed. It had an urgency to it. I couldn't make out the words, but from the intonation it was clear he needed assistance. Then I heard shouts. Both Wingsy and I turned a hundred and eighty degrees and ran up the next flight of stairs to our colleague.

Wingsy was faster than me and was just in front, slightly blocking my view. I saw him reach inside his jacket and pull out his asp, so I realised it was serious, then my Airwave confirmed that Jim had pressed the panic button on his radio set. I could hear the control room mustering immediate response. Whatever I thought of him, Jim wouldn't do that lightly – and Wingsy wouldn't have pulled out his asp unless he was prepared to use it. An asp was an extendable piece of metal. A potentially lethal piece of metal.

As I ran behind Wingsy, I saw that Jim was on the floor at the open door of a flat and another person was on top of him. I knew Wingsy wouldn't rack his asp for fear of extending it straight into my face, so I pulled out my own and opened it. The sound of our running footsteps, police radios and shouting gave the man with his hands around our colleague's throat a few seconds to react. He looked up in our direction and made a run for it towards the nearest exit – straight towards us. Wingsy, slightly taken by surprise, tried to grab him but missed and was moving too fast to stop. By the time Wingsy got to Jim's prostrate body, the man legging it away from our assaulted colleague was level with me. I had half a second to think how I was going to stop his escape.

I tripped him up. He went down hard and fast. I heard a crack. The thing that stuck in my mind was that he was wearing a lanyard around his neck and the ID pass attached to it hit him in the face as he fell. And now he was on the floor.

Three uniform officers had run up the stairs and joined us. I'd heard the sirens in the background, but it was only now the red mist had lifted and I could think rationally again that I made the link that they were coming to help us. Two of the three stopped and cuffed the man screaming on the floor. As they turned him over, I saw that the crack I'd heard had been the sound of his nose breaking as it hit the concrete corridor floor.

I turned my attention to Jim and Wingsy. Jim was sitting up against the outside wall of the flat next to the open front door. He had his head tilted back and was prodding his neck with his left hand. Wingsy was crouched down next to him. I had to turn away again so that they couldn't see me smile as I heard Wingsy say to him, 'You're welcome. You may be a Spunk Bubble, but you're our Spunk Bubble.'

'Alright, Jim?' I asked when I could keep a straight face. He nodded at me.

'What happened?' I asked.

Jim coughed then cleared his throat before saying, 'As I turned the corner, there was a bloke coming out of the premises. I told him I was a police officer, asked him his name and if there was anyone else indoors. He grabbed me and pushed me to the floor.' Jim shut his eyes for a second. 'No idea what his problem is.'

'Best we take a look in this flat, then,' I said, as much to myself as to anyone else. I went to step over Jim's outstretched legs towards the door. Wingsy, asp still in hand, stepped in behind me. Jim got to his feet to follow us inside.

Less than a minute had passed since we'd come tearing up the stairs to help Jim, but it was enough time for anyone inside to have run out. There were no other exits from the flats. They didn't have individual fire escapes, so, if someone else had been inside, they'd have heard us. And they'd be waiting.

14

From the doorway, I could see along a passage leading to a dimly lit living room. An archway to my left led to a cramped kitchen. It was empty, that much I could see at a glance. Another door after the arch appeared to be a cupboard. I gestured that I was going to open it and then called out, 'Hello, it's the police.' No reply. It contained a hoover and three or four black bags of junk. No room to hide in there.

The three of us stood in the hall, peering into the room that had the curtains drawn and the lights off. I felt along the wall inside the doorway for the light switch. My fingers made contact with it, but there was something not right with the surface. As I snapped the light on and pulled my hand away, I guessed without examining my fingertips that I'd pressed a light switch swathed in blood.

What was left of a smashed white mug lay on the carpet. In the now-illuminated room, dark patches were visible under the china fragments on the floor. A sound made me whip my head towards my right. I guessed the bedroom. I put my hand up to halt the two chomping at the bit to get past me.

'Mind that,' I said to Jim and Wingsy behind me, pointing down to the broken pieces littering the floor. Having little time to worry about scene preservation if there was either someone injured on the premises or an offender about to make good their escape, I stepped over the remnants and moved towards the bedroom.

'Police,' I called again. I pushed the door open with my asp before rushing forward to the figure on the floor. 'Call an ambulance,' I shouted to Wingsy.

An elderly man of about eighty was lying on his right side inside the bedroom door. A large laceration on the left side of his head was bleeding. Against the whiteness of his hair and the paleness of his skin, the blood was stark. He had on a white shirt, too, and the contrast of the blood seeping down on to the material was all the fiercer.

Without any hesitation, he was my priority. Preservation of life. It was a fundamental policing principle but also a human instinct. It was extremely difficult to fight it; it was why people tended to run towards a car accident. That said, I had to make sure no one else was in the room. A very speedy recce told me that the bed was pushed up against the window and the wardrobe door was ajar. Two £20 notes were sticking out of the bottom of the wardrobe. An old-fashioned dressing table on legs and a wooden chair with a red leather seat and back were the only other items in the room.

Bending down beside the old man to feel for a pulse, I was relieved to hear him moaning. I was also pretty pleased to hear Wingsy come into the room and say, 'An ambulance is on its way.' Then I could hear him giving an update to the control room on the victim's approximate age, condition and injuries. Once my temporary patient had opened his eyes, I tried to explain that I was a police officer, but I didn't think he was taking any of it in. Once again I could hear the sounds of sirens in the distance; the paramedics would be here shortly.

Wingsy and I made the old man as comfortable as we could without allowing him to get up. He didn't seem to have any injuries other than the one to his head we could already see, and eventually he told us his name was Walter McRay. I could hear Jim moving about looking for any contact details for Walter's family, and any medication he might be taking, ready for the imminent arrival of the paramedics.

Once Walter had told us that he didn't think he had any other injuries, Wingsy asked him what had happened.

'I had my lunch,' he said, 'cleared up and heard a knock at the door. When I went to open it, I could see a bloke outside with some sort of pass on a string around his neck. He waved it at me and said that there was a problem with the water in the block and he'd have to come in and check that the pressure was OK.' Walter paused at this and took several short breaths. 'Told him I'd just washed up and it was fine. He said it was for fine for short bursts, but I'd need mine looking at. Like a silly old fool, I let him in.' Lying on the floor, Walter's eyes welled up and he raised a hand to his face to wipe the tears away. 'Turned my back on him, heard noises from the wardrobe there and there was a second fella inside the flat. The first one must have let him in. He was going through my wife's jewellery box. It's all I've got left of her.' He tried to move his head in the direction of his furniture. A wince gave away how restricted his movement was.

The sound of paramedics coming into the flat drowned out Walter's next words. I could hear Jim giving them a summary of what had happened, refusing any medical attention for himself and then showing them the way to the bedroom. Wingsy and I left them to it.

'Poxy artifice burglars,' I said to Wingsy when we were back outside on the communal balcony. The misery they inflicted on the vulnerable had always got to me. I let out a sigh and looked over the railings to where the uniform patrol was putting the prisoner into the back of their car. Even from two floors away, I could tell that he wasn't enjoying his day so far.

I felt the railings give a little as Wingsy lent next to me. 'I heard Walter say that the other one must have taken his dead wife's wedding ring. It had an inscription inside the gold band.'

'What scum does that to the elderly?' I said watching the patrol car drive away. 'That's why they pick on old people, isn't it? They get confused and find it difficult to identify them. No doubt the cash and property are long gone with his accomplice. He must have got away before Jim got there.'

'You know what you, me and Jim should do, don't you?' said Wingsy.

I turned to look at him. 'Well, since I hate to think that you might be suggesting a threesome, Baldy, I'm going with we have to go back to the nick to write a statement. That'll make a change.'

15

Often, everything worked out. I would have loved to be able to say that Allan Ragland, the man arrested outside Walter McRay's flat for burglary, assault on police and GBH of Walter, was taken to the police station, a Section 18 PACE search conducted of his home address and his accomplice found, arrested, searched and the stolen wedding ring recovered and returned to a grateful Mr McRay. That didn't happen.

Ragland, distraction burglar, was arrested, made no comment in interview and had nothing to say regarding the £4,775 found hidden in the loft of his home address. A uniformed search team seized the money anyway and, under the Proceeds of Crime Act 2002, he was unlikely to get it back. Nor the Audi A3 on his driveway. He had no job, no income and didn't appear to be landed gentry. It was a greater punishment for him than the custodial sentence the courts were likely to hand out to a man who had nineteen convictions for thirty-two different offences. It cheered me momentarily, until I thought it through. Ragland would be released from a short prison sentence and revert to type. He would scour the streets for the homes of elderly people and steal their life savings. With no compunction, care or thought for those in his wake, he would pocket the tiny bit of cash his victims had put away month after month, possibly going without heating in the winter. This was the cash he would take to enjoy an easy lifestyle enhanced by the comfort of his brand new luxury car. It was like shooting fish in a barrel for him.

Wingsy and I set about completing our paperwork to hand over to a harassed-looking DC who had landed the job of interviewing Ragland, charging him, remanding him and putting him before the next available court in the morning. We finished doing what we had to do before making good our escape for the night. Assisting in the arrest of an artifice burglar added to the mixed feelings I was having about my eight-hour days. At least I was earning a few extra quid, even though I could have fallen asleep at my desk.

Wingsy and I finished much later than we should have by the time we'd got everything completed. It was dark, and the rain began to fall again as we left the station. We shouted our goodbyes to each other as we ran to our cars. Despite the rain hitting my head and back as I made haste towards my BMW, I ran an eye over the interior of my car before getting inside. Old habits died hard.

By the time I'd turned the engine over and begun to pull out on to the ring road, I was cold, damp, tired and feeling pretty cheesed off. It had been a tougher day than the one I'd expected when I'd hauled myself out of my bed that morning. Or, to be more precise, Bill's bed.

Driving in the direction of Bill's home, I crawled through the traffic, watching the people on the pavements on their way back to loved ones. I thought how good it was to have someone to go home to, but I still couldn't ignore the urge I'd had to go to my own house, shut the door and be alone for a while. The slow-moving traffic did little to improve my mood, so I was looking forward to a relaxing evening. I shouldn't be so ungrateful for my temporary place of refuge at Bill's. I was the one staying at his house, and he could ask me to leave. I was physically able to go home and live by myself; it was just that I didn't really fancy the idea very much.

Pulling on to the driveway, I saw the light on in the hallway and smiled at Bill's thoughtfulness before he'd left for his late shift. Letting myself in with the key he'd given me weeks previously, I saw that he'd Sellotaped a handwritten note to the mirror hanging opposite the front door. *Nina, call when you get in. It's urgent. Your mum's been here today.*

Momentarily puzzled whether I should call Bill or my mum, and wondering what the crisis was, I opted to call Bill first.

He answered the phone by saying, 'Hello, Nina.' There was no 'sweetheart' or 'darling'.

'Hi, Bill,' I said. 'What's the problem with my mum?'

I caught sight of myself in the mirror. I had my free hand in my hair, tearing at a clump of my damp locks, and it was only when I saw myself that I felt the pain in my scalp. I put my hand down by my side and listened to the sounds of Bill's police radio at the other end of the line.

'She wanted to know where her money was this month,' said Bill.

'Oh,' I managed to say. 'I'd forgotten about it.'

'Were you going to tell me about that?'

'No, Bill, I probably wasn't ever going to tell you.'

'Right. Well, when I get home tonight, Nina, I think we need to talk.'

My stomach lurched at this prospect. No one liked the 'we need to talk' talk. I knew what he was going to ask me. And I didn't want to tell him the answer.

16

As I wondered whether I should open a bottle of wine and warm up for the heated debate I knew would begin when Bill got home, my phone started to ring. Willing it not to be my mum, I saw the name 'Stan' on the screen.

Smiling with relief, I answered the phone.

'Hello, Stan,' I said, going to the kitchen in search of a corkscrew.

'Hello, Nina,' he said. 'I got back from holiday yesterday and wondered if you wanted to come over this evening for dinner if you're not busy. I realise that it's late and short notice, but – '

'Love to, Stan. What time do you want me there?' I asked, putting the corkscrew, which Bill had hidden under the food processor blades, back in the drawer.

'Well, any time, really, but I was planning on having dinner in about half an hour.'

'OK, I'll have a quick shower and head on over. See you soon, Stan.'

'Bye, Nina.'

Twenty minutes later, I was heading towards my old friend's house. It was the best I'd felt in a number of days. The effort of returning to work and fitting in with Bill's lifestyle, plus the sudden burst of energy during Allan Ragland's arrest, were all beginning to wear me down. The latest problem to blight my life was a financial pressure from my parents that I knew I couldn't meet at the moment. I'd been off sick from work for months, and that meant no overtime.

I'd never considered my police officer's pay either fantastic or particularly low. Some days were so brilliant, I felt a bit guilty even taking a wage. Other days were so low that trebling my salary would not have been enough. One New Year's Eve was spent arresting a suspect with HIV and hepatitis B who spat at me and tried to bite me. Great memories.

My trip down memory lane brought me, literally, to Stan's house. I pulled up on his driveway and walked up to the porch. A black cat ran in front of me and stood waiting by the door. I rang the doorbell and edged inside the porch, encouraging the cat with my foot to go in the other direction. Stan opened the door as I was attempting to push its feline face away from the door.

'Hello, Miriam,' said Stan.

It took me a second to realise that he was talking to the cat.

'Let her in,' said Stan. 'Hello, Nina. It's great to see you.'

I gave up my battle with the cat and watched Miriam run straight inside towards the kitchen. Stan gave a chuckle and said, 'She must think we're having chicken. She's always here on poultry night.'

'Getting a bit hacked off here,' I said. 'You look more pleased to see the cat than me.'

My words served their childish purpose. I got my hug, and very welcome it was too. My face pressed against the motif on Stan's jumper, I relaxed for the first time in a while.

'Miriam pops in from time to time,' I heard Stan say through the ear that was not full of lambswool. 'I may even have a cat flap put in.'

I pulled back to say, 'Have you got sunstroke from your cruise or has retirement from the police finally sent you senile? It's not your cat.'

'Enough about the cat,' said Stan, peering at my face. 'You look exhausted. What's bothering you? Money, or Bill?'

I felt like crying. I had to put my hand across my mouth to stifle a sob. I struggled to meet his gaze and covered my eyes, just too late to stop Stan from seeing the tears threatening to escape.

17

In Stan's kitchen, tears drying and wine breathing, I felt pretty foolish. My old friend and confidant allowed me to regain my composure and muster what dignity I could with bloodshot eyes and Hallowe'en mascara, before speaking.

Even then, his question was, 'How many potatoes do you want?'

'Three, please, and it's both Bill and money.'

I watched Stan's profile as he got out plates. I'd known him nearly forty years, since the day he'd rescued me and my sister from our childhood kidnapping. He had never let me down, not once. He'd been the reason for me joining the police, and even now I relied on him.

He brought the food to the table and sat opposite me. I felt compelled to fill the silence.

'My mum came round today when I was at work,' I said across the steaming dishes of food. 'She told Bill that I give her money to help out with my sister. I'm so annoyed with her. She shouldn't have discussed it with him. It's none of his business.'

To avert my eyes from Stan's, I concentrated on heaping peas and carrots on to my plate.

'Or are you actually annoyed with yourself for the guilt you still feel for your sister's mental health?' asked the ever-perceptive Stan.

His words hit home. The result was that my wavering hand shot diced carrots over the tablecloth.

'Nina,' said Stan, 'I know I'm treading on eggshells every time I try to raise the subject, but your sister was affected by the kidnap in an entirely different way from you. What she endured was not the same thing as you did. You should never feel guilty about that.'

'Yeah, I know,' I managed to say, seeking out a cube of carrot from behind the gravy boat. 'My mum still shouldn't have told Bill about the money. He's really hacked off that I didn't tell him. He knows I'm struggling without any overtime – I moan about being broke often enough. I can see why he's annoyed with me.'

'Perhaps after all these years you really should stop giving her money. How much do you give her?'

I concentrated on cutting my steak. I acted as if it was particularly troublesome although it was cooked to perfection and Stan knew it. But it meant I could look at my plate as I said, 'Four hundred pounds a month.'

I could hear Stan's intake of breath.

'How can you afford that?' he asked.

'I can manage as long as I don't go out much. All I buy are clothes and wine.'

Stan left it there. He knew I didn't want to say any more about it. He was the one who had rescued us all those years ago, had been the one I'd looked up to ever since, and had guided me down the best paths in life. He'd always kept updated on my sister's progress, from her initial ambulance ride to hospital all those years ago, to the fifteen days in a coma, to the months she spent in one hospital after another being retaught to walk and talk before finally going home to our parents, where she'd lived ever since. She'd made a great deal of progress over the years but her life would never be what it had once promised. Did I have feelings of anger that her life shouldn't be this way, coupled with a deep-down sense of shame that I was relieved it wasn't me? Yes, and that was why I would always feel so guilty. The man responsible for our kidnapping was currently locked in prison and justice seemed to be done, but I had to live with my own selfishness.

However, once again, I buried those thoughts and acted as normally as I could in front of the world.

We chatted for a while about his cruise and why he was now feeding a cat called Miriam that wasn't his. Eventually I sought his advice on work matters. I did this often and usually just talking the matter over was enough to resolve the issue.

By the end of our meal I'd explained about the shooting, my visit to see Joe Bring, and the information he'd given me about the Rumbly family. Stan asked me a couple of questions to fill in any details I'd skated over. When I'd finished, Stan pushed his plate away and sat back in his chair, arms folded across his chest.

'The name Leonard Rumbly rings a bell,' he began. 'If he's the same one I'm thinking of, he's a particularly unpleasant individual. A couple of colleagues of mine when we were all still in uniform had to travel down from the Met to an estate on the outskirts of Wickerstead Valley to nick him. Rumbly had bitten someone's thumb off in a fight in New Cross.'

'How can you possibly remember that?' I asked. 'You haven't been in uniform for decades.' I was impressed, but also a bit worried Stan was losing his mind.

'Well, it would have been some time in the Sixties. I remember it because Rumbly tried to bribe them. They had to nick him for that too, of course. He seemed to think that he was outside the law and could buy whatever he wanted. I also remember it because some of their equipment went missing – a truncheon, that sort of thing. There was always a big fuss when stuff like that happened, in case officers were selling them to make a few bob.'

'Police corruption was more of a problem in the Sixties, though, wasn't it?' I asked. There was no hint of accusation in my question: not for one moment did I think Stan himself would have been involved in anything untoward, and he knew that.

'Yes, that's true.' He uncrossed his arms and picked up the half-full bottle of Côtes du Rhône, moving to top up my glass.

'No, thanks, Stan,' I said. 'I'd better be getting home. Bill will be in soon. We've got a row scheduled for about half an hour's time.'

I pushed my chair away from the table as I stood up, gathering plates and bowls as I went. The two of us cleared the table, filled the dishwasher and removed the debris from the meal in a contented silence. The only sound was of plates being scraped, and a noisy, attention-seeking cat.

When I couldn't put it off any longer, I said my goodbyes and drove home to Bill's house, defences on full alert.

18

When I got home, the row I had been expecting was waiting for me.

Bill was sitting in the armchair in his dressing gown, fingertips drumming on the side of his coffee cup.

'Hello,' I said, coming into the room, coat still on.

'Why didn't you tell me you were giving your parents money?'

'You'd have been annoyed.'

'Not as annoyed as I am now.'

I wasn't about to get tearful twice in one evening, so I got angry.

'Who the hell are you to tell me what to do with my money, Bill?'

'Please understand me, I'm not trying to tell you what to do. But you didn't tell me the truth.' He put his cup down and stood up. 'We're in this together. You won't talk to me about your sister. You've never even told me what's actually happened to her. I can accept that you'll tell me when you're good and ready, but I don't want you to feel you have to keep things from me. I've got to be up at four for a drugs warrant so I'll sleep in the spare room. Goodnight.'

He walked past me, pausing to kiss the side of my face. I wanted to stop him, go with him, tell him that I didn't mind that he'd wake me in only a few hours when his alarm went off. I did none of those things, but remained where I was until I heard him close the spare room door.

The next morning, I woke with a feeling of domestic disharmony, despite the now still and peaceful house. I took myself off to Riverstone police station. The car park was packed when I pulled in a few minutes before eight. I reversed into a tricky corner space perfect for vehicles like mine that wouldn't look any worse if another passing car left a scratch or dent.

As I opened the rear door of the station and made my way through the patrol officers' wing, the unmistakable stench of cannabis greeted me. It was accompanied by the sound of rustling paper exhibit bags and two uniform officers wading through a couple of hundred exhibits. Mid-wave, I caught sight of Bill walking towards me with a petite blonde CSI whose name I couldn't remember. She had a camera in her hand ready to photograph the cannabis plants seized from the latest haul.

Figuring it was safe to stop and talk to Bill, as he was too polite and professional to show his disdain for my financial predicament in front of others, I went towards them.

'Getting up at four o'clock paid off, then?' I asked, gesturing towards about twenty cannabis plants.

'Yeah,' said Bill. 'They're skunk plants, and we've got about another hundred or so still on the premises.'

'Right, Bill,' said the very pretty CSI, as she busied herself with her camera. 'I'll photograph these and put the pictures on the same disk as the ones of all the plants taken in situ, and you let me know what samples you want sending off to the lab. Get one of your officers to drop me the HOLAB form when you're done.'

I thought it best to remain on neutral territory so asked, 'What was the address of the drugs warrant?'

'It was at 37 Park Road, Kilnchester,' said Bill, with no hint of animosity. 'Management are all patting themselves on the back, but it was as a result of information from a member of the public, apparently. Whoever it was had been on our website and read up on how to spot cannabis factories.' He leaned closer to my ear and said, 'From what I can gather, it was a resident in the street who noticed the lights were always on at the premises, the windows were blacked out, and the types of people coming and going with large bags of soil didn't look as though they'd be growing tomatoes.'

'Anyone in the bin for it?' I asked, feeling that at least talking about work was, at the end of the day, talking.

'Yeah, there are two in custody. Some fella called Nathan Samms and his wife. One's being booked in now. Anyway, I'll see you tonight, Nina.'

He strolled off to speak to the two officers on the floor bagging exhibits.

I left the area, leaving behind the aroma of drugs, and headed onwards to the cubbyhole that was the Cold Case office.

The door was open. Wingsy sat on one side and Jim Sullivan on the other. Both were engrossed in whatever was on the computer screens in front of them. Neither of them looked up as I entered the room.

'Morning, fellas,' I said, as I went to a desk and prepared to start work for the day.

'Hi, Nin,' said Wingsy. 'Got much on today? Only asking because there's a couple more things that we need to take care of in relation to our mate Allan Ragland, from yesterday. Then I thought that I might head off to Magistrates' Court for his remand hearing.'

'Course, Wings,' I answered, taking off my coat. 'It's either that or a fifty-year-old train crash. You've got my undivided attention.'

As we were talking, Jim got up and left the room. I watched Wingsy scowl at his back as he went out into the corridor. 'He's a donkey's dangler,' said Wingsy. 'I'm going to get my own back.' He got up and went over to Jim's desk.

'Can't you just leave it?' I asked. 'He's grassed you up once and, to be fair, he had little choice, with the chief constable involved.'

Wingsy paused with a roll of Sellotape in one hand and a pair of scissors in another. He stared at me.

'You of all people are taking Spunk Bubble's side in all this?'

'In all what, Wings? You're about to Sellotape over the mouthpiece on his phone? I want no part in "all this".'

I ignored my friend as he carried on covering the mouthpiece of Jim's landline with clear tape.

Firing up the laughably slow computer, I logged on to my account and checked my force email. I had the usual notifications of various servers and databases going down and then being magically restored while I'd slept, blissfully unaware that the Betterjax Matrix was experiencing problems. I had truly no idea what half of the databases used by our police force did, and was never entirely convinced that one or two weren't made up.

At last I got to an email of interest from HMP Pensworth. Slightly aghast that a burglar could email me on my police account from the comfort of his incarceration, I hesitated for only a second before opening it. I told myself Joe Bring was the man who had saved my life first and a burglar second – or something like that.

Detective Nina, Miss,

    Thank you for coming to see us in here. Got a few other things to tell you. I know I am no angle but can you come see us again.

    Ta very much

        Joe

PS I did twat that fella with a plant pot for you.

That made me smile, especially the part about being 'no angle'. I must still have been smiling when I looked up at Wingsy. He was holding the phone and staring at me.

'What's up with you?' he asked.

'I've had an email from Joe Bring,' I said. 'And put that phone down before Jim comes back. What are we going to do today after court?'

'Did a bit of digging and spoke to Mac in the Intel unit. He seems to think that the stolen jewellery from the artifice burglaries is being sold on at the Noël Coward estate gold shop.'

'That came from Intel, did it?' I asked, stacking my forearms on the desk in front of me. 'I worked that out about twenty-four hours ago.'

'Yeah, but what you don't know, smart arse, is that someone saw them going in with a load of stuff that looked moody and they're supposed to be going back today with more. They're due in there at midday.'

This grabbed my attention. 'You and I won't be sent, though, will we?' I said. 'We're Cold Case. We've got other stuff to do. They'll send a couple of DCs from the main CID office, surely?'

'You're totally correct, DC Foster,' said Wingsy. 'Doesn't stop us being in one of the shops opposite, though, to see who turns up. At least we know it won't be the bloke arrested yesterday, Allan Ragland, as he's still in the cells, then on his way to court. You must be at least a bit curious as to who it is. I know I am.'

I weighed up what he was saying. Mac really shouldn't have given Wingsy the information he had, but, for a detective constable, the chance to watch the arrest of a burglar without being left with hours of paperwork was too tempting an opportunity to pass up. Even so, we'd have to write a statement and provide an innocent explanation as to why we were there in the first place.

Wingsy then said the words that were most likely to entice me me into trouble, whatever the outcome.

'Thing is,' he said twirling the phone cord in his fingers, 'we may well get Walter McRay's wife's wedding ring back.'

19

Unable to resist dropping in at the Magistrates' Court en route, we left feeling pleased, as Ragland's bail was refused by the Bench.

Cheered by this, we made our way to the Noël Coward estate. Wingsy and I discussed in which one of the shops in the parade we were least likely to appear conspicuous. I tried to persuade him to eat at the Golden Goose café. He shook his head from side to side for about thirty seconds at this suggestion.

'Are you having some sort of fit?' I asked, leaning across to steady the wheel.

'No. Mel's told me to cut down on fat and not to eat processed food. I had porridge for breakfast and that will see me through to lunch.'

'Don't talk crap,' I said. 'Porridge is processed.'

'No, it's not. It's a natural product.'

'Well, you don't have porridge fields or porridge trees, do you, so it must be processed. Have a fry-up and don't tell her.'

'She'll know and then there'll be hell to pay. It's just not worth it for a sausage.'

When I'd finished laughing at Wingsy's comment, he added, 'That was very childish. You know what I mean.'

'Yeah, I do know what you mean, and the real reason that Mel will know is that the last time we went for a late breakfast you dropped egg yolk on your navy tie and she didn't talk to you for three days.'

'That's true.' He pulled the car over around the corner from the shops and looked off into the distance as if mulling over good times. The corners of his eyes crinkled as he lost himself in the memory of his wife sending him to Coventry.

A short while later we were trying our best not to look like two detectives in the hardware shop opposite the gold shop. Wingsy got himself into a blokey conversation with the man in overalls behind the counter and they seemed to be comparing hammers. I found it most amusing, but played the part of the bored female in tow and spent most of the time looking out of the window at the gold shop.

I saw a couple of people come and go. The window gave me what all police officers were taught at training school to call 'a clear and unobstructed view' of the portly bloke in the shop across the street. He was behind the counter, weighing and pricing goods. Without thinking about it, I estimated the distance between me and the man I was watching, the amount of daylight, and any obstructions such as passing cars and pedestrians. I also made a note of the time I'd started to observe him. You didn't do this stuff for eighteen years without it becoming part of your waking thoughts, even if there was a hilarious conversation taking place feet from you about hollow wall anchors. For a moment I thought I'd misheard and it had turned nasty.

As it was getting to the point where we would soon have to leave the shop, following Wingsy's meagre purchase of gate hinges and brackets, I saw a male in a high-visibility jacket strut his way along the street as only those with a tiny IQ could. I liked to call it 'the geezer walk'. They looked ridiculous but were unlikely to ever find out, as those who recognised this particular gait as belonging to a moron didn't want their teeth knocked out for delivering constructive feedback.

The ringing of the cash register, a sound I hadn't heard for many a long year, signalled that Wingsy was finally finishing his transaction. I heard the rustle of the bag containing his purchase as he came up behind me. Leaning close to my ear, he said, 'Who's that? I recognise him.'

'Dunno,' I said, shaking my head. 'I can't say I know him, but he looks a likely candidate.'

The man in the high-vis jacket carried on walking past the gold shop, glancing in both directions as he did so. Continuing his bounce along the street, travelling from left to right from our point of view, he picked up speed. A small black Polo had parked about a hundred metres up the road ahead of him. Although I couldn't see anyone inside the car, as the man got to it, he opened the front passenger door, jumped in and the car made off at speed away from us. Neither Wingsy nor I were able to get a look at the driver or anyone else in it.

Turning to Wingsy, I kept my voice low, as the ironmonger was now wondering why after Wingsy's heady spend of £5.99, we hadn't left his shop.

'What do you think, mate?' I asked.

The sound of a police car with its siren blaring blocked out whatever his reply was. It came past us at an incredible speed, heading after the Polo. Curiosity getting the better of us both, we went outside to see whether the car making off had been stopped and what the outcome was. The ironmonger followed us and stood in the doorway, peering after the racing vehicles. I also noticed that the man from the gold shop had pressed his face up against his glass window. There were bars on the inside, presumably because Riverstone Council didn't want them on the outside ruining the 1960s concrete ambience. As the chubby shopkeeper squeezed his face close to the glass, I had visions of his head getting stuck between the bars.

Blue lights in the distance showed that the Polo had been stopped at an angle across the road, halting the traffic in both directions. This being an estate full of community-minded people, a small, curious crowd was already gathering. Wingsy and I headed towards our uniform colleagues in case they were in need of any assistance.

By the time we got to the assembled group, one man was handcuffed in the back of the police car, and one officer was searching the Polo while the other kept his eye on two other men who had jumped out of it and seemed to be doing their best to distract him. Wingsy and I made ourselves known and offered to lead one of the men away so he could search the other one unhindered. As luck would have it, he indicated that we take the strutter with the high-visibility jacket.

'What's this all about?' he shouted. 'I've not done fuck-all.' While he ranted, he started to put his hands into his pockets.

Wingsy and I moved as one to stop what he was about to do. We had no idea what was in his pockets. We didn't fancy finding out the violent or foolish way, either.

'Hold it there,' Wingsy said to him. Picking up on the conversation going on between our two colleagues, who were still within earshot, we got the gist of the reason for the stop-check. Strictly speaking, we weren't adhering to PACE – you weren't supposed to form the grounds for a search from a whispered conversation in the corridor with an old mate who was now in Intel, nor from a uniform patrol's conversation – but these two had been stopped by our uniform colleagues, not by us. At the end of the day, we knew our reasons, and our grounds – and we knew we had the public's best interests at heart, even though that hadn't ever been a part of PACE.

Our man in the reflective got louder and louder. This could be a sign that he had something to hide. But he might just be a dickhead. His friend, the driver, was keeping very quiet. Almost too quiet. Up until this point, I hadn't taken much notice of him. He was being given the same grounds as his more vocal friend while the PC went through his pockets. I tried to see what was happening. The other PC was looking in the boot of the Polo, Wingsy was turning out chopsy Hi-Vis's pockets, and the PC searching the driver only had one pair of eyes.

That was when I saw the driver's hand move towards the kerb. Roughly where the drain was.

I had to hand it to the PC searching the car, he must have caught a movement out of the corner of his eye. He moved faster than I had in months towards the outstretched hand. I caught a glint of gold. Within a second of the man's palm opening, the PC was underneath the falling items. The only way for him to stop them going down the drain was to throw himself to the ground over the opening. I also moved towards the drain and the officer on the ground, but he had it covered – literally.

We had both had the same thought but he was quicker than me. We both wanted to prevent the loss of someone's prized possessions. Prized possessions like Walter McRay's wife's wedding ring. That thought took the edge off the sharp pain shooting through my abdomen. I hadn't moved far and I was too slow, but it had been a sudden jerking action that had wrenched my insides.

A heavy bracelet hit the PC in the face, a pair of earrings bounced off his head and some sort of watch went straight over the top of his head. I thought he shouted something out, but it might just have been air being expelled from his mouth as he hit the ground. Within seconds, the sound of a woman saying, 'Did you see what he's done?' was almost drowned out by the noise of another patrol making its way on blues and twos towards us.

Some time later, the three in the Polo were under arrest, names and addresses taken from any witnesses willing to give them, and searches completed. Wingsy and I drove back to Riverstone police station to write up the necessary paperwork explaining how we happened to be in the area.

Once we got back to the station, we offered to book the suspected stolen items into the property store, then arranged for them to be photographed, for identification by burglary victims. The gold items were logged as yellow-coloured metal, the reason being that if the police took your jewellery from you, if it had been described as gold, then you should receive gold back. If it turned out not to be gold, the police could be sued. In any case the Rolex was our best bet: apart from having unique identification, it was likely to have fingerprints somewhere on it. The owner wasn't likely to be too pleased to find fingerprint powder all over it, but at least they might get their watch back.

When we returned to the Cold Case office to finish our statements, the room was deserted. Wingsy and I each sat at a computer in silence as the machines booted up. After a couple of minutes, Wingsy muttered something about a 999 call. He was staring intently at the screen showing his emails. He clicked on an attachment and the room was filled with the digital record of an emergency call: first the dialling, then the operator speaking to the caller, a voice of reassurance to a panicked person.

Operator: 'Police. What's the emergency?'
Male caller: 'Someone's been shot. They've been shot, twice. Oh, God...'
Operator: 'OK, sir. Where are you?'
Male caller: 'Outside Screwfix, London Road. Oh, God, oh, fuck.'
Operator: 'Who shot him? Are they still there?'
Male caller: 'I don't know. Oh, God, they're coming back.'

The sound of a gunshot reverberated through the cheap speaker system of the police computer. Then the line went dead.

Wingsy looked up at me. 'You alright, duchess? You look very pale.'

My throat was very dry and the room seemed to have got extremely warm. Thing was, I recognised the voice. I knew who had called the police and paramedics. The voice belonged to Richard, Annie Hudson's son. He'd been present when his own father was shot.

20

My friendship with Annie had far-reaching consequences. Now I had the information, my job
wouldn't allow me to ignore it. And attempted murder
was attempted murder at the end of the day. Richard knew
something about the shooting of his father and there was
no way that I wasn't going straight to the Incident Room
with the knowledge I had. I'd face the personal backlash
another time.

'Bloody hell, Wingsy,' I said, thumping my elbows on
the desk and putting my head in my hands.

'What's wrong?' he began. 'Do you know who that...'

He trailed off as the door opened and Jim appeared.

Wingsy was up and across the tiny room, blocking the
door, by the time I'd turned my head from one side of the
room to the other. 'Give us ten minutes, Jim, yeah?' he
said.

Jim's weasel face poked around the doorframe at me.
He looked momentarily puzzled, then nodded before
disappearing. I could hear him whistling tunelessly as he
slid off up the corridor.

'What's going on, Nin?' Wingsy took the chair opposite
me.

I cleared my throat and said, 'The male caller who
dialled three nines...' I sighed and then said, 'It was
Richard, Annie's son.'

Wingsy ran his right hand through his thinning grey hair and uttered only one word. 'Shit.'

'Suppose I'd better go and tell the DCI.' I stood up, hoping the action would energise me. It didn't. 'Annie's never going to talk to me again,' I said, feeling a little resentful towards my job.

Wingsy looked up at me. 'She may never find out.'

I appreciated the effort he was making to cheer me up but we both knew that was ridiculous. Richard had been present when his own father got shot, had called the police but fled before they arrived, and had failed to come forward and identify himself as being within earshot of the gunfire. Had he acted differently at the time, he might have been treated as a witness. Running made him look as though he had something to hide.

Steeling myself for the unpleasant task ahead, I walked to DCI Janice Freeman's office on the other side of the station. It was technically still the CID wing but, with Riverstone police station being an older building, it had add-ons and bolt-ons to the original building. The result was about eight staircases all over the building, some seeming to lead to empty corridors. The part of the station where Freeman had taken up temporary residence was located up from the conference room and across from the division's superintendent.

When I got to Freeman's office, I could see the back of the superintendent as he leant against the door jamb, talking to someone inside the room. I thought of warning her about getting grease from the hinges on her white shirt but, while I stood and waited for my presence to be acknowledged, I reckoned I had more important things to worry about.

The superintendent eventually turned to me and smiled. 'Hello, Nina,' she said. 'How's your first week back been?'

'Yeah, you know, ma'am,' I said, returning the smile, 'no peace for the wicked. I wanted a word with Mrs Freeman if she's in.'

A voice called out, 'Come in, Nina. I wanted to talk to you anyway.'

It was incredibly warm in the office, despite the tatty blinds swaying from the breeze of the draughty windows. The heating went on in October and it went off in May. Probably the equivalent of two full-time PCs' wages was leaking out of the building every year.

Freeman was sitting behind her desk. I moved towards her. She appeared friendly enough but there was a sharpness to her I found unsettling. She scrutinised me as I stepped across the uneven beige carpet. The station's floors had warped too over time. I came to a stop beside the vacant chair, waiting to be told to sit.

After a couple of seconds, she said, 'Sit down.'

Freeman wanted me to talk first. That suited me: I needed to get the information out there. I said, 'I've just heard the 999 call for the shooting of Patrick Hudson. The unidentified male caller is his son, Richard.' I could have left it there but I felt the need to be as detailed as I could. 'I've known Richard for a number of years and, although I only see him from time to time, I spoke to him a few months ago. It's him. It's definitely him.'

Discomfort oozed from my pores as I told her this. The more I rambled, the more my composure left me. All credit to her, she seemed to mellow towards me. She leaned across, face softening and said, 'That's what I wanted to tell you. This morning, Patrick Hudson died, and we arrested Richard for the murder of his father.'

21

'Who's with Annie?' I managed to say.

Freeman looked at me and tried her best to smile. 'We're looking after her and she has her sister staying. Patrick died in the early hours of this morning. We'll know more later from the hospital but there were unforeseen complications.' She paused before adding, 'I know that you're friends with Annie and, despite there being no love lost between you and Patrick, this must come as a shock to you.'

Freeman had got up and walked towards the hot drinks dispenser in the corner underneath a whiteboard with various operation names written on them in red. None of them meant anything to me. 'Tea?' she asked.

I really didn't want one but thought that, if she was offering me a drink, she was expecting me to stay and finish it. That might mean I would get some information from her, but it also could mean that she would get information from me. It was going to be a battle of wills and I wasn't sure I was up for it. Still, I rarely turned down a cup of tea. I nodded at her.

As she put the drink capsules into the machine, she began to explain that they had had little option but to arrest Richard.

'We had trouble locating Richard at first, but then we spoke to him at length after the shooting, while his father was still alive. Richard told us that he hadn't seen Patrick in years.' She came back to my seat with an instant tea and put it in front of me on the desk before sitting down again. 'We know that's not true from the prison records we have. There were a couple of other things, too.'

DCI Freeman looked down at her side of the desk as she reached for her cardboard cup.

'I can't discuss all the information with you. I know that you won't try to find out the extent of the evidence we currently have on Richard Hudson, but I do know that you and his mother go back a long way. I don't want her putting you under any pressure to pass information back to her.'

What I was being told was that I should stay away from Annie. I knew they couldn't force me to give my friend a wide berth in her hour of need, but life could be made fairly uncomfortable for me if I didn't co-operate.

'I get what you're saying, ma'am. Can the family liaison officer pass a message to her for me? I don't want her to think I've washed my hands of her.'

'Of course he can,' came the reply. 'It's Pierre Rainer. I'll get you his number.'

'No, no, that's fine,' I answered. 'I've got his number from my Operation Guard stint with Serious Crime. I'll give him a call.'

We nodded at each other and, leaving the rest of my tea, I left the office. At least I felt happier knowing that Annie was in good hands with Pierre. I'd truly hated Patrick Hudson but I felt a touch empty knowing he was dead. My concerns were with Annie. I smiled at the hell she was probably putting Pierre through, and went to the canteen to call him. It was always quiet there at this time of day, just after the midday rush and well before the mid-afternoon office workers' tea break. Squirrelling myself away in the farthest corner I could find, I called Pierre and hoped it wouldn't go to answerphone.

'Hello, Nina,' he said.

'Hi, Pierre,' I began. He knew why I was calling. Even though I'd never spoken to him about Annie, she would no doubt have told him that I was an old acquaintance and that I had kept in touch with her over the years. My visits to her had been a fortnight or so apart but I'd never totally abandoned her, just as my old friend Stan had never abandoned me.

'I'm at Annie's, Nina,' said Pierre. 'She's out in the kitchen so I may have to end the call. She's OK. I know that's why you're ringing. How are you?'

'Not so bad, ta, Pierre, but I'm not the one whose ex-husband's been murdered, possibly by their own son. This is a mess.'

'I know what you mean. The point is that she's convinced he didn't do it.'

There was a pause: Pierre was probably deciding how much more he could tell me.

'It's OK,' I said. 'I know you can't discuss the evidence you have against him, even if you weren't at the suspect's mum's house. But can you tell her that I'm thinking of her and… well, you're eloquent – make something up.'

I heard him chuckle as the sound of Annie's voice carried across the ether towards me. 'There you go, love. There's some Belgian chocolate ones there too. They're my Nina's favourite.'

Ordinarily, I'd have been put out that she'd given the best biscuits to Pierre when she never offered me any. Any feelings of annoyance, though, were squashed by her use of 'my Nina'.

22

The goings-on of the last couple of days had left me feeling exhausted. There seemed to be little I could do, or would be allowed to do, as far as Annie and Richard were concerned.

Making an effort to concentrate on something else, I thought of Joe Bring. He'd emailed me, somewhat weirdly, from prison and asked if I'd visit him. The irony was, if I wanted to talk to him officially, I'd have to fill in a form and get it signed by a detective inspector. For a fleeting moment I toyed with the idea of going to see him in a personal capacity instead, but I ruled that out as very dangerous: I was already friends with a murder victim's ex-wife, so visiting a burglar in prison was going to get me attention from those of rank, and the Professional Standards Department, for all the wrong reasons.

Lumbering my way back up to Cold Case, I passed the uniform sergeants' office. I thought I'd stick my head in on the off-chance that Bill was still at work. He was in the process of signing off duty, and seeing him brightened my day. I hoped that he wasn't still angry. I was all out of emotion.

'Hi, beautiful,' he said winking at me.

My heart lifted.

'You've had a long day,' I said. 'I'm already tired but you must be cream-crackered.'

'You could say that,' he said, turning off his Airwave radio and securing it in his locker. 'Two of my team have been asked to stay on and do scene preservation and house-to-house for a suspicious death. A young woman, aged in her twenties by all accounts, has just been found, overdosed on heroin. That's the third drug OD this month. They all seem to come from the Noël Coward estate, too.'

'Three?' I said. 'One was a friend of Joe Bring's son. I hadn't heard about the second one. Is there a CAD record of that and today's sus death being linked anywhere?'

'Probably there is, but you'll have to search for it yourself. I'm off to get some sleep. What time will you be in?'

'Not late. I'm going to look at this and then arrange to go back to prison to see Joe.'

Bill was giving me his most displeased look. It was the one he usually reserved for when he thought I should lay off the wine and put the kettle on. I gave him my look reserved for when I wasn't about to be given orders.

'OK.' He sighed. 'I'll see you at home.' Bag over his shoulder, he headed towards the exit.

When I got back to the Cold Case office, I began to scan the CAD reports for the initial calls from members of the public and police attendance to deaths from drug overdoses. The first one I found easily enough. Joe had told me that the boy's name was Daryl, so it was a simple task of searching for male juveniles called Daryl on the intelligence system. It only gave me three, and two of them were still very much alive. Daryl Hopkins was very much not. He was known to us for shoplifting at the age of ten and for public order offences at the age of fourteen. By the time he was eighteen, he had injected so much heroin into his system that he was dead.

I read the report over and over. Heroin was normally a drug used by older addicts, not teenagers. I was only reading through scant details, but something wasn't right.

Something had caught my eye on the first read-through but I couldn't put my finger on what it was. It crawled across my brain the entire time I sat looking at the CAD reports for other linked drug deaths. The one for today was still being updated as I was reading it. This gave me little in the way of usable information as it was such a work in progress: there wasn't, at this point, even a name for the victim; she was being referred to as 'unidentified white female'. I minimised the screen of live calls and continued to search historic ones for the last few weeks.

Finding the third drug-related death, I got to the part I wanted, which logged the caller and the information they'd given to the emergency services. An ambulance was requested by a man giving his name as Errol. Errol said that his friend had taken drugs and now wasn't breathing. As I scanned through the report, I saw that the unconscious friend was named as Sidney Manning, aged eighteen. But the part that reached out from the computer screen and grabbed my face, pulling it to within inches of the lettering, were the words typed on by the call-taker in police-speak: *Caller states that drugs were supplied by people known to the Rumblys.*

For a moment I wasn't able to move an inch. This had to be the link that would lead us to the Rumbly family. I didn't question for one minute that someone would have reviewed this call for further lines of enquiry and asked Errol to clarify and expand on what he'd said – I was looking forward to finding out his version of events.

As I continued to read, though, I realised that there was only one problem with that. Errol was dead.

23

Harry, my DS, came into the room while I was submerged in the CAD reports, picking my way through last month's calls relating to deaths of young people due to drug overdoses. He took a seat beside me as I continued to trawl through the information amassing on the screen.

'How's the historic train crash investigation going, Nina?' he asked, pointedly.

'Been looking at this,' I said.

'I can see that. Any particular reason you're not doing the job you're supposed to be doing?' he asked, rubbing the stubble on his chin with his hand.

'Yeah, Harry. Because I never do what I'm told to do. It's the wondrous unpredictability of me. Take a look at this.' I pointed at the screen to the call made by Errol at 18.56 on the twelfth of the month. 'When patrols and the ambulance were en route, Errol Chandler, the lad making the call, said that his mate was unconscious and had been sick. He was near to hysterics. When the patrol arrived at the same time as the ambulance at 19.02 hours, Errol was dead on the floor, shirt off on a particularly cold evening, having suffered a cardiac arrest.'

I turned in my seat to look at Harry and to tell him to stop rubbing his stubble. The noise was putting me off. His answer was, 'Stop moaning,' followed by, 'I remember this call being discussed at one of the morning meetings. There was a lot of confusion, as the kid we'd originally thought was going to die, Sidney Manning, was found unconscious but after a hospital stay he was discharged home to his parents. Errol Chandler, meanwhile, was dead on arrival in A&E.'

'But he'd been alive minutes earlier, shouting and swearing into the telephone. Doesn't that strike you as a bit odd?'

Harry began his chin-scratching again. I slapped his hand.

'Well, you've heard of Acute Behaviour Disturbance?' Harry asked.

I didn't have the foggiest what he was talking about but didn't want to admit it. I shifted my weight to the armrest furthest away from Harry and nodded as wisely as I could manage. 'Don't forget that I've been off for a while and clearly expect that, as my supervisor, you should fully appraise me of the situation.'

With a look full of malevolence, he said, 'Cut the management bullshit. There's enough of that from management. It's also called Excited Delirium. Basically, it's often mistaken for a violent person resisting arrest. The person has no control over themselves or their state of mind. Often the subject strikes out and just snaps. Some of the signs are that the person who's been bingeing on drugs is confused and disorientated. It's often associated with cocaine-users.'

I sat listening to what Harry told me. So much stuff was heaped on us daily in the form of emails and electronic updates covering things like changes in stop-searches, dealing with victims of sexual abuse, who was now in charge of maintenance and servicing for police vehicles, the latest booking-in procedure for property... and that was without keeping up-to-date with the local thieves and handlers. Although, in fairness, they didn't usually change too drastically. Half of it I never bothered to read. I didn't think I was alone, either. If you took the time to read everything that was expected of you, you'd never get any work done.

When he'd finished explaining, I thought it through. The paramedics had been summoned to a call from one man who had been swearing and abusive, so they'd called the police to make sure they weren't being left to face a violent junkie and his dead, overdosed mate. When they'd got there, the caller was already in cardiac arrest but his friend had been brought out of his heroin overdose by a shot of Naloxone.

'Am I right in thinking, Harry,' I asked, 'that Naloxone is personal issue for opiate users who are at the highest risk of overdosing?'

'Yep.' He nodded, putting his hand up to his chin. He put it back down again when I glared at it. 'It's prescription-only. It's mostly for those who've gone back to drug use after a period off the stuff and now have low tolerance.'

'But if it is personal issue, surely there'll be some sort of batch number on it, or identification linking it to the owner, like any other prescription?' Something most definitely didn't feel right about this.

'Dunno, Nin. If you want to know more, speak to Michaela Irving. She's the officer in the case for it.'

'Yeah, think I will. Thanks.' I locked the computer terminal and stood up.

'Er, I don't know where you think you're going but you haven't looked at the work you've been allocated all week. And I've had to give the house-to-house you left unfinished to someone else.'

'OK, Harry. I get it. You're my sergeant and, even though neither you nor I actually give a damn about doing what we've been told to do, as my supervisor this is you telling me that I'm behaving badly so that, if the proverbial hits the fan, you've given me a warning.' I gave him a smile that I really didn't mean and left the room to the sound of him shouting something about my staff appraisal being out of date.

I was hoping that Michaela Irving was going to shed some light on Errol Chandler's death and help remove the nagging doubt I was feeling about the whole thing.

24

Michaela was sitting in the Divisional CID Major Crime office. The idea behind the latest set-up of crime allocation was that the detectives in her office picked up the crimes in the local area that needed more time and investigation than a single robbery or GBH but not as much as a Category A murder. The crimes within their remit fell between the two, and Errol Chandler's supposedly accidental drug overdose was just such a crime. Even if it was thought to be non-suspicious and no one else was implicated in his death, that didn't mean an investigation wouldn't take place.

'Hi, Kayla,' I said, walking up to her across the empty office.

'Hi, Nin. I'm sorry I haven't come to say hello. I only got back from Northern Ireland a couple of days ago. How's it going?' She glanced in the direction of my stomach – I hoped because of the stabbing and not my weight gain.

'OK, ta. It's the usual happening: too much crime and not enough police to investigate it. You went home for a while, then?'

'Yeah, I saw the folks. Caught up with friends. They told me that I've lost my accent and to stop talking like a Londoner. Said I've gone soft.'

'Did you tell them that we can't understand you half the time?'

'Oh, aye.' She laughed. 'So what brings you to our office?'

I'd taken a seat beside her and was eyeing up a blue case file that was open in front of her. A mess of paperwork was strewn across the cheap wooden desk. I could recognise the Manual of Guidance forms at fifty paces, I clocked a couple of handwritten witness statements on the top.

Michaela tapped the statement on the top and blew out her cheeks. 'That one's from Errol Chandler's mam,' she said. 'When she last saw her son alive.'

I let out a sigh. Wordlessly we both focused on the sheets of paper, contemplating the words of a tortured mother attempting to express the feelings of every parent's living hell. Death engulfed like nothing else. To lose a child was beyond my comprehension.

But we had a job to do. We looked at each other as I said, 'I could do with your help if you have time.'

'Always time for you, Nin. I miss our time when we worked together. Great fun, it was.'

I wasn't sure which particular memory was making Michaela smile as much as she currently was, but I had dozens of my own. 'Are you talking about that call we went to for the man who hadn't been seen for a couple of days? His neighbours were worried and called the police?'

She threw her head back and shrieked. 'Aye, and when I looked through the letterbox he was wheeling himself down the hallway on a chair, dressing gown open and his bollocks out?'

'That's right,' I said, laughing. 'I was also thinking about the warrant we went on and you searched the bedroom but failed to spot the man asleep in the bed.'

'Well, it was five o'clock in the morning,' she said, chuckling subsiding. 'And we were looking for stolen car radios, not fellas fast asleep.'

'Just as well, as we'd have come back empty-handed. Anyway,' I continued, trying not to get off track as always with Michaela, 'there's something bothering me about the death of Errol Chandler, so I thought I'd ask you.'

She tilted her head to one side, shoulder-length brown hair framing her face as she raised an eyebrow and waited for me to explain.

'Right,' I said, looking towards the ceiling to avoid the intensity of her blue eyes, 'Errol called the ambulance service but, by the time they arrived barely a few minutes later, he'd suffered cardiac arrest and died. The other lad, Sidney Manning, had been unconscious but was given a shot of Naloxone by the attending paramedics...'

I'd trailed off to face the bold blue eyes. I could see her shaking her head at me as I spoke. Clearly, I had said something that wasn't true. It was my turn to raise an eyebrow at her.

Michaela held three sheets of paper up from the case file. Waving them at me, she said, 'The paramedic who attended states quite clearly here in his statement that, when he got there, the Naloxone had already been administered to Sidney. He couldn't risk giving him more, and the toxicology report for Sidney confirms that it was in his system before he arrived at A&E. Someone had already injected him with it before the emergency services arrived.'

Daytime television really had dulled my senses. I was struggling to understand what she was telling me. This must have been evident to Kayla but then again, we'd worked together on and off for so many years; she knew how slow I could be to catch on. She was nodding at me, coaxing the thoughts from me.

'So... someone *else* injected Sidney but we don't know who that someone was...' More nodding from across the desk. Encouraged, I forged on with my guesswork. 'Are we saying it was unlikely to have been Errol because of his own physical incapacity?'

'Aye,' said the ice-eyed detective. 'The Naloxone syringe and wrappings were sent for fingerprinting. They came back with a negative result. There wasn't one single fingerprint anywhere on it. If you were trying to save someone's life by administering a drug under obvious pressure, would you take the time to wipe your fingerprints from the bottle and wear gloves?'

'Only if I was hiding my presence at the scene of someone's death,' I answered.

'Or,' she added, 'if you were in some way responsible for that death.'

25

My mobile phone began to ring, dragging me away from Michaela and the unease I felt about Errol's death. I saw the word, 'Wingsy' on the display and gestured silent apologies to Kayla as I left her office and headed towards my own.

'What's up, Jug-ears?' I asked.

'Word of warning, Nin: Ian Hammond's been looking for you and wants to know how you're getting on with Joe Bring and your next prison visit.'

'Oh, bollocks. I'd forgotten about that halfwit.'

'When you say halfwit, are you talking about Ian Hammond or Joe Bring?'

'Yes,' I answered, taking the stairs towards the office. 'I honestly planned to set up another prison visit to Joe in the next couple of days.'

'Nin,' said Wingsy, 'are you walking up the stairs?'

'Yeah. How did you know?'

''Cos you're out of breath, love. You wanna lay off the Rioja.'

'Listen, Baldy, don't make any plans for the rest of the day. I've got some stuff I want to go over with you. I'll be back in the office in two minutes.'

When I got back to Cold Case, Jim had also reappeared and was on his phone shouting at someone in Forensic Science about an exhibit. I wasn't surprised to hear him say that it seemed to be a terrible line. Wingsy was trying hard to keep a straight face.

Rolling my eyes, I sat next to my friend and brought him up to speed with the conversation I'd had with Janice Freeman, and that I was to play no part in the investigation into Patrick's shooting.

'Listen to this, though, Wings,' I said, when I had exhausted the topic of Patrick Hudson. I shifted on my chair to get into a more comfortable position. Wingsy mirrored my movements. 'In the last few weeks in the division, there have been three fatal drug overdoses. The first was Joe Bring's son's mate, Daryl Hopkins, aged eighteen, the second was Errol Chandler, aged twenty-one, and the last one was discovered today. I haven't had much of a chance to look at that one but the CAD describes the victim as a young female, approximately twenty to twenty-five years old.'

'How exactly does this relate to Cold Case?' asked Wingsy, crossing his arms. This wasn't a movement I'd executed: we were clearly finished with the tandem body language. I got what he was saying without him having to put it into words – leave it alone. But it was like an itch that just had to be scratched, and I wasn't going to be happy until Wingsy was scratching too. My determination showed on my face.

Sighing, Wingsy resigned himself to helping me. From experience he knew that, if he didn't, I'd wear him down with my personality in the end.

'OK,' he said, 'I'll take a look through this lot, but you at least get on and book another visit to see Joe Bring while I get up to speed. The DI is going to do his nut if you don't sort it out.'

I pushed the paperwork from the three drug overdoses towards him and logged back on to the computer to fill out the paperwork to see Joe. When I'd finished filling in my application, I pressed the print button. No sooner had the form whirred out of the printer than DI Hammond came into the office.

Knowing full well that the form didn't show the time printed on it, I made out that I was looking through the paperwork on my desk for it. The DI stood for a moment or two, probably totally unconvinced by my amateur dramatics. While I searched, he asked, 'Do you think you're likely to get any more from Joe Bring? We're not getting any closer to arresting Leonard Rumbly for the murder of seven people so far.'

Glancing up from the *faux* forage, I saw that Ian Hammond's face was grey. I had put him in his early forties, but in the bright strip lighting of the office he looked nearer to fifty. This job did have a tendency to make people age faster than they should. Senior-ranking officers breathing down your neck for performance figures didn't help. My premature ageing was down to alcohol, late nights and a tendency to enjoy myself. Still, I did feel a bit sorry for DI Dandy. He was still wearing those bloody shiny cufflinks, though, and his tie had some sort of waving, smiling cat on the bottom. No doubt he found it amusing. I hoped I'd never get stuck in a lift with him.

'Dunno, boss,' I said, getting up and going to the printer. I felt a bit mean now, pretending I didn't know where the form was. I handed it to him for signing as I said, 'Not sure where else to go after nearly fifty years. Shall I start going through the list of passengers? I'm interested in speaking to those who made statements and gave accounts the first time around, but even more so in those who didn't for some reason.'

He handed the prison visit form back to me with his signature at the bottom and said, 'When you've finished reviewing the entire file, show Harry a list of actions you think necessary. Bring me the ones you consider a priority and we'll talk about what you can do. Perhaps Wingsy or Jim can help out on enquiries.'

'Jim's really busy,' Wingsy jumped in. 'I can probably help her for a day or two.'

'That sounds like a good idea,' said Hammond, already on his way towards the door. 'Run that by Harry and get him to come and see me when he gets back in the office.'

'Where is Harry? I only saw him a couple of hours ago,' I said when Hammond had gone.

'Some training session at Headquarters for something. Wasn't really paying attention,' said Wingsy. 'Tell you what has caught my attention, though, Nina – this CAD report you printed off.' He waved a sheet of paper at me. I'd highlighted the date and time of the call but that was about as far as I'd got. Wingsy, it seemed, had scrutinised it, and was about to impart some information to me.

'Well, go on, then,' I said. 'What have you found?'

'Only a vehicle that was seen by neighbours making off from the scene where Daryl Hopkins' body was found. It was a black Polo, and a bloke in a high-visibility reflective jacket was in the passenger seat.'

'Bloody hell, Wings. You think it's the same vehicle that was stopped on the Noël Coward estate by the gold shop?'

'Let's have a look at the ANPR and find out. It seems that we may have just discovered who sold the drugs to Luke Bring's recently departed friend.'

26

Despite knowing that those involved in burglary, theft and selling on a victim of crime's cherished possessions were often the same people as those responsible for dealing drugs, and keeping the suppliers' pockets lined, I still felt angry. But I had a job to do, so I got on with it.

It took some time to trawl through and find what we were looking for but, once we had the registration number of the Polo that the uniform patrol had stopped by the Noël Coward gold shop, we found out where else it had been over the last month. Despite the public's growing concern that there were too many CCTV cameras covering the entire country, they didn't always come up with any useful information. They also needed someone to look at the thousands of hours of footage. It was often a laborious task, picking out a grainy figure or car in the background, taking weeks or months, and I for one didn't have the patience for it.

Eventually, Wingsy shouted at me as I kept leaning across him and pressing buttons on the keyboard while he tried to print out the Polo's movements around the times of the three recent drug deaths. 'Nina, will you sod off and read through that train crash file? You're getting me down now.'

'Alright, misery guts – just for that, I'll stop helping you. When you've done, go and see Michaela. She's the

OIC. She'll be interested in that. Oh, and make sure that you put in an intelligence report on the vehicle.'

'Thank you, and I'll get some eggs to suck on my way back too.'

Wingsy got up from his chair, snatched the pages from the printer and left the office.

A snort from the corner of the room made me look over. I'd forgotten that Jim was still in the office.

'Lovers' tiff, you two?' he wheezed.

I chose to ignore him. Instead, I turned my attention to the file. I couldn't keep putting it off, and I had to have something to ask Joe Bring about, as well as to show Harry on his return.

I had previously run an eye over the entire file and had taken a fair amount of detail on board. Grabbing a new investigator's notebook, I began to make a list of the enquiries I thought might lead somewhere. This included a list of all those who had been interviewed the first time around, and those whose details had been taken but no further account elicited from them. I was so engrossed in the task, I didn't look up as Jim left the room. I leafed through the handwritten pages of officers' reports from those on duty, duty statements from officers attending the scene, and the handful of witness statements.

The handwritten notes of a contemporary interview with Malcolm Bring, Joe's father, were in among the yellowing pages. He seemed to have been asked a number of questions during an interview but there was no record of his having been arrested. Over the years, older colleagues, some now retired, had regaled me with tales of their arrests and interviews pre-PACE. I had never fully believed all the stories I'd been told about what went on in the old days when a police officer was unconstrained by the 1984 Police and Criminal Evidence Act. Some seemed to thrive on embellishing their stories, but no doubt some of those stories had substance. I made a note to check the Police National Database for any other arrests of Malcolm Bring after the crash.

My attention span not being what it once was, I was beginning to lose interest and fantasise about a chicken salad sandwich, when the words I had just read clanged together in my mind. I might be hungry, but I needed to take stock of what I'd been reading and slot a couple of things into place.

According to what Joe Bring had told me, there had been three football players on the train. The file contained a list of passengers with their details next to them, including occupation. Scouring the pages for details of those Leonard Rumbly meant to disrupt, I found the names Jimmy Crow, Charles Fitzhubert and Thomas Ross on the list, all with the words 'footballer' next to them. Crow and Fitzhubert had supplied statements to the police, but Thomas Ross had not. While I couldn't rule out that it had merely been an oversight or that the statement had been lost during the last fifty years, I could find no mention of it anywhere in the file.

Sometimes, it wasn't what you had in an investigation or what someone told you, it was what you didn't have, and what someone had chosen to leave out. Thomas Ross was now at the top of my list of people to visit.

I continued to trawl through the file, making notes, photocopying some of the pages and highlighting the salient points and areas I wanted to check. The next hour passed quickly enough as I read and reread the file, still wondering where the fruit and veg had gone and adding to the list of enquiries I'd drawn up for Harry. I drew up the list of people to see, placing Thomas Ross very much at the top, underlined and in bold.

Then I did the obvious thing and went online to look up Thomas Ross. It seemed that in the last twenty years the footballer had slipped from the public eye. Yes, he was getting on a bit now, but, even so, little had been seen or heard from him since his wife, Shona, had been hit by a car in 1989, leaving her paralysed and needing twenty-four-hour care. This, unsurprisingly, had eaten up all of his time and most of his money. He had left behind a football career, radio commentating and later television presenting to look after his wife. After some more searching, I found that Shona Ross had died three months ago.

Here was a man who at first appeared to have had it all. He had been a first-class footballer in the early 1960s, with high hopes of playing in the 1966 World Cup. Every English person knew the ending to that one – even someone like me with a feeling of total indifference to football – and I wondered if Ross had ever got over the disappointment of not being selected that year. Still, it was a long time ago. Perhaps he was over it now.

Next on my list, after Thomas Ross, was Jimmy Crow, then Charles Fitzhubert. Something struck me as very odd, though, as I started making notes about where each passenger was at the time of the crash: the three of them hadn't been sitting together. Fitzhubert and Crow were in their allocated part of the train, but Ross was not only sitting apart from his team mates, he was also four carriages further away from the point of impact when the crash happened. This was recorded in notes scribbled by a long-dead police officer who was one of the first on the scene. My mind ran amok with a conspiracy theory as to why Ross was so far down the back of the train. I gave the train's plans the once-over and my terribly suspicious mind came up with a very prosaic probable reason – the nearest toilets were towards the rear of the train.

Slightly defeated, I carried on working my way through the mass of paperwork, engrossed in its detail until Wingsy's return. 'Think I'm getting somewhere, Baldy,' I said as he came back into the office. He walked behind my chair and leaned over me to read the now lengthy list I had spent some time compiling.

'You're gonna have to be bloody good to speak to Crow,' he said. 'He's dead.'

'Oh, for heaven's sake,' I said, throwing my pen down. 'That's annoyed me. And you've had cheese and onion crisps. I can smell them on your breath. You didn't bring me any?'

'No, I didn't, and yes, he's dead. Don't you read the newspapers?'

'Not the part where it lists dead footballers, I don't. Right, I'm going to get some food. I was only waiting for you to come back. Thanks very much.'

I was annoyed that Wingsy hadn't brought me a snack but I also knew that I was, once again, being very childish. My stomach was hurting and I had a headache but I had been determined not to show weakness and go home. Besides, Bill would be at home. I decided to give the crisps a miss as it was late on Friday afternoon and I had a weekend of arguing with my boyfriend to look forward to. Before I left, I quickly cobbled together a plan for the following week's enquiries that I could go over with Harry on Monday morning, in preparation for throwing myself into my job. There was also the small matter of visiting Joe again. That was bound to be entertaining. I had managed to arrange that for Tuesday.

Logging off the computer, I gathered my belongings, signed out in the diary and made for Bill's house, thinking positive thoughts all the way.

27

Just as I thought we were about to get through our Friday evening without a cross word, Bill dropped a bombshell.

'Your mum called earlier,' he said from the safety of the armchair farthest away.

'Oh, yeah?' I answered, my grip on my wine glass tightening. 'Everything alright?'

'Completely alright.' Bill gave the nervous little throat-clearing cough which always gave him away. 'She invited us round for dinner tomorrow. I've said we'd be there.'

'You did, did you?' I said, wildly searching out the wine. He was across the room, filling my glass before I'd even located the bottle. I could fill my own bloody glass, I wanted to say, but accepted the refill nonetheless.

As he backed away, looking like an over-attentive waiter, Bill held the wine bottle as if he was offering it to me for my approval. The fact that it was now only a third full should have given him some sort of an idea.

'I told your mum we'd be there at six o'clock.' He studied the label on the bottle as he spoke to me. 'Said that we probably wouldn't stay long either. You get tired easily.'

'I get tired easily, do I?' This was incredible. Now he was telling me when I got tired. I was about to start a row when I yawned, and that spared us both from another barney about nothing. I did the decent thing and went to bed. It would appear that my Saturday was going to be an emotional one.

I got ready for dinner at my parents' with the usual feelings of dread and regret. It was always tense when we all got together, probably made all the more so by everyone expecting an atmosphere. This particular evening started amicably enough with a pre-dinner drink and small talk about the weather before we moved on to the subject of mortgage rates. My stomach lurched at the mention of money. I knew what was coming.

At the top of the table, my dad sat helping himself to green beans while my mum unfolded her napkin, smoothing it over her lap.

'Things are getting more and more expensive for us,' sighed my dad, heaping vegetables on to his plate. 'I'm not too sure how we'll pay the mortgage this month.'

My mum continued to smooth the napkin. I sipped my wine, looking at the top of my dad's bald head as he shook it. Out of the corner of my eye, I could tell that my mum had looked up at me but was still needlessly brushing her lap.

For thirty-eight years I'd played this game with them. My part in it was to feel as guilty as possible, but recently the rules had altered. I thought it only fair to tell them of the latest change in my status.

I took a deep breath.

'Me too,' I said, looking my mum straight in the eye. She looked back at her lap. 'I don't know how I'm going to pay *my* mortgage. I've not earned any overtime for several months. I can't pay my bills.'

My mum stood up, letting her serviette fall to the floor. 'Forgot the mustard,' she mumbled, leaving the dining room to rifle around in the kitchen cupboards for a condiment no one wanted.

'You've upset your mum now,' said my dad, moving on to the carrots. 'We can't look after your sister on our own all the time, you know that. We love that your sister still lives here but we need help – and we need a break sometimes. I know we get some help, but decent private carers and homes cost money.'

I knew this only too well, and one of the reasons I had never begrudged the money was because Sara did so well from a respite stay in the clinic. My sister didn't require long-term residential care but, at a cost to my parents – or, in fact, me – she went there from time to time for a long weekend, like this one. It was a nice enough place with cheerful staff, but it was a care home, with patients who had a wide range of mental health issues. However, it always seemed to do her good and meant that she coped a little better with day-to-day tasks. I gained too, as I much preferred seeing her away from our parents. They meant well, but my mum fussed, and I always thought that my sister would have improved quicker if my mum didn't try to do everything for her.

I bit my lip and said nothing in reply. I'd tried to tell them I was broke but they hadn't listened. I wasn't up to this. I needed time to get better before I could face another onslaught.

'It could easily be your sister sat there and you in her place,' said my dad. 'Do you ever stop to think about that?'

Of course I do, I wanted to scream. The only positive aspect of anyone asking me that question was that it showed I masked my feelings better than I thought possible. But then that made me appear selfish. I would never win. Never.

I couldn't afford to tell the world that not a day went by when I wasn't grateful it was her and not me. I battled every day with what a terrible person it made me, but I liked being a grown woman with a career, boyfriend, my own home. I didn't want to swap places with a forty-six-year-old woman who couldn't fully grasp that she was no longer a child.

The first time I'd admitted this to myself, I'd felt a relief I hadn't imagined possible. I rarely said Sara's name and I only had one photograph of her, and that was taken when we were both children. If I didn't look at her every day, I could picture how things might have been.

At some point Bill was bound to say something. It was the whole reason he'd arranged this hideous evening. He'd thought, the poor misguided fool, that he was doing me a favour by trying to clear the air, and I supposed he'd had the crazy notion that I would rock up and tell my parents that the gravy train was on the last leg of its journey. My parents, however, thought that Bill was their saviour and was about to add some first-class carriages to the locomotive. They saw his arrival in my life as one of financial benefit to them both.

I wasn't conjuring up these feelings from spite; they had form for it. The only lasting relationship I'd managed in the last ten years had been with the store manager of a national supermarket chain. On the second occasion Marcus met my parents, my dad asked him for a loan. The embarrassment was too much for both of us and we split up shortly afterwards. Facing facts, though, the relationship hadn't really been going anywhere, so I couldn't entirely blame my parents for the break-up. And I still bumped into him from time to time when I was shopping. I needed to buy food, and he managed a shop which catered for such needs. Now he was married with a toddler and another on the way. Life had worked out pretty well for him. What had become glaringly obvious in the last ten minutes was that, despite my grumblings about Bill's over-attentiveness, kindness and other annoying tendencies, I wasn't about to lose him as easily as I had Marcus. So, whatever Bill was about to say, I was going to back him all the way.

'The thing is, Derek,' said Bill to my dad, 'Nina doesn't have that kind of money any more. Police officers, like lots of other people, have had a three-year pay freeze. The cost of living has gone up. Most people are struggling to pay their bills.'

I could have said that, but it would have fallen on deaf ears. My mum came back in with the mustard, sniffing into a tissue.

'Have you thought of getting a job, Sue?' said Bill.

No one moved. No one said a word. I'm not sure if anyone even breathed.

At last my mum spoke. 'You know I'd love to get a job.' She sounded almost convincing. 'But I have to look after Sara. Who else is going to do it?' She turned to me, glowering, then she sat back down, unscrewed the mustard jar and passed it to me. I ignored her. I was over forty years old and had never liked mustard. Would she ever take any notice of anything I did?

Bill was sitting opposite me. His mouth was hanging slightly open. In spite of everything, he carried on cutting up his chicken pie. My dad was managing to eat his dinner without too much putting him off, either. I'd picked at some of mine but I had no appetite.

Just when I thought the atmosphere couldn't get any worse, though, I was about to be stunned all over again.

'I suppose Stan McGuire put you up to this,' huffed my mum.

I rarely used Stan's name around my mum and she avoided it at all costs. Anyone would have thought that the man who had rescued her two children from certain death decades ago would have held some kind of deity status in her home and heart. Instead, she seemed to feel nothing but contempt for the retired detective chief inspector whom I had always looked up to and idolised. I put my mum's attitude towards him down to a very childish jealousy.

I bristled at her use of his name but made no comment.

'He wasn't happy enough with finding you and Sara and getting himself promoted from the glory. Oh, no – he wanted you to go and live with him and his wife, too.' I spun in my seat and looked round at her. She was picking over her food, head on one side. 'Oh, yeah,' she continued, 'wanted you to move in, he did. I must have told you that.'

She knew full well that she had never told me anything of the sort. I sat dumbstruck. I struggled for something to say. Her words had ambushed my world, though I recognised them for what they were: she was being spiteful. Things weren't going her way and so she was trying to make me feel bad for being alive and healthy.

I put my fork down and said, in a voice barely above a whisper, 'Bill, I'm very tired. Can you take me home, please?'

A noise very much like a humph came from my mum as she stabbed at her food. My dad continued to shovel his meal into his mouth as if nothing had happened.

As Bill and I got up from the table, it seemed to jolt my mum from the carrot-impaling taking place on her plate. She looked up at me from under her blonde fringe. 'You've not finished your dinner,' she said. 'It's typical of you to make a fuss and storm out.'

'Goodnight, Mum. Goodnight, Dad,' I said. I wasn't

going to give her the satisfaction of a row. Over the years, they'd led nowhere. I followed Bill from the dining room to the kitchen where we'd left our coats. He held mine out for me and I pulled it around me to fasten the buttons. He wrapped his arms around me and kissed the top of my head.

I only heard him say the one word: 'Sorry.'

28

The rest of the weekend held no joy for me. I knew that the courageous thing to do would be to call Stan and get to the bottom of it. He wouldn't lie to me; I'd been certain of only a handful of things in my life and Stan's loyalty to me was one of them. What was bothering me was my mum's attitude. Even after all this time, she hadn't forgiven me for coming out of it all apparently unscathed. Some wounds were invisible and I'd gone to great lengths to keep them that way, primarily where my own family were concerned. But, even more, I was worried about facing Stan in case he told me that my mum had been telling the truth and he had wanted me to live with him and Angela.

My mum could be spiteful but she didn't usually lie. Even the spitefulness I put down to frustration at how her life had turned out. She had probably pictured herself as a doting grandmother by this stage in her life. Not for one moment did I expect she had foreseen that her sixties would be spent taking better care of my sister than she had when we were children, with her only break coming when Sara stayed at the clinic.

The thought of Stan and his wife wanting me to live in their home was crushing me in a way I had never thought possible. I had carried guilt around with me for longer than I ever could recall. Trying to remember any other emotion before the shame wrapped itself around me was all but impossible. Now I was covered in a new blanket of horror – regret that it hadn't happened.

Never had one word been uttered about this in all the time I'd known my friend. In thirty-eight years, during all of the meals, drinks and chats we'd shared together, he hadn't mentioned one word of it. I trusted Stan with my life. Well, if someone saved your life, I supposed that was only to be expected.

I went home with Bill and wouldn't discuss my mum's revelation. I would talk to Stan about it, but not tonight.

I would only ever admit to myself that my real reason for not wanting to face Stan was because it had made me feel so sad to think it might have been true and that I'd missed out on a whole better life. The thought of Stan looking after me as his own daughter showed me a new world of lost opportunities – feelings of loss I knew I'd never shake. I had kept secrets for decades. One more wouldn't matter.

My Sunday was spent sleeping, reading, watching television and catching up with anything and everything to avoid making any decisions or confronting any issues. I felt more tired than I had in a long time.

29

Monday morning saw me ready to return to work, glad of the distraction from my private life.

When I got to the Cold Case office, Harry was already busy at a terminal compiling overtime and staffing figures for a meeting to justify Cold Case's existence. Wingsy walked in seconds after me, while those about to go off to Crown Court were busy discussing the jury's imminent return with the Barry Oakes verdict.

'Morning, Nina,' said Harry from his side of the office. 'Managed to come up with a priority for the train crash? And by the way, you look dreadful.'

'Thanks, Harry,' I said, peering around my computer screen at him. 'Yes, I have. I'd like to visit Thomas Ross. He lives in West Sussex. I've got an address for him from the Voters' Register, but no phone number. I was planning on going this morning. Can I see if Baldy's free to come with me?'

'Yeah, you can. Leave me the address and call me later if he has much to say.' Harry returned to compiling a list of how the budget had been spent so that he could go fully prepared to the morning meeting where a senior officer would ask him why he couldn't release some of his staff to other areas of police business. Knowing him of old, he would fight for his staff and return in a foul mood. I'd been a police officer long enough to know that it was a good idea to keep out of the way of anyone attending such a meeting, to give them a reasonable cooling-off period. I figured that a trip to Sussex and back should be plenty of time for my detective sergeant to calm down.

I looked expectantly at Wingsy and gave him my best Monday morning smile.

'I'll make the tea; you sort out a vehicle and we'll head off,' said my companion for the day. 'I've got a sat nav as well.'

I busied myself getting the paperwork and travel logistics sorted. As we were about to leave, Wingsy said, 'I'll see you in the car. I've got to get my packed lunch salad out of the fridge.'

'Packed lunch salad?' I asked. 'You are some sort of super-tart. I was hoping that we could find a café or sandwich shop.'

Wingsy looked at my stomach.

'What?' I said before I could stop myself.

'It's up to you what you eat, Nina, but I've got enough salad for two.'

'Then it's not really a salad, is it? A whole lettuce and a pound of tomatoes aren't enough to see someone through the day. I'll see you in the car park.'

I flounced off down the stairs in the direction of the back yard, arms full of paperwork, checking the key fob for the vehicle registration. At the entrance to the patrol wing which led to the car park, I almost collided with Pierre Rainer coming through the door. He was flicking through his family liaison officer's log book as he walked.

'Hi, Nina,' he said, voice full of cheer.

'Hi, Pierre,' I answered. 'How's Annie?' As I uttered these words, I remembered that I hadn't thought to check with anyone how Richard was. Annie's son had been arrested for the murder of his own dad and I'd been so wrapped up in myself, I hadn't even thought to ask after him. I was a terrible friend.

Carrying out mental PACE arithmetic, I worked out that if Richard had been arrested on Friday and was still in custody without charge, he would either have been taken to the Magistrates' Court for a Warrant of Further Detention at some point over the weekend, or released on bail. I should at least have found out whether he'd been charged or not.

'Annie's doing OK,' said Pierre. 'She's pleased to have Richard home.'

'When was he released?' I asked.

'Early Saturday evening, a couple of hours into the superintendent's twelve-hour extension. I didn't interview him, but I do know that he answered all questions. He said he went to see his dad in prison to warn him to stay away from Annie once he got out. He also said he was there when his dad was shot because he was making sure Patrick kept his word and steered clear. There wasn't enough to charge him, but it may be a different story when he returns on bail.'

It might have been my imagination, but Pierre seemed to remember who he was talking to. He glanced at his watch. 'Look, I've got to go,' he said as he began to walk away. 'I'll let Annie know you were asking after her.'

'OK, thanks,' I said, making towards daylight. 'Tell her I'll be in touch soon.'

I headed across the yard to the unmarked police car I'd managed to get my hands on for the day's enquiries. As I loaded the stuff into it, I wondered what exactly I would be saying to Annie when I saw her next. I had the same amount of enthusiasm for facing her as I did for facing Stan. Fortunately, I had a drive of over a hundred miles each way to work out what I was going to do.

Wingsy's swearing interrupted my reverie as he made his way towards me, dropping his Tupperware box of salad as he tried to hold on to everything he was carrying. The lunch box hit the floor, the lid came loose and the adjacent parking bay was adorned with cucumber and radishes. As if the sight of Wingsy's healthy meal on the tarmac wasn't funny enough, the look on his face made me hold on to my sides as I hooted with laughter. He looked furious but I couldn't help myself.

When I'd finished laughing, I carried on giving the vehicle a quick check-over for faults: cracked glass, low tyre pressure... All of our police vehicles were supposed to be checked every Monday morning. I hadn't bothered for months before my time off, and probably wouldn't have taken the trouble now, had it not been for wanting to give Wingsy time to calm down after decorating the car park with his lunch. I knew that he'd sulk for a bit but then cheer up. Especially now I was going to be able to justify stopping for a pub lunch somewhere.

'Ready, mate?' I asked, pretending to check the vehicle's oil.

'You didn't even wipe the dipstick when you checked that then,' he said, leaning against the side of the car.

'That's because I don't have anything handy to clean it with,' I answered him. 'Unless you've got a spare lettuce leaf I can use?'

'Can we get going, if you've finished taking the piss?'

At least he was laughing as he said it.

I drove as Wingsy put the destination into the sat nav. As we settled into the journey ahead, we began with our usual ramblings about nothing. He told me how Mel, his wife, was on at him to decorate the house but wanted to move closer to her parents so what was the point? I told him about Bill and my visit to my parents over the weekend, leaving out the details of the row; I told him it was about money and left it there. Our journey was uneventful and we made good time on the way there. When the sat nav told us that we had fifteen miles to go, I gave Wingsy a bit of a run-down on what I was going to ask Thomas Ross.

'He was on the train but he should have been sitting in the carriage with the other two players. For some reason he was four carriages away from them. Which was also four carriages further away from the impact of the train hitting Malcolm Bring's lorry.'

Wingsy shifted in his seat to look at me. 'So, do you think that he knew the train was going to collide with something? That's why he moved further down the train?'

'It could have been,' I answered. 'He also may just have wanted a wee. The toilets were towards the back of the train.'

'What's your plan, Nin?'

'Thought I'd go for a very general who I am, what the purpose is and that there is new evidence being investigated. Strictly speaking, that's true, although it's currently in the guise of Joe Bring and his dead father.'

'I know a bit about Tommy Ross,' said Wingsy. 'He played for the equivalent of today's Premier League sides and was tipped to play for England in the '66 World Cup. Due to injury, he didn't play for a time before the squad was picked – that was why he didn't get to represent his country in 1966. He wasn't thought to be fit enough. That, and the corruption charges.'

'Corruption?' This I hadn't expected.

'Good lord, Foster. Are you telling me that you didn't know about his convictions? How much research did you do on this fella?'

'About as much as a detective would deem necessary to visit a seventy-three-year-old former professional footballer who was an innocent member of the public back in 1964 when the train he was travelling on crashed.'

'Well, I'd tell you all about it now,' said Wingsy, 'but, knowing your attention span, especially if the topic is sport-related, I'll let Ross tell you and fill in anything he leaves out.'

The sat nav saved us from further bickering by telling us that we were metres from our destination. The road we were travelling along was wooded on both sides and we hadn't seen a building since turning into it.

Seconds away from accusing Wingsy of inputting the wrong post code, I bit my tongue when I saw a partly hidden entrance on the right. Large black iron gates were open on to a driveway, a plaque on them showing the property's name as 'Five Wents'. The trees hanging over either side obscured the house I presumed I was driving us towards.

Five Wents was remarkable in that it was unremarkable. I hadn't known whether Thomas Ross was going to live in a flashy house or a modest home, because of the more moderate earnings of footballers in the 1960s. Ross had subsequently enjoyed a career on radio and television but, again, it was difficult to gauge how well he had done from it. The large house was set back from the road along a driveway. All the windows were closed and, despite the lateness of the morning, the curtains in the bedroom windows were still shut. That struck me as a bit odd: who was Thomas Ross trying to stop from peeking inside? There wasn't another building in sight, and no one was likely to be passing by.

I pulled up outside the house, facing the car towards the exit – just in case – and we walked to the front door.

I hoped Thomas Ross was at home, since we had come all this way. I had no idea if he'd be surprised to see two police officers at his front door to talk about a historic accident or pleased with the company, living as he did in the back end of nowhere.

There was only one way to find out. I rang the doorbell.

30

We stood on the doorstep for less than thirty seconds before Wingsy said, 'I'll go round the back.' Police officers were seldom patient people.

Despite the huge iron gates to the driveway, security was most definitely not Thomas Ross's highest priority. There were no fences or gates encircling the house itself, allowing Wingsy and me to walk around it. An enormous conservatory at the back of the house faced an overgrown garden. As we approached the door, I saw that it was ajar and someone was sitting in the conservatory. I could make out the outline of a man, hunched at a table, a drink held to his mouth.

He looked in our direction, having spotted us perhaps in his peripheral vision as we made our way across his garden. Warrant cards in hand, Wingsy and I stood outside the conservatory waiting for him to get up.

'Mr Thomas Ross?' I asked as he came to the door. The images on the internet I had seen of him portrayed him as a dark-haired, carefree young athlete with his entire life ahead of him. Time had savaged him. His hair was almost entirely white, his eyes were bloodshot and his cheeks and nose were covered in small red veins. I was looking at a very heavy drinker. If I'd been in any doubt, a faint whiff of morning-after alcohol wafted my way from the former footballer. The man who might once have played for his country in England's only World Cup victory liked a drink or two.

'We're police officers, but please don't be alarmed,' I told him. 'We're here in relation to a very old matter.' This explanation was something I always used for non-emergencies. During my years of policing, I had never got used to the look of horror and dread worn by every law-abiding person I'd visited at home, on production of my warrant card and introduction. Parents immediately thought the worst for their children, partners and spouses worried for their other half's safety, and those with loved ones of any description dreaded what they were about to be told.

But Thomas Ross had already lost everything. I couldn't have brought anything to his door that hadn't already chipped away at his heart.

Introductions made, I shook his hand. I couldn't fail to notice a slight shake as he took mine. He led us into his kitchen. I glanced at the calendar on the wall next to the fridge. He had two hospital appointments in the next two weeks, and a letter from his doctor's surgery was stuck to the fridge with a magnet.

Leading us from the kitchen to the front room, Ross turned and said, 'Sorry, I wasn't expecting company. I haven't cleared up yet.' He went over to the window and drew the curtains, flooding the room with light. The room was cluttered with papers, empty bottles and dirty glasses. I had been in much more untidy houses but there was something very depressing about the room. I put it down to his lack of caring rather than a choice to live with so little joy in his life. Thomas Ross seemed to have given up on himself, and everything else along with it.

'Please, sit down,' he said, smiling and gesturing at the large sofa. It was covered in dog hair but no other traces of a pet were obvious in the house. It was a neglected home.

'Is there anyone else living here, Mr Ross?' Wingsy asked.

'No, there's not,' came the reply, with a slow shake of his head. 'My wife died recently.' He looked down at an empty whisky bottle as he said this. 'The dog died the same week.' Thomas Ross gave a dry laugh. 'Sounds like a blues song, doesn't it?'

I smiled politely, although I found nothing funny about this man's misery.

'This may not be the best time for us to spring this visit on you and ask about this, so we can come back another time, Mr Ross.' I said. I studied his face as I spoke. He oozed sadness from every pore, as well as forty per cent proof spirits, but his face was open and friendly, waiting for my explanation.

'New information has come to light about the 1964 Wickerstead Valley train accident,' I explained.

The muscles in his face tightened. It was a flash tensing of his jaw. Thomas Ross started to grind his teeth. I had expected him to say something obvious such as, 'Haven't thought about that in years.'

The words that did pour forth were not the ones I could have predicted.

'That bloody train crash was no accident,' he said, sinking down into an armchair, head bowed. 'My life started to go downhill from the day of the crash. Everything went to shit afterwards. I had it all – a great career, a reputation – but I threw it all away. I was greedy and weak. Now I have nothing. My wife's gone...' He trailed off, wiping a tear spilling from the corner of his eye.

He threw himself back in the armchair, sending a small dust cloud up into the air. He sighed and then, staring straight at me, said, 'A few months ago I wouldn't have told you this, but I've nothing to lose now. It's all gone. I'm not even sure if he's still alive, but I'll do what I can to help. I have to make amends somehow.'

I thought I'd missed something. Feeling myself frowning, I asked, 'If who's still alive?'

'The man responsible for the crash,' he said. 'Rumbly – Leonard Rumbly. He organised the train crash.'

31

For several seconds, I sat motionless. I was completely dumbstruck. Nothing was ever this easy in life. Certainly not in police work. A straightforward enquiry into what Thomas Ross had seen or heard on the train when it crashed, and why he hadn't made a statement at the time, was about as much as I could have hoped for.

'Leonard Rumbly?' said Wingsy. 'You're sure about that, Mr Ross?'

'Oh, yes. He can't hurt my wife or me any more. If he's still alive, he needs to face what he's done. He should be held to account. I avoided speaking to the police at the time by making out I was too badly injured and couldn't remember anything. No one questioned it. Now I know I need to make up for it... What do you need me to do?' Ross glanced from Wingsy to me and back again, a look of peace taking over his features. 'You'll have to be quick, though,' he said, nodding along at us.

I glanced at my watch and was about to suggest that we come back another time when he interrupted.

'No, no,' he said. 'The time of day isn't important. I have cirrhosis of the liver. I'm running out of time.'

'What can they do for you?' I asked, as tactfully as I could manage.

'Not much.' He shrugged. 'If my wife was still here I might have had treatment, but I've drunk myself to death.'

His honesty was uncomfortable. He was torturing himself on a daily basis and now he was paying the price he felt was appropriate for whatever he had done in his past.

'She was in a wheelchair, you see.' Ross smiled at me. 'She never blamed me, either.' He put a shaky hand up to his forehead, rubbing his brow, I thought to shield his waterlogged eyes.

I had read on the internet about his wife, Shona, being knocked over on a quiet country road on her way home one day from a local stables. I had a sinking sense of dread that he was about to confess to trying to kill his own wife twenty-five years ago.

'I was supposed to pick her up from her riding lesson but I got held up in the pub. This was well before every man and his wife had a mobile phone, so she started walking. Unlit country roads, no footpaths. She didn't stand a chance. It was amazing she didn't die. There were probably days when she wished she had, but she never gave up hope. She was a remarkable woman, in spite of what I put her through.'

Wingsy asked the question I was trying to formulate in my head.

'Did the police catch the driver?'

'Depends how you look at it,' Thomas said. 'They made an arrest. Problem was, he had an alibi. Shona was certain that the man driving the car that hit her was Andy Rumbly – Leonard Rumbly's son. But the police never found the car, and a friend of his said he was at a restaurant in Oxford at the time.'

'How well did she know Andy and Leonard Rumbly?' I asked.

'Well enough to name him. He'd been here on a couple of occasions. I'll have to tell you the story from start to finish. It's not a pleasant one, but it starts well.'

Thomas Ross got up from the armchair and went towards a large wooden display cabinet. The upper, shelved part of the unit was full of trophies and football memorabilia. He opened the door on the lower left-hand side and took out a photo album. It was a black hardback album filled with pages of stiff black card. He handed me the book, and the scent of nostalgia wafted towards me. There was something about old photo albums bursting at the sides with black and white snaps, held in place at their corners by white picture mounts, that I found deeply comforting. Perhaps it was all the years I'd listened to an older generation tell me about how wonderful their youth had been and how the world had degenerated since their heyday. Seeing a better, lost world in tangible form gave me a longing for a time of innocence. Until I remembered that this was a generation getting over a world war. Innocence had long since lost its way.

As I turned the pages, the white tracing paper laid between each page to protect the memories held within crackled. One or two of the photo mounts had come loose but otherwise the contents were intact. I glanced up to see Ross watching my every move. His fingers twitched as if he was stopping himself from leaning forward and snatching back the album.

I turned each page by its edge, glancing at the photos but wondering why on earth he was showing them to me.

As if he was reading my mind, he said, 'I wanted you to see a glimpse of how happy my life was before I messed up. That page you're on now has a picture of me and Leonard Rumbly. We were friends once. I left that in the album to mark where my life started to go wrong.'

I studied the photo, with Wingsy leaning across my arm to get a better look. We both stared intently at a young man in football strip with his arm around another man dressed in a suit and tie. All the other pages had held two or three photos, but this particular picture had a whole page to itself.

The next page was full of wedding photographs of Thomas and the recently departed Shona. Happiness radiated from every face caught on camera. They made a very handsome couple. The final page held a newspaper article dated September 1965. The headline simply read 'Footballer Thomas Ross charged with match-fixing'.

'You've seen the highlights of my life,' said Ross. 'Now I'm going to tell you the low points. Before I do that, I need a drink.'

Left alone while Ross attended to the drinks – we'd asked for tea and hoped he'd stay sober long enough for a lengthy statement to be taken – Wingsy and I had a whispered conversation about how long we should stay. Ross clearly wasn't a well man, and getting as much detail as we could against Leonard Rumbly was our priority, but we had to weigh it against his welfare. However, neither of us wanted to take the chance that, if we didn't commit what he had to tell us to paper now, he might not be alive for our return visit. Heartless, but we had a murderer to convict.

I allowed Wingsy to broach the subject of Thomas Ross's health. I'd murmured to Wingsy that I thought he should bring it up, as he was much more tactful than me. Really, it was because I was a coward.

Ross returned with two mugs of tea and a tumbler of whisky. By now it was lunchtime so I wasn't going to judge. He'd brought garibaldis too, so he had something to soak up the booze.

Once we were settled back in our seats, Wingsy picked his mug up and said, 'We know that we've descended upon you without any notice and we're asking a lot of you, and there is no sensitive way to ask this, Mr Ross, but have the doctors told you how long you've got?'

'Few months at the most without treatment.' He took a swig of his drink. 'I know you're wondering if I'll live to see out a trial.'

Wingsy and I both looked at our feet, and I for one was about to utter some sort of noise expressing incredulity, when it struck me that this man was no fool. He deserved our honesty. I said, in a tone I hoped conveyed compassion, 'Mr Ross, seven people died in the Wickerstead Valley train crash. Some sort of justice for them is important, but so is your health. It's not our intention to affect what time you have left.'

He stared at me and rubbed his stubbly chin with his free hand before downing the rest of his drink. 'Please, call me Tommy, and it would be great to have something to live for again. How do we do this? You write and I'll sign. I've every intention of being here for a trial. Leonard Rumbly gave evidence at mine. I feel it's only polite that I return the compliment.'

32

Intrigued as to what Rumbly had said at the trial, but not wanting to jump ahead, we let Tommy Ross talk. I'd already made up my mind when he let us into his house that I liked him. My feelings about him were of course totally immaterial, but they made my task feel easier. I sat, notebook balanced on my knee, scribbling notes as Wingsy asked the correct football questions. Well, I presumed he asked the correct football questions because I knew very little about the game. Wingsy covered what teams Tommy had played for, what dates he had been at each club and who his team mates had been, as well as a few questions I was sure he asked purely out of curiosity. Eventually, Wingsy asked him about Leonard Rumbly and their relationship.

I watched Tommy take a deep breath before he said, 'I'd known him for about three or four years before he asked me if I'd like to make some extra money. We were due to play a side that we always got beaten by. Leonard asked me if I thought we'd win this time. I remember laughing at him and saying, it would probably be like the last four or five matches and we were bound to end the game three- or four-nil down. He said, in that case, I could go along to one of his betting shops and place a bet against my own team to lose. The odds were good and he told me that, if we did look as though we were going to score, I could pull a player down for a penalty. I laughed to begin with but I could tell he meant it.'

Tommy paused to rub at his face again. I could see the tears forming as he told us his tale of shame. With his hand over his eyes, he continued, 'It's not an excuse, but our weekly wage was very low and I found that I could make hundreds of pounds simply by putting one bet on. So I did it again, and again.'

He took his hand away and gave me a sad smile. 'I never fixed a match, though, despite what was said later. Despite what Rumbly said about me in court.' His grip tightened on the glass he was holding in his other hand. 'He made sure I wouldn't tell by threatening to hurt Shona. Just before she was run over, I'd approached a couple of publishers about writing my biography. It was my warning from him. He sent his son to do his dirty work and no doubt Shona knew it too, but she never blamed me. Not once.'

This time, the tears did flow. Tommy waved away my packet of tissues and continued. 'The Wickerstead Valley train crash was Rumbly's fault. He told me that he was going to slow the train up and delay it so that the match was called off. He never told me he was going to make the train crash, but I know he arranged for a lorry to be on the line. I'd gone to another carriage to find a reporter I knew and thought was on the train, otherwise I'd have been several carriages closer to the impact. I've never been sure if that saved my life or meant I was in the wrong place and got concussion when I was knocked out. That's something I'll never know.'

Time was getting on, I was tired and, more importantly than anything else, after several hours of talking, Tommy was waning. I watched him slump further and further into his chair, and pause to think for longer and longer each time Wingsy asked him a question. As I was about to suggest we call it a day, my friend said, 'Tommy, can we come back and see you in a day or two? We have so much information here, and we're very aware that this has been a lot for you to take in.'

Tommy's reaction was to pick up his crystal tumbler, which had been empty for over an hour, and turn it around in his palm before he said, 'I'm going to put the kettle on. Want another drink before you leave?'

We declined and told him that we would call him the next day to see if he was up for us to return and get more details or whether he would prefer to speak on the telephone. Eventually we would need him to read and sign his statement, but there was certainly no harm, in these circumstances, in getting what we needed, typing up his account of the train crash complete with evidence against Rumbly, and then bringing it back for him to read and sign. As we packed our notebooks and paperwork away, I said to Tommy, 'Here are both my and John's mobile numbers, as well as our direct office number.'

He looked down at the card I handed him. He closed one eye. I think he was struggling to focus. I knew the signs well, having displayed them myself a number of inebriated times. Perhaps that was why I liked him.

I was unsure of how I was going to say what I needed to without alarming him. But it had to be said.

'Tommy, if you have any concerns at all that there's a problem out here, don't hesitate to call one of us. But... if you're threatened or worried for your safety, call 999.'

I felt uneasy warning him in case it panicked him, but I couldn't leave it unsaid. I had nothing on which to base the concern I had for this lonely soul, living in an isolated house with only scotch and a crippling conscience for company. Rumbly wasn't going to find out Tommy had been talking to police for a while, if at all, depending on the evidence we could accrue. It was highly probable that he would know once he'd been arrested, though. I was looking forward to that day. I was building up a picture of Leonard Rumbly, complete with his criminal network and destruction of the lives of others, and I doubted that I would be warming to him. Tommy on the other hand, had suffered enough, and had a pitiful existence to show for it.

Tommy tapped my business card to his chest and said, 'I don't even know that Rumbly's alive, so I doubt he knows where I live. Do you think there's any chance I'm in danger?'

'No.' I shook my head. 'I don't. At the moment, only the three of us know you've had anything to tell us. However, if we get to the point of arresting him, that will change things, and we'll need to assess what happens from there.'

With a few more words that we hoped were reassuring, we left him to it. I was quiet in the car as we drove away from Tommy's property.

'What's up with you, duchess?' said Wingsy at last. 'You've said nothing for about five minutes. You're never silent for that long.'

'It's an odd job we do, isn't it, Wings?' I said, trying to put into words how our departure from Tommy Ross had made me feel. 'We bowl up, knock on his door after decades, ask him some questions that have released all sorts of demons, then we drive off and say we'll be in touch.'

As Wingsy pulled up to a Give Way sign at the junction, he glanced over at me, before checking for traffic. He pulled away and said, 'You back to normal yet?'

'What's that supposed to mean?' I overreacted.

'Nin, girl. You were stabbed, in case you've forgotten. It's gonna take time. It's not only your stomach that needs to return to normal – it's your mind, too.'

'What's wrong with my stomach?'

'Don't be so touchy. Are you hungry?'

'Of course I'm hungry. The garibaldis were stale. I can't help feeling that we've left Tommy in a vulnerable position. We should speak to the local police and at least get him a panic alarm fitted. He's in the arse end of nowhere.'

'Very true. You ring Harry, update him and see what he can sort out. Ian Hammond should know what we've got here.'

I made the call as Wingsy drove us to a sandwich shop he told me he'd been to before. Harry Powell answered his phone by saying, 'Hello, Detective Sergeant Powell. How can I help you?' I didn't know why he did that. He knew it was me because my number was stored in his phone's memory. I could only guess that he was with senior management and didn't want to answer the call with his usual, 'Alright, Nin?'

'Harry, are you free to talk?' I began with the standard question whenever police officers made a call.

'Can I call you back in ten minutes?' he said.

'Course you can.' I ended the call as Wingsy turned right towards a sign that took us in the direction of a village called Little Knobbler.

'Little Knobbler?' I asked. 'Interesting name.'

'It's got a great sandwich shop and restaurant. It used to be a pub and it's been turned into an eatery. The menu's fairly amusing – the breakfast special's called the Ultimate Knobbler, and for the lighter appetite they have the Little Nibbler.'

'How come you know so much about it?'

'Me and Mel have driven out this way to see her family from time to time and used to stop off there now and again. There's a B&B next door, too, if you and Bill fancy a dirty weekend.'

I was stopped from saying something telling about my love life that I knew I would regret later, even if it was only Wingsy, by a return call from Harry.

As I answered the phone, Harry said, 'Alright, treacle?' I gathered he was out of his meeting.

'Yeah, great. I need to give you the heads-up on a very interesting conversation Wings and I have just had with Tommy Ross.'

Harry listened in silence as I summarised the morning's conversation.

'Ross is prepared to put it in writing and give evidence stating that Leonard Rumbly was behind the Wickerstead Valley train crash,' I said. 'Rumbly put Malcolm Bring up to delaying the train by leaving his lorry on the line.'

'Coupled with the information your mate Joe Bring is prepared to give us,' said Harry, 'we may, after all this time, have an arrest to make. Oh, and one more thing: your staff appraisal is now well overdue. Come and see me about the outstanding objectives before I start getting an earful from the DI.'

Settled a short while later in the sandwich shop, tea in front of us, huddled in the corner farthest from the other customers, Wingsy and I discussed what we had so far.

I topped up my cup, letting my toasted sandwich cool. Dropping my voice so that Wingsy had to lean forward, his tie narrowly missing his baked beans, I said, 'We've now linked Leonard Rumbly to several deaths from the train crash corroborated by Tommy Ross and Joe Bring, but there's also the recent deaths of eighteen-year-old Daryl Hopkins, Luke Bring's friend, who got his drugs from Andy Rumbly, plus twenty-one-year-old Errol Chandler whose drugs were supplied via the Rumblys. If that's not enough, there's the death of a third person in the division that we haven't even looked into.'

'Are you still on about that woman who was found over the weekend?' Wingsy flipped his tie over his shoulder so that he wouldn't drop juice from his jacket potato topping all over it. The pattern was so hideous, I doubted it would have showed.

'They haven't had the post mortem results yet, then?' I muttered, looking over at the old lady who was sitting at the table nearest to us. She glanced at us, making me want to change the subject.

'They haven't done it yet,' said Wingsy. 'Thought you knew that she'd been identified as Lea Hollingsworth, aged twenty-seven. She went missing a couple of days beforehand and then her body turned up. Apparently no sign of previous drug use. It's all very odd, especially as she had a two-year-old at home.'

Few things put me off my food, but I put my toasted sandwich back on the plate. My empty hand went straight to my stab-wound scar. I was going soft. Tears were gathering.

I heard Wingsy make a noise as if he was about to say something. I hoped it wasn't going to be words of concern. As I looked back across the table at him, the beans stacked on his fork fell off on to the front of his white shirt.

Whatever he had been about to say came out as, 'Oh, for fuck's sake.'

Cheered me up, anyway.

33

With me insisting on taking my turn at driving, we headed back to the office, making plans for the rest of the week.

'It's only Monday and I'm shattered,' I said to Wingsy.

'When's your next prison visit to Joe?'

'It's tomorrow. I need to get what he has to say in writing. It may take a bit of time.'

'If you're going to be out all day, I'll call Tommy back in the morning and see how he's fixed for another visit on Wednesday.'

'That'll be three days taken care of,' I said with a sigh. 'We're working Saturday too, though, aren't we? Five more days to go before a lie-in. I'm getting too old for this.'

We settled into a companionable silence for the last hour of our journey, which gave me time to think. I needed to find out more about Lea Hollingsworth's death. I had little concern over the quality of its investigation and doubted it would be carried out in isolation from the other drugs deaths, but I wanted to satisfy myself that they were all linked to the Rumblys. It was sounding very much as though the family was behind more than a train crash. I was going to make it my business to get to know as much about them as possible. I planned to find out what I could from the various databases available to me, pester those with access to the ones I didn't have authority to use, and finally glean as much as I could from Joe Bring. Only then would we have enough to arrest Leonard Rumbly, with his son Andy and grandson Niall thrown in for good measure.

My musings were broken by the sight of the M25 stretching out in front of me. It was a road guaranteed to jolt you to your senses. If that wasn't enough to bring me back to reality, my personal phone started to ring in the centre console. I glanced down to see that Annie was trying to get hold of me. My personal phone wasn't connected to the car's hands-free and I wouldn't have wanted Wingsy to overhear our conversation anyway. Even though they'd now met each other, I still wanted to treat these units of my life as separate. The two should never have crossed in the first place.

The phone bleeped to tell me it had a message, which I would pick up when I was good and ready. I'd have to face her some time, though. I could feel an impending sense of exhaustion threatening to get the better of me. My financial situation was dire, I had more work to do than anyone would have envisaged when they gave me a historic train crash to look at, my boyfriend was measuring my units of alcohol, and now I had to call Annie for what would undoubtedly be another barrage of abuse. Could be worse. At least I was still alive. A close brush with death did that for you: it made you take stock and be grateful for when things were simpler. I'd had my wake-up call. Life was far too precious. Its preservation was number one. Something to remember at all costs.

Finally we got back to the police station and parked in the yard. I smiled to myself as I reversed into the spot next to the mobile incident room, costing thousands of pounds, with signs on the side stating, 'Warning. Not to be moved.

Long-tailed tits nesting inside.' It never failed to cheer me up that we owned such an expensive bird box. Joe would have liked it, too.

'Something amusing you, doll?' said Wingsy. 'Or have you got wind?'

'I'm not the one with baked beans down my shirt. And what's with that awful tie?'

'My mum bought me this.'

'She thinks you're a twat, too, then? How much longer are you staying at work for today?' I asked, noticing the time on the dashboard clock as I jotted down the mileage from our journey into the car's log book.

'Well, as we're already on overtime and Harry said not to take liberties with the budget, I was going to call it a day. You?'

We got out of the car and, gathering our paperwork, made our way through the patrol wing to the Cold Case office. 'I may stay for a bit,' I said. 'Plan what I'm going to ask Joe tomorrow.'

By the time we'd got to our office, Jemma and Mick were turning off the computers and lights. There was a buzz coming from the two of them which could mean only one thing: a guilty verdict.

There really was nothing which came close in comparison: an investigation you'd worked on for so long, managing to bide your time and watch the evidence amass until you knew you had the right man or woman. Then came the part where you had to almost try the case to get it past the Crown Prosecution Service. The charge was authorised and then the games began. The accused's legal team didn't provide a defence statement protesting their client's innocence as they were supposed to; defence didn't ask for any unused material they required as *they* were supposed to; and witnesses, understandably, got very nervous about giving evidence. As a police officer it could be daunting. For a member of the public, it could only be petrifying. Getting a case to court was a massive task, and seeing it through to a verdict was exhausting. I had run up and down the stairs in the Old Bailey hundreds of times.

That thought made me realise how unfit I was. The way things were at the moment, I'd need to take the lift every time.

Jemma's face was illuminated. Micky's was still ugly but he had a glow. 'We're off to the pub,' said Jemma. 'Jury was only out twenty-five minutes. Me and Micky bought a cuppa and never even got to drink it before the tannoy called us back in.'

Her voice dropped and she added, 'Suzanna was there when the jury came back. She'd refused to be screened from Oakes when she gave her evidence. He stared at her the whole time. He's such an utter wanker.'

'Cracking woman, Suzanna,' said Barry, face softening. 'We asked her if she wanted to join us for a drink but she's got a husband and three-year-old. They wanted to get home to their little boy.'

Now I knew I was getting soft. I wanted to cry again. I soon got over it when Jemma said, 'How about you two coming for a drink?'

Happy to jump on the back of any celebration that had ended in victory, even one I'd played no part in, I shoved my paperwork in my tray and got ready to join them.

Wingsy tilted his head to one side and said, 'Thought you were staying to do a bit of planning for your prison visit, Nina.'

'And miss out on toasting a rapist being sent down? Not likely. Oh, and Jemma, you're right. Where he's going, he will be an utter wanker.'

34

I woke up with a vague recollection of Wingsy dropping me home the previous evening and a twinge of concern that I had no way of getting to work. While I had been in the pub, Bill had been kept on at work, and once again had done the decent thing and slept in his own spare room when he'd eventually got in. I had no idea when that was, but it was long after the room stopped spinning.

As quietly as I could manage, I got ready for work and checked my job phone for messages. I had only one new one, which read: *Be ready at 7.30am. I'm coming to get you. Don't puke in my car.*

A few minutes later, Wingsy pulled up outside Bill's house.

'Do you feel OK?' he asked as I got in the car.

'Yeah, terrific,' I lied. 'What time did you drop me off last night?'

'About eleven,' he replied as we got to the end of the road. Pausing at the junction, Wingsy glanced at me and then did a double-take.

'What?' I said.

'You look awful.'

'Thanks so much. Thought you were my mate.'

'Really, Nin. You're going to have to take it easy. Stop putting so much pressure on yourself to appear normal to the outside world. You've had a bad time and you're allowed to let your hair down from time to time. Just try and make sure you haven't got lumps of last night's kebab in it.'

'That's so funny. At least I have some hair. And I don't have kebab in it, thank you.' I paused, partly to reflect on what kind of kebab I actually ate, as it was a little hazy, and partly to sound sincere for what I wanted to say next. 'Thanks, though, for the concern, but I'm fine. Really I am.'

He looked over at me again. 'When you want to admit that you're not actually fine, let me know.'

I reached my hand out and briefly touched his arm.

Some time later we got to the station and, to show Wingsy that I appreciated his concern, I went to the canteen to get us both overpriced lattes. Nothing said 'thanks for being a friend' like a three-quid coffee in a paper cup.

I sat at a computer and got my paperwork in order for the questions I had for Joe. Mostly I wanted to fill in a couple of blanks surrounding things he'd given me scanty details on, but on the whole I had the statement mapped out in my head. That was if he was ready to put what he'd told me in writing and sign in the right places. It wasn't a particularly difficult one: anything and everything Joe could tell me about the Chilhampton Express train crash that his father had told him before his death, what type of man his father had been, and what Joe knew about the Rumblys and their involvement in the train crash. I mulled over whether he would stop short of telling all regarding any other criminal associations he knew the family had. He did, after all, want to send Leonard Rumbly down for a long time. As the saying went – might as well be hanged for a sheep as a lamb. The phrase had popped into my head in relation to Rumbly, but I couldn't help but ponder how much it would also apply to Joe. No one liked a grass. This would make Joe a marked man.

There were ways of protecting someone's identity if they wanted to give information to the police anonymously. Joe had made it abundantly clear to me, on my initial visit to him, that he would stand up and be counted for what he was doing. I couldn't fathom out if this was because Joe had a death wish or if he merely wanted his son to know what he was doing for him. Still, there was no honour among thieves and I couldn't see him exactly getting preferential treatment on the wing for his actions. Far from it.

Joe, the unlikely hero, had saved my life not so long ago. As I packed my paperwork together into my folder, I racked my brains wondering how I could take the information Joe was giving me, use it, but somehow manage to return the enormous favour I owed him. Exactly how did a police officer set about saving an incarcerated burglar from getting the beating of his life in prison? I must have missed that class at police training school.

Of course, there was the added complication that I was supposed to surreptitiously be Luke Bring's guardian. Without some kind of reassurance that I would do this, Joe was unlikely to sign a statement. I knew that this left me on shaky ground: police officers couldn't offer incentives to people to hand over information, unless they were prepared for it to come back to haunt all parties at Crown Court. Informants were supposed to be registered and handled correctly. I wasn't trained for that, and I wasn't sure I was the correct person to be dealing with Joe. Professional ethics told me that this was all wrong, but my personal morals wouldn't allow me to walk away from him. For now, I could justify it to myself by saying that Joe hadn't given me any information yet and I had done nothing for him or his son.

Folder under my arm, car keys in my hand, I set out on my second visit to Joe. Many lives had been ended by the train crash and many more ruined. What was clear to me was that nothing I did or Joe said was going to alter any of that. Niggling in my brain was the more present danger Leonard Rumbly was causing to the population of Riverstone, and the class A drugs causing death on the streets. My hopes had been pinned on convicting him for the train crash, but the way Rumbly conducted business, even if it wasn't his drug-dealing, perhaps it would be his links to other parts of the criminal network that finally brought him to justice.

My mind was full of my next task of the day, so much so that I almost walked straight past Ian Hammond. He said my name, but a combination of too much to think about plus a fuzzy head from the night before meant that it took me a few seconds to register what he was saying. My stomach lurched as he repeated what he'd said.

'Janice Freeman will meet you this afternoon at Riverstone Mortuary. Harry told me it's been on your appraisal objectives for some time to go to a post mortem. Janice was the SIO on call over the weekend when Lea Hollingsworth was found. It'll be a Home Office PM, so you're bound to learn a lot. See her there at four o'clock.'

He looked pleased. I didn't doubt that I looked green.

35

Once more I found myself being led to a booth on the far side of the prison's visitors' hall. Joe was standing up, watching me walk towards him, prison officer leading the way. I was relieved to see that Joe had his hands inside his blue bib rather than his pants. He had a slightly less cocky air about him today, and nodded at me as the prison officer stood aside after opening the door. I went in.

'Miss,' was all he said.

I waited until I heard the door shut behind me before I said, 'You OK, Joe?' My tone was laced with more concern than I wanted to show, but my feelings were genuine. There was something bothering Joe that hadn't shown on his face six days ago.

He hooked the chair towards him and sat into it, leaving his feet where he'd been standing. It was the kind of gesture a child would make when trying to appear annoyed. It also looked as though it was putting stress on his spine, but bad posture was probably the least of his worries.

'Nah.' He sighed, looking up at me. 'Didn't sleep very well. It all kicked off in here last night. We had a lockdown. Some bloke went into one and smashed up his cell.'

Joe straightened up, dragging his legs under the table separating us. He stretched his arms out to the side and gave a yawn, exhaling some terrible breath in my direction.

'Geezer found out that his girlfriend died of a drug overdose. They've got a little 'un together, too. It's bollocks. Now you know why I want you to keep an eye out for my boy.'

Despite the warmth of the room, I felt goosebumps on my arms. This was not a coincidence; this was the same dead woman. 'Was she the girlfriend of one of your cellmates?' I asked, as casually as I could manage.

'Nah, George's missus is still very much alive and no one wants to shag Fat Frank, the ugly bastard. It was another bloke's missus. He's well cut up about it. Swore she never took drugs even though he did. Told me he owed quite a few quid to someone too. She was apparently always going on about how she was going to get him out of trouble. He's got no reason to lie to me; I couldn't give a fuck. I've only spoke to him a couple of times during the few days he's been here. He got moved from Mill End.'

The whole time Joe was talking, I was nodding, appearing to accept what he told me at face value, but really I was storing the information away. There was clearly more to Lea's death than a simple drug overdose. My problem had been finding the time to look a little further into it, but in a couple of hours I was due to attend her PM. I was finding my return to work enough to cope with on its own, let alone trying to look into suspicious deaths that were really nothing to do with the Cold Case team.

Still, I wasn't about to walk away from it. And, right at this moment, the only way I could get Joe Bring to make a statement was to help him out with covert babysitting for his fourteen-year-old son so that he would give me information on the Rumblys. Why was nothing ever easy?

'What's the fella's name?' I asked. A frown creased Joe's forehead at my question so I added, 'I'm curious. It comes with the job.'

I could tell that he didn't want to tell me so I left it there. It shouldn't be very difficult to find out. It amused me that Joe was willing to tell me as much as he could about the Rumbly family and make himself a marked man for a train crash before he was born, but he wouldn't tell me the name of a prisoner whose girlfriend had died from a drug overdose and was now suffering the consequences of smashing up his cell. The irony of what people were prepared to tell police officers and what they drew the line at was always fascinating.

'Fruit and veg,' said Joe, leaning towards me.

'Pardon.'

'You know, fruit and veg,' he repeated. 'That's where this all started. My old man worked for Randalls. They had a stand in the Borough Market, up town. You been there?'

I nodded. I'd been to London for a day out the previous summer and paid the market a visit. I'd loved the coffee shops, stalls and food vendors. I'd been taken by the cheerfulness of the place.

'It's shit now,' he said, shaking his head and hardening his mouth into a grimace. 'Fucking tourist piss-take, that's what it is. A fiver for a sausage in a roll. Anyway, the old man, he used to go to the Borough, and another couple of stalls, one in Brighton I think, and one in Brentford, and sell fruit and veg he picked up from farms down in Kent. Bushels, half-bushels, quarter-bushels, whatever – he brought them back full and took them to markets in Essex and Sussex, as well as the Borough.'

At this, Joe paused and shook his head at me. He pointed across the table as if he was about to impart fantastic news.

'Know what, though?'

It was my turn to shake my head.

'They didn't do spuds! In them days, your potato, well, that come from specialist firms, and the spuds, they were in hessian sacks.'

As I began to wonder if Joe had suffered from a blow to the head, he said, 'You're wanting to know why I'm telling you this, aren't you, miss?' Without giving me time to answer, he said, 'The takings used to drop drastically in September, see. The prices were so cheap at that time of year. Well, the old man told me that he used to struggle around then. Some stuff was out of season, like the soft fruits – strawberries, cherries – you couldn't get hold of them, and the fresh veg you could get your hands on was cheap and competition was fierce. That was when he turned to other ways of earning a living.'

All the while Joe had been telling me about his dad's legitimate self-employment, he'd appeared pleased to share information with me. Now, he didn't seem to be so animated. At some point in the Bring family's past, pride must have had its place, but now it was replaced with drugs, death and incarceration.

'His gambling debts got bigger than he could cope with,' continued Joe. 'He dug himself out of the hole the only way he could think of: he did someone a favour and they was wiped clean.' Joe paused to run his fingers through his messy hair. 'Problem was, he never got over what he did. He was only supposed to delay the train, perhaps cause a bit of an accident. My old man, the stupid fucker, didn't reckon on a 1948 five-ton Bedford truck being such a sturdy old beast and knocking the train straight off the track.'

I had been writing furiously as Joe spoke. As I caught up with him, I glanced up to see that he was watching me write down his last few words. I knew that Joe could read and write from the many occasions I'd interviewed him for shoplifting. I wrote one single word on the top of the next clean page in my notebook – *Who?*

He gave a short laugh. 'I think you know the answer to that already,' he said, 'Leonard Rumbly was behind it all. The question you should be asking me is, how are you going to prove it.'

'And how's that, Joe?' I asked, pen poised.

'I can give you the names of five or six people who knew the Rumblys' business and would have known that it was pre-planned that the truck was on the railway line. Most are still alive and some may not help you, but you probably only need one or two. Am I right?'

He grinned. I nodded.

'Thing is, miss, you know I'm not going to do that unless you do something for me first. And you're probably not going to like it.'

36

Joe was right. I didn't like it one little bit. I left the prison without giving him an answer. I had to speak to Clint Stirling before I went any further, and I wasn't about to make promises to banged up burglars.

I found Clint in his office. He shared it with another DI but she wasn't about. I waited at the door, about to knock, when he looked up.

'Hello,' he said. 'Take a seat.'

That seemed a good omen – we were making a break from sign language. I shut the door behind me and sat facing him. I'd spent the entire journey back from prison wondering how I was going to formulate the words that would stop Clint from laughing in my face and telling me to sever all ties with Joe. I owed Joe, and I was keen to get my hands on the list of names he was prepared to swap for my assistance.

'I've been to see Joe Bring today,' I said.

Clint raised an eyebrow. I guessed that he was wondering why I hadn't gone to Ian Hammond with the update.

I shifted in my seat. 'The reason I haven't gone directly to Mr Hammond is that I could do with your advice.' Clint had once told me on a disastrous date that the best way to get someone to do something for you was to make them feel valued, and asking for their advice usually did it.

Clint nodded. He had a short memory; I had not.

'Whatever you need,' he said.

'Joe's offered to give me some information in exchange for something a little unorthodox.'

'Not money, then?'

'No. He wants me to make sure his son doesn't get into trouble, particularly where drugs are concerned. He thinks that there's a way around that.' I paused, took a deep breath and told Clint what I'd spent the last half-hour going over in my head. 'Joe seems to think that if I get his son enrolled on a training boot camp for juveniles it'll show him some discipline and in some way protect his boy.'

I studied Clint's face. It remained unchanged. I'd dropped this ludicrous bombshell, so I thought I needed to fill the conversational gap.

'I have pointed out to him that I can't simply arrange it. I'm well aware that these courses are few and far between and cost the earth. Am I asking something ridiculous here, or is it doable?'

Clint nodded, pondering, I suspected, how he was going to tell me not to be such a gullible fool, without using those actual words.

At last, he spoke. 'I'm guessing that, even if Joe didn't actually remind you that he saved your life, you're feeling torn between helping him somehow and not getting yourself into bother for arranging favours for his kid.'

I couldn't have summed it up better myself. 'In a nutshell, yeah.'

Clint glanced at his watch. 'Got your purse on you?'

'Of course.'

'Come on, then, let's get a pint and we can talk it over properly.'

It was a little early in the day but I wasn't one to argue with officers of rank. We walked over to the Dog and Gun. I wasn't comfortable having an alcoholic drink so I stuck to orange juice, much to Clint's surprise. He ordered himself a pint of bitter. Once settled in a quiet corner of the pub, we discussed Joe's request. We both agreed that we couldn't do what he asked: there was no way police officers should be doing favours for criminals in any circumstances. Clint had a bit of a faraway look in his eyes as he listened to me insisting that there was no way we could do it. He had joined the force about ten years earlier than I had, so I wasn't sure if his dreamy look was due to nostalgia for a bygone time in policing when deals could be struck, or whether he was bored with my company. I didn't think I'd like the answer to either question, so I asked for his professional opinion. This seemed to follow on nicely from asking for his advice.

'As you've pointed out, we can't give him what he wants, and we want the list of names he has about the train crash. Do you think what he actually wants is a reduction in his prison sentence?'

I took a sip of my fruit juice, regretting my choice of beverage. 'No, I don't, and I've told him that won't happen. I get the feeling that he doesn't want to get out at the moment. He has nowhere to go, anyway. I think he wants to help, but he's had the information all these years and made no attempt to pass it on. Why now?'

'His son,' suggested Clint. 'Joe gets banged up and then people start overdosing all over the place, including his son's mate. It would be enough to make anyone take a stand. Some people need a catalyst to do the right thing.'

'Do you reckon?' I asked. 'Joe did the right thing when he helped me last year. I doubt that anything was driving him then. All that he got for his troubles was eighteen months inside.'

'Perhaps he's found God.'

We both laughed at that.

'Best plan of action,' said Clint, finishing his pint, 'is for you to make a statement covering your visits to Joe and everything he's told you, including what he's asked you to do. Then put in an intelligence report stating that Joe has asked you to arrange a week at boot camp for his son in exchange for information. Leave the rest with me. Don't visit him again on your own.'

I knew that Clint was right, but it seemed like a massive backside-covering exercise without actually achieving anything. After eighteen years, though, I shouldn't be surprised any more. And I didn't have time to think it over for too long: I had a post mortem to get myself to. Despite my hangover being long gone, I was feeling a bit nauseous at the thought of it.

37

I arrived at the hospital in plenty of time and found my way to the mortuary. I didn't really want to do this. I pressed the buzzer, gave my name and walked in. It wasn't what I was expecting.

There was no smell. I'd been in mortuaries many times in the first couple of years of my service, when I was a probationer, and I remembered what it was like. I couldn't call it the smell of death or anything as drastic, but nevertheless it had been thick in the air. It probably simply came down to those experiences being in very old and badly ventilated buildings, and this was in a brand new one with air-conditioning. I hadn't expected the radio to be playing so loudly, either, blaring out a cheery song about love and forgiveness.

I was greeted by the attractive CSI I'd seen Bill talking to on the station a couple of days ago after the drugs warrant. She introduced herself as Elaine Day. I chatted to her as she laid out the pots, evidence bags and paperwork she needed for taking the samples. I noticed a silver band on her wedding finger.

'This is my first post mortem,' I felt the need to confess.

She smiled and said, 'You'll probably find it fascinating. If you feel a bit ill, take yourself outside to one of the offices the other side of the door. It does happen from time to time. I like coming to them, but the first one can be overwhelming. There's not that many Home Office PMs, so you were lucky to be on duty for this one.'

Right at that moment, I wasn't feeling very lucky.

I heard the outside door open and Janice Freeman's voice. She was talking to a man and it was clear that they knew each other. He was asking her about the sentencing at Crown Court of the murderer of another victim he'd carried out the PM on. While I waited for them to come in, I had a look around the room. It was about fifty feet by forty and held four empty fixed metal tables, all slightly larger – funnily enough – than a body. Elaine had covered one with syringes, bottles and bags. The rest of the room housed sinks and equipment, knives, and a set of silver scales suspended on a trolley.

'You may want to put your stuff outside,' said Elaine, pointing at my handbag. 'It'll get blood on it in here.'

I glanced down at the floor. Although spotless, it was still wet from the last PM. I was still trying to act casual about the whole thing but I didn't think Elaine looked easily fooled.

Janice Freeman smiled when she saw me. 'Hello, Nina. This is Dr Philip Fleischer. He's carrying out the PM today. Shall we all go and have a couple of minutes before we get started?'

The doctor and I exchanged nods, not before it registered that he was a very good-looking man. That was a totally inappropriate feeling, especially as I saw a mortuary assistant right behind him, wheeling in a trolley. On the trolley was Lea's shrouded body.

We ran through some paperwork, such as suspected cause of death and who was going to be present. By this stage we'd been joined by Jo Styles, senior CSI, and the coroner's officer, a middle-aged woman whose name I never found out. She was very pleasant and filled me in on what was going on throughout the whole procedure. Then the time came for everyone to fulfil the role they were here to do. All except me. I was here because I had previously expressed an interest in learning more about forensics and recognising causes of death, and had made the mistake of putting it on my staff appraisal. I had also been determined to find out what had happened to Lea Hollingsworth. What I hadn't banked on was the two meeting in the mortuary.

Elaine handed me a pair of plastic overshoes and a plastic apron. I glanced down at my feet. I'd worn heels. What had I been thinking? I didn't doubt it would be only minutes before I went straight through the coverings and got blood all over my Marks and Spencer shoes.

The first half-hour consisted of the pathologist examining Lea's body in the body bag and Jo taking a number of photos. All the while this went on, Elaine got her exhibit bags ready, Janice Freeman caught up with her endless paperwork and I stood transfixed.

Three and a half hours later, I was grateful for the shoe protectors but cursing wearing high heels. The whole thing held a morbid fascination for me and I surprised myself by not feeling sick, but my determination to see it through was born more from a desire to find out what had happened to Lea. I watched as the doctor frequently stopped to make notes on his clipboard and from time to time called over Jo to take photographs, or Elaine to hand him a pot, bag or syringe so that he could deposit a sample from Lea. On a couple of occasions he beckoned to Janice. I was shifting from foot to foot, as my knees were locking up from standing still for so long, something I didn't think had happened since I was in uniform – and then I'd been wearing Magnum police boots.

The post mortem had got to the part that everyone warned me about. I had seen the hand-held electric rotary saw brought out by the mortuary assistant, connected to a huge, wheeled mobile power base. He'd plugged it in underneath the trolley holding Lea. The same trolley that was being constantly hosed down. I had already refreshed my first aid knowledge from the sign on the wall warning what to do in case of an electrical shock, and was torn between watching what the doctor was doing to Lea's head and hoping he wouldn't also end up dead from standing in a puddle while operating electrical equipment. I figured Health and Safety didn't drop by all that often.

I was so mesmerised by the sound of the drill on Lea's skull and the trickle of water on to the trolley, sluicing her blood to the drain on the floor, that it took me a second to realise that the doctor was calling Janice over to the table once more. I edged closer. Philip Fleischer was pointing to the inside of Lea's skull. As he moved his hand away, I saw that there was more blood to come.

'What this indicates,' said the pathologist, 'is that she suffered massive head trauma. Can you see these marks here? They show that her skull was hit by something with a rounded or tapered end. Someone or something struck her on the head, possibly a number of times.'

38

The doctor's revelation seemed to come as little surprise to anyone in the mortuary, except myself. The pathologist peered very closely at Lea's skull and then stood up straight, looking around the room. He caught Jo's eye and waved her over. This got everyone's attention.

'Here, by the larger abrasion to her head, you can see a small fragment of something,' he said, eyes so close to Lea, his breath must have been on her skin. He stood back to allow the CSI to photograph the fragment, before removing it and passing it across in an evidence bag.

I watched Janice as she made a couple of phone calls, no doubt attempting to summon some staff to work on the suspicious death of Lea Hollingsworth. She glanced my way a couple of times as she spoke into her mobile. She was too far away for me to hear what she was saying, leaving me unclear whether she was talking about me or wondering if I was about to faint. I had taken to fidgeting about, but it was due to my legs aching, and I had to be honest, I was wondering how much longer this was all going to take. I felt truly awful about Lea's death, which was looking now like a murder, but I had worn the wrong shoes. I wanted to go home.

While the mortuary assistants saw to affording her some dignity again, I looked away and got ready to park what I'd witnessed as Janice went off to speak to the doctor about the cause of death. I threw my plastic apron in the hazardous-waste bin, along with my shoe covers, and made a call to Bill. I told him that I wouldn't be much longer, and, much to my shame, that I was hungry and would like some dinner.

'How about we go out to eat?' he suggested. 'I thought it would do both of us good to get out and have a meal, spend some time together.'

I really didn't have to think about it. 'Fantastic idea,' I said. 'Do you still fancy the new Thai restaurant?'

'Good idea. I'll see if I can get a table for nine o'clock. Will that give you enough time?'

I glanced down at my clothes. 'Make it half-nine. I think I may need it.'

I rushed home to Bill, pleased that we were managing at least half a night out together. He ordered a cab as I dashed from bathroom to bedroom, trying to remember the last time we'd gone out for a meal. And before I knew it we were sitting next to each other in the back of the cab, holding hands in a comfortable silence.

As we walked into the restaurant and a rush of aromas, I heard Bill say to a beautiful waitress wrapped in red and gold silk, 'I've booked a booth at the back. Bill Harrison.'

I couldn't fail to notice that the restaurant was almost full and the booths at the back were few in number. I got the feeling that, despite Bill having given me the impression this was last-minute, he had in fact had booked the table some days ago.

The meal, restaurant and evening were all but perfect, and, even though we had room for another two people at our table, we sat inches apart. Bill told me about a backpacking holiday around Thailand that he'd gone on when he left school. I hadn't thought of him as the sort to sleep in hostels and tents, but it reminded me that there was a lot we didn't yet know about each other. I was having such a relaxing time, I didn't even pretend to insist that I contribute when the bill was brought over.

We opted to stroll home, once more hand-in-hand, barely exchanging a word as we made our way through the warmth of the night. An evening free of arguments and terrible television couldn't have come at a better time.

39

Feeling relaxed and content after an evening with my boyfriend, I went in to work the next day looking forward to another shift with Winsgy. We were due to see Tommy Ross to get him to make a statement covering everything he had told us, filling in as much detail as he could manage. I liked Tommy. He had suffered enough, partly because of his own foolishness, but it had come back to him tenfold. We all made mistakes. Some of us drank too much and went to work feeling slightly the worse for wear; other people covered up train crashes and murder. It put my problems into perspective. There was always someone worse off.

On the way to Tommy's, Wingsy and I talked about how we would use the former footballer's evidence if he didn't make it as far as a trial: whether we'd be better off recording him on DVD in case he didn't live long enough, and whether it would be admissible in court. Wingsy had made some enquiries with the Crown Prosecution Service but they had seemed to think that a statement was the correct way forward. We went along with what they wanted and hoped it was the right decision in case we didn't get a chance to do it any other way.

As we pulled up outside the front of Tommy's house, a cat sat by the front door, meowing loudly. 'I don't remember seeing a cat when we were here on Monday,' I said as we grabbed our stuff from the back seat. When had everyone taken ownership of a cat?

'Perhaps Tommy was so pissed, he forgot he had one.'

I stopped myself from laughing in case Tommy was watching from one of the windows. I needn't have worried about being spied upon by our witness. It took him a while to come to the door, and when he did eventually open it I was temporarily stunned into silence at the sight of him. He hadn't looked the picture of health two days ago, but today he looked as if he'd joined the living dead. Despite the coolness of the day, he was sweating, and his skin had taken on a grey hue. As he welcomed us inside, I noticed the increased tremble to his hand as he held on to the door latch. The cat ran inside straight to the kitchen, cutting across our paths as it did so. I hoped it was a good omen.

'Sorry for my appearance,' he said. 'I've not been out of bed long. I've had trouble sleeping since your last visit.'

'We're sorry if we unsettled you, Tommy,' said Wingsy. 'That was never our intention.'

Tommy waved a shaking hand in our direction. 'No, no,' he said. 'The reason I've had problems dropping off is that, since you were here, I gave what you said a lot of thought and I want to make sure I see a trial out. I've not touched a drop since you left here on Monday.'

I wasn't sure how to respond to this. For some reason this chilled me more than his acceptance of death and refusal of medical treatment. I wasn't the best person to give alcohol consumption advice, but I felt sure that sudden withdrawal could be medically dangerous.

Tommy led us through to the living room where we'd sat two days ago before he headed off to the kitchen to put the kettle on. I raised my eyebrows at Wingsy as we got our notebooks and paperwork out. He replied with a shrug. Keeping my voice low, I said, 'What do you reckon about his abstinence? Isn't it dangerous?'

'What do you suggest we do, pour vodka down his throat? We'll speak to him before we get started. I think he should at least see his doctor or something.'

We left our whispered concerns there as Tommy returned with three mugs of tea. As he placed them down, I noticed that he'd only half-filled them. I put that down to his tremors and the cat which nipped in front of him as he tottered across the room. This was a man who didn't need any more obstacles in his way, especially darting feline ones.

'Tommy,' I began, 'it's not that we don't appreciate that you've helped us out by keeping clear of the booze, but isn't it dangerous?'

'I feel fine,' he said, though his complexion, and the nails digging into the arms of the chair, said otherwise. 'I've got a doctor's appointment in the morning. I've decided I want to see this out.'

I smiled as genuinely as I could manage, but it was difficult. The hopelessness was coming off him in waves. He was a grown man and I couldn't force him to go straight to the hospital but he was making me feel uneasy. Enough people had already lost their lives over the years; I didn't want to add another name to the casualties.

His mind was made up, though, so we let him talk. Wingsy wrote and I asked the questions. Well, to be more precise, I asked the question, singular. The only words I spoke were, 'Tell us about Leonard Rumbly and the train crash,' and he talked for an age.

Once Tommy got going, he relaxed more into himself, sitting back in the chair and reducing the chances of wearing away the upholstery on his recliner's arms. He began by recapping what he'd already told Wingsy and me forty-eight hours earlier, but giving more details this time around. He was a near-perfect witness, apart from the rotting liver that threatened to take his life at any point. Most of what he had told us was already typed up and saved on Wingsy's laptop. The object of this visit was to get as much detail as we could, add it to what we already had, print the statement off from the mobile printer and get Tommy to read and sign it. Simple. Or it would have been if he hadn't looked like death warmed up.

'I've already told you how I met Leonard,' he said. 'The most important part, the part you want to know about, is how and why the train was derailed and why I kept quiet about it. It's important that you know I had no direct involvement in the accident. I was on the train. It wasn't supposed to derail, but be delayed by a few hours. Rumbly had a small team around him then. He couldn't afford any more loyalty than one or two minders. If they're still alive, the men you want to speak to are Lance Phillips and Martin Withey. They're about Leonard's age and came from the East End. Haven't seen them in years either. They would have known about any plans he had. There was nothing those two didn't know, although they didn't have the brains between them to organise anything, just turn up and look fierce.

'Rumbly's genius plan was to delay the train to postpone the football match we were on our way to. If the match was off, the bets were off and he wouldn't have to pay up. He'd have to give the stake money back, but he wouldn't be out of pocket. In the meantime, he used the money for other matters, laundered cash through his bookies and returned the cash he owed. He thought it was foolproof. Only trouble was, it went wrong – terribly wrong.'

Tommy paused at this moment and reached for his mug of tea. As his unsteady hand picked it up, he let out a sigh. I wasn't sure if that was due to reliving the horror of the train crash or because he had forgotten he was drinking tea and not whisky.

'Leonard Rumbly got a fella called Malcolm Bring to leave his fruit and veg lorry on the track and put in a call to stop the train. There was a problem with that: Malcolm Bring was not only an unreliable idiot who left the call too late, but Bring might have had an ulterior motive. Bring's girlfriend, Marilyn, was on the train.'

I knew I looked surprised at this comment. I could feel the creases in my own forehead.

'Malcolm Bring's girlfriend was pregnant, and someone told Bring that Leonard Rumbly was the father of the unborn child.'

40

'Do you need a break?' Wingsy asked, looking up from his note-taking.

Tommy answered with a shake of his head. I could see the damp creeping through his hairline. On a brighter note, he no longer looked like a living corpse and actually seemed to have a bit of colour to his cheeks, other than grey.

'You see, Bring knew that his girlfriend was cheating on him with the very man he was in debt to,' continued Tommy. 'I didn't know any of this until some time later, you understand. As far as I knew, the train was just going to be held up, or I wouldn't have been on it. Martin Withey – he was the henchman with two brain cells rather than one – he told me that Bring had been reluctant to be a part of any of it but desperately needed his debts cancelling. It was his only way out. He knew his girlfriend was going to be on the train, and he'd been told she was carrying someone else's child – it might have been enough to make him do it.'

Tommy paused to stare miserably into his cup. 'Marilyn was taken to hospital and nearly lost the baby. Apparently Bring was beside himself at what he'd done: the deaths of innocent people, the near-death of an unborn child. He found out the truth from someone, I was never sure who told him, and he went to have it out with Rumbly and got the crap beaten out of him by Withey and Phillips. It's the only reason I know about it.'

Tommy had begun to turn the cup round and round in his hands, studying the pattern. Eventually, he put it down on the carpet and wiped the back of his hand across his clammy forehead.

When I thought I'd given Tommy enough of a pause to compose himself, I carried on. 'What we need, Tommy, is something a little more substantial than you telling us that Rumbly was behind the crash. Malcolm Bring is dead, we have no forensics, which we rely on these days, and any documentation would probably be long gone. Can we start with how you know so much about Leonard Rumbly's business?'

After several seconds, he answered me. 'I was in Leonard Rumbly's debt by then too, you see. Not the kind of debt Bring was in, but Rumbly had me where he wanted me. I'd placed bets on matches I was playing in and he had something on me. That's what he did: he gained my trust and then I couldn't get out. He used to invite me to his warehouse in Deptford to drink, chat, play cards with him, Phillips and Withey.' He gave a dry laugh and carried on, 'Withey always talked too much when he drank. Sometimes it was innocent fun, you know? Other times it got out of hand.'

'Out of hand?' I echoed.

My question was greeted with a small shrug. 'That's all water under the bridge…'

Tommy trailed off, avoiding my gaze, and for the first time I thought that he was hiding something. Nevertheless, I made myself concentrate on what we'd come here for, making a mental note to ask him again on another occasion.

'Where will we find Withey?' I said.

'I'm not sure. He and Rumbly had a falling-out about money a few years later. He may help, if you can find him. If you get no joy from him, Malcolm Bring's ex-girlfriend may talk to you. Her name was Marilyn Springate but she's married now. Reckon she'd want to help, since Rumbly ruined her life as well as many others.'

I had so many more questions but I could see that Tommy was struggling to hold it together. We'd been in his house for over an hour and I was worried that we were wearing him out. As much as I was reluctant to leave and return again another day, it might be better than exhausting him now, and there would be other questions further down the line.

As if he'd pre-empted what I was about to suggest, Tommy said, 'I'd rather get this finished today, if you don't mind. It's not that you're not welcome here any time and I'll assist you in any way, but I think it would be better if we got this done. You never know, do you?' A sad smile tugged at his mouth.

'I'll add what you've been saying to the statement on the laptop,' said Wingsy, 'while you two talk. We can get out of your way then.'

Tommy eased himself out of his chair. 'May as well put the kettle back on,' he said, moving to pick up the cups.

'Want a hand, Tommy?' I asked.

'No, thanks, love,' he said. 'You can have a look through the photo album again while I'm making a brew. There's a couple of newspaper clippings of the train crash in the back. They may be interesting.' He shuffled over to the sideboard to get the album he'd shown us on our previous visit before going to his kitchen.

I flicked absentmindedly through the pages of memories, some showing glimpses of the happiest moments of the lives they portrayed, some capturing the sadder times. All of them pertinent to Tommy, and, once, to his wife. I was aware of the noise of the keyboard as Wingsy typed next to me, as well as the sounds of tea-making from the kitchen. But then every outside distraction faded. I was staring at a page from a newspaper dated 20th June 1964. It was a black and white photograph of the derailed Chilhampton Express. The photo showed a view the police pictures hadn't. It was the impact of the engine and Malcolm Bring's lorry. The lorry had a gaping hole in the side. Where I expected to see crates of carrots, cabbages, apples, I saw an empty mangled wreck. Where exactly was the fruit and veg? It should have been strewn all over the crossing and ground.

This thought had flitted through my head some days ago but had got lost in the ether. Now it meant something else – the crash must have been pre-planned. Even Malcolm Bring wasn't stupid enough to waste money by filling his lorry with stock if he knew he was about to use his vehicle to derail a train.

41

The sight of Tommy's cat trying to get into my handbag brought me back to the present moment. That, and Wingsy whispering, 'What the fuck's the matter with you?'

'The cat is in my handbag and there's no fruit and veg in this lorry.'

'Can you hear yourself?' said my friend, trying to shoo the cat away and leaning in for a look at the newspaper cutting.

'The lack of food strewn on the railway line has always bothered me,' I said. 'It shows Malcolm Bring always planned to derail the train, not simply delay it.'

'Not sure that's going to make too much difference anyway. He's long since dead.'

'Yeah, I know that, Wings, but the point is that surely this will in some way show that Leonard Rumbly knew it too.'

Wingsy paused from tapping on the keyboard to mull over what I'd said. I paused to tip the cat from my bag.

'Not necessarily,' he said, scratching his balding head with the biro he had put behind his ear. 'It could still just have been Malcolm Bring's decision. We've got to show that Leonard Rumbly had something to do with it if we're going to charge him with conspiracy to commit murder, and, besides, even if he wrote off Bring's debts to derail the train, it would have been up to Bring whether he wasted his own money or not. Rumbly wasn't involved in Bring's legit business, was he?'

'Yeah, fair point.' I was silent again, looking through the memorabilia of tattered lives while Wingsy carried on with his typing. It was miserable reading when I thought it through too deeply. On a lighter note, the cat had made itself scarce.

Tommy returned with more tea and we chatted about football while Wingsy finished typing up his statement. At last, when I'd looked at every family photo Tommy had to offer and made as much conversation as possible about a sport I knew nothing about, Wingsy announced he was finished. He explained the process to the sweating, fidgeting Tommy and began to read the statement from the laptop, making amendments where needed as we went.

Eventually, we were all happy with the content and, most importantly, Tommy was happy to put his signature to the statement. Wingsy set up the printer, produced a paper version of Tommy's words and asked him to read and sign. As soon as he'd done what had been asked of him, Tommy waned. It was so slight, I almost missed it. He looked as though someone was letting the air out of him, bit by bit.

'We'll be on our way soon,' I told him as Wingsy dismantled the printer and shut down the computer. 'Can we get you anything before we leave?'

'No, thanks, love,' he said. 'Everything I want has long since been out of reach.'

I looked down. I couldn't face his expression.

We packed up our equipment and paperwork and went through to the hall. As we opened the front door, I turned to our witness and said, 'We'll be in touch, and see you very soon, Tommy.'

'Hope so, love. God willing.'

42

I opened the back door of the car to let some air inside and threw my handbag on to the back seat. As I'd been rummaging through it for the car keys, I'd found a piece of chicken kebab in the compartment designed for mobile phones. That would probably explain why the cat had tried to climb inside it.

Wingsy opened the boot and stowed the computer and printer. As he slammed the boot shut, I distracted him by saying I thought I'd just seen a peacock in the field. He turned away from me to look and I quickly flicked the piece of kebab over my shoulder.

'That's not a peacock, Nina, it's a blue carrier bag caught on a nettle.' He shook his head and got in the passenger seat. I got in the driver's seat.

'Are we going straight back to Riverstone?' I asked.

'Yeah,' he said. 'I've got a stack of paperwork to catch up on. And I thought Hammond was chasing you for an update on Joe Bring.'

'I've got to say, there's never a dull moment, is there?' We turned out of Tommy's side road and back on to the main road.

We'd been travelling about twenty minutes when Wingsy said, 'The car seems to be making a strange noise.'

'Does it?' I said.

'It might be best if you pull over and we take a look.'

'Brilliant idea,' I said. 'Apart from the fact that neither of us really has a clue what we'd be looking for – and don't make out that you would – how do I know you're not going to drive off and leave me here in the wilds of Sussex.'

'The wilds of Sussex! You just thought a carrier bag was a peacock. What do you know about – '

I held my hand up to quieten him.

'I can hear a cat,' I said. 'It meowed.'

Wingsy made an abrupt shift in his seat to look over his shoulder. 'Bloody hell,' he said. 'Tommy's cat's on the back seat. It's got its head in your handbag.'

'It's after the chicken.'

'What chicken?'

'The doner from the other night. I found some chunks in my bag. We're going to have to take it back.'

'You really are a muppet, Nina.'

'It's not my fault that the poxy cat got in the car. Why weren't you looking out?'

'What for? How often does a cat jump inside someone's motor? It's not the type of thing you expect to happen.'

Wingsy kept a cautious eye on the stowaway as I made a hasty about-turn in the next layby we came to. He seemed very jumpy with the animal's company and must have been straining his neck. I'd never really thought about my friend as being the nervous type, but it was good to have something to wind him up about later.

Eventually we were on our way back to Tommy's with his stowaway pet. We were undecided whether we should stop at the top of the drive and let the cat out so Tommy didn't see us, or take the cat to the door. It clearly didn't have enough sense to stop itself from getting in the situation in the first place, however, so we couldn't guarantee it would ever find its way back to the house.

'What do you reckon?' he said.

'Well,' I said, 'we've been gone too long to say we found his cat at the top of the road and brought it back. We're going to have to knock.'

'I don't fancy knocking and saying, "Sorry, Tommy, but we seem to have driven over thirty miles without noticing your cat was chowing down in my colleague's handbag." He's going to think we're idiots.'

'This does put us high up the halfwit chart. How about we pull up and, if he comes out, we say, we thought we'd left something behind but now we've found it.'

It was too late for him to argue with me, as I was driving and we were almost back where we'd started forty or so minutes ago. Wingsy was out of the car before I'd even turned the engine off. I smiled to myself at his reluctance to open the door and release the savage tabby cat within. I went around to his side of the car so that, if Tommy was watching out of the window, the position of our car meant that he wouldn't see the cat bolt from our vehicle.

As the feline shot across the patchy grass masquerading as a lawn, I glanced up at the upstairs windows. Convinced that when we'd got to the house earlier that day the bedroom curtains had been closed, I was now struck by something odd about their position. Had they simply been open, I probably wouldn't have given it further thought, but the front main bedroom curtains were open on one side and closed on the other.

Wingsy stood beside me and looked up at the window.

'That's strange,' he said. 'You knock; I'll go round the back.'

He moved out of sight to the back of the property as I went to knock at the door. Something wasn't right at Tommy's house. We'd been gone less than an hour but a lot could happen in that time. We'd passed no other vehicles for some time so, whatever the problem was, I was sure it was already in the house.

I knocked as loudly as I could and shouted out 'Tommy!' several times before Wingsy opened the door to me. His face had taken on a serious look I could only recall seeing on a few occasions. Even more concerning was that he had taken his asp from inside his jacket.

'No one down here,' he said leading the way upstairs. I followed, listening out for sounds of movement. The only noise I heard was that of laboured breathing, growing louder as we hurried to the first floor.

43

The door to the main bedroom stood open. The sunlight came straight through the window where the curtain had been pulled back, illuminating the figure on the bed. Tommy's ashen, clammy face looked even worse in the harshness of the sunshine. His eyelids fluttered as if he was trying to open them but couldn't manage to do that as well as wheeze. I preferred that he put all of his efforts into breathing; seeing could wait.

I quickly checked the room to make sure that no one else was there as Wingsy moved from room to room. I was sure that Tommy's physical state was caused by a medical emergency and not an intruder, but nevertheless we weren't taking any chances. I saw the phone next to the bed and made a grab for it, calling out Tommy's name as I did so, telling him who I was. I had no idea if he could hear me but it seemed the right thing to do.

I made the call from the landline, knowing that dialling 999 from a mobile was likely to connect you to the wrong county, and I couldn't recall whereabouts in Sussex we were. I was already going to have to explain who we were and why we had returned to our star witness's home address having inadvertently catnapped his moggy. I could feel my own heart rate increasing as I looked at Tommy, praying he would keep breathing. I told the operator I wanted an ambulance and, as I was being connected, I watched the tormented face of Tommy as he tried to get more air into his lungs. Wingsy was shouting Tommy's name at him and gently shaking his shoulder in an attempt to get some response. I put the call on speakerphone and explained to the operator that we were police officers and knew only a little of Tommy's medical background. The calm, reassuring female voice never faltered and kept asking the right questions and giving instructions. I didn't feel anywhere as calm as she sounded, but I knew that panicking wasn't going to help. Several minutes went by, with me watching the timer on the phone's display as it ticked away the seconds and Wingsy watching the shallow breathing of the man on whom we were pinning our hopes for a successful conviction against the Rumbly family – and whom we had come to like.

Eventually we heard the noise of an ambulance's siren heading in our direction, and relief hit me. Wingsy ran down to the front of the house to wave the paramedics towards our patient, and within seconds I heard someone crashing up the wooden stairs. Wingsy was explaining the little we knew about Tommy's condition and was offering to look for medication and any relevant notes. Tommy was still breathing, although he was struggling, and there was little else we could do. I hoped it wasn't too late. I heard the second paramedic coming into the house, and went to the top of the stairs to let her know where we were. Once I'd explained who I was and that I had no idea if there were any next of kin, I announced to anyone who was listening that I was going downstairs to find an address book or recent contacts for family and friends. I didn't think that anyone heard what I said but that suited me fine. I wasn't comfortable around death, and the thought of watching Tommy take his last breaths did nothing for me. I headed for the kitchen, figuring that most people kept assorted paperwork in the room with the tea and alcohol. I felt I knew the patient well enough to guess this was likely.

One of the stranger parts of my job was looking around other people's homes. Sometimes they were literally fleapits which left us scratching, but other times they were just untidy, and this was true of Tommy's house. The former footballer's house needed a little in the way of dusting, but it was far from the worst I'd ever been in.

As I sorted through address books and scraps of paper, I could hear the paramedics talking to Wingsy upstairs and the creaking of floorboards. Eventually, I heard the sound of a trolley being taken up to the bedroom.

Tommy was being taken to the hospital and, from my fruitless search of his personal papers, it looked as if he had no one in the world to sit beside his bed waiting for him to wake up.

44

Wingsy followed the ambulance to the hospital, trying to keep up with it on its blues and twos. We had an unmarked car and no need to drive at speed, and, without justification for exceeding the speed limit, police officers were as liable to a speeding ticket as anyone else. Besides, we had a black box fitted to the car to record speed, and the police passenger was supposed to grass the driver up if they were driving too fast. Some days, my job got me down.

I decided to call the office and let them know what Wingsy and I were doing. And, just when I thought it couldn't get any worse, Jim answered my call to the office number. His voice provoked the same reaction in me that fingernails down a blackboard would. Nevertheless, I persevered with my message that we were accompanying Tommy to the nearest A&E, which fortunately was the same hospital where he was due to receive his treatment, meaning his notes should be easier to locate. Having a lot of experience of hospitals over the years for both personal and professional reasons, I knew that the interdepartmental liaison was sometimes shocking.

'He's not been nicked, though, has he?' asked Jim.

'Who?' I asked, wondering where we were going with this.

'Your bloke – the one on his way to the hospital,' said the office dickhead.

'No, he's not been nicked,' I answered, wanting to end the call.

'Doesn't matter, then, does it? It's not a death in custody. At least you're off the hook.'

'Jim, there have been few times in my life when I've met someone who is as much of a nutsack as you are. Tell Harry to give me a call when he's free and that me and Wingsy are going to the hospital. I don't know when we'll be back.'

I hung up. Wingsy said, 'What's with the dramatic sighing?'

'It's that idiot Jim. He gets to me.'

'He gets to us all. Is it only that, or is it also because you've taken a shine to Tommy Ross?'

'Bit of both, really, bit of both.'

I was quiet for the rest of the journey to the hospital. I'd grown very fond of our witness over the last couple of days, and it wasn't merely because he was the best hope we had of putting Leonard Rumbly inside or getting some sort of justice for those killed in a train crash that so easily need not have taken place; it was simply that I thought that Tommy was a decent bloke. He'd been stupid and weak with the match-fixing scandal, but temptation was one of the things that made us human. Tommy had never felt able to do the right thing before, but, with his wife dead and us turning up out of the blue, he had a chance to redeem himself. The thought that he might not do that was causing me more concern than it really should have. Quite why that was, I wasn't sure, but now it was in the hands of the medical staff.

We pulled up in one of the police bays of Worthing hospital's A&E entrance and went inside to find out whether Tommy Ross was likely to see another day.

45

Once we'd got past reception and been sent in the direction of the nurses' station, we saw the paramedics who had brought Tommy in. They were completing their handover to those on duty in A&E. One sister was listening intently to one of the paramedics as he updated her. They saw Wingsy and me approaching and made brief introductions, but the only thing that was important to me was the wellbeing of the man who had just been wheeled away on a trolley. As keen as I was to check he was OK, he wasn't going to improve by me peering around a disposable NHS curtain at him, so I stayed where I was and made some notes instead. I was trying to find out as much detail from the paramedics' update, along with the next-of-kin details from Tommy's hospital records, when my mobile rang. The sister glowered at me. She looked very cross but then I supposed working in a busy Accident and Emergency unit would do that to you. On the other hand, maybe she simply disliked the police.

Instead of pointing out that we'd probably saved Tommy's bloody life, I walked around the corner from her and took the call. At least I'd managed to get next-of-kin details from her before I put a supporting wall between me and her. I couldn't see Wingsy flirting with *her*.

'Nin, where are you and Wingnut?' said Harry's voice in my ear.

'Didn't Knobhead tell you?' I answered. 'We're at the hospital with Tommy Ross. We had to go back for something and he'd collapsed.'

Harry listened as I told him as much as I could about Tommy. 'OK, then, treacle,' he said when I'd finished, 'get as much information as you can about how he's doing, tell the hospital that you'll be in touch tomorrow, give them contact details and make your way back. Oh, yeah, and did you get the next of kin?'

'I most certainly did,' I said, sounding a bit more smug than I really should have: as I was reading the name out to him, it hit me why it had sounded so familiar when I heard the sister read it from his notes. I'd been distracted by the day's events but really should have been paying better attention. I was supposed to pick up on these things. 'It's Charles Fitzhubert,' I said, adding with a little more hesitation in my voice, 'He's one of the other footballers who were on the train when it derailed. Rather strange that Tommy should have him as next of kin.'

'Well, presumably you got an address for him along with his name? No guesses what you'll be doing tomorrow.'

'Actually, Harry, depending on how Wings feels about it, I'd rather go tonight. We're halfway there anyway.'

There was a brief pause and Harry said, 'OK. Don't be too late off. I'm getting a hard time about the overtime budget again, and you're supposed to be taking it easy.'

Harry was right, but I needed to pay Fitzhubert a visit and I didn't want to leave it any longer. I needed to know why he was named as Tommy's nearest and dearest, and exactly how much he knew about Leonard Rumbly. This might make all the difference to our evidence against Rumbly, but of more importance was why Tommy had failed to mention he was still in touch with Fitzhubert. I only hoped he would wake up to tell us the answers to those questions.

46

Twenty minutes later, Wingsy and I had left the hospital and were on the road to Portsmouth, heading for Charles Fitzhubert's address. The sister had offered to call ahead, but we wanted to try to speak to him first.

Wingsy was driving so I took the time to leave a message on Bill's mobile, telling him I didn't know when I'd be home, and then I picked up my voicemails. I had one from my mum asking when I was going to visit my sister, and one from Stan asking if I was planning on going over on Sunday as usual for lunch and to put the world to rights.

I hadn't allowed myself to think too much about Stan. While I wanted desperately to get the truth from him, I was exhausted. My days off were in sight but I was aware of how much we had to do in the meantime. I was working on Saturday so I couldn't visit my sister this weekend, which was a relief, although I felt guilty about it. It wasn't that I didn't love seeing her, but afterwards I always felt totally drained. If most of Sunday was spent at Stan's, no matter how uncomfortable our conversation might be, I still had to fit in some time with my boyfriend and also for the laundry – I was one pair of clean knickers away from catastrophe.

I realised Wingsy was talking to me. 'Are you listening to anything I've been saying?' he asked.

'Yes. Of course I was. You said something about food.'

'No, I bloody didn't. I asked you if you wanted to ring Fitzhubert to make sure he doesn't leave before we get there.'

I dialled the number as Wingsy continued to go on about how I didn't listen to a word he said. I wasn't paying full attention, as I was listening to Fitzhubert's answerphone message. As I ended the call, Wingsy looked in my direction, momentarily taking his eyes off the road. 'Why didn't you leave a message?'

'When we were talking to Tommy, didn't he tell us that Malcolm Bring's former girlfriend's name was Marilyn?'

'Yeah, he did. Marilyn Springate, I think it was, but she got married. What about it?'

I was dialling the number again but this time from Wingsy's phone, which was set up on the hands-free. 'Listen to this,' I said.

As the sound of ringing stopped and the message cut in, a man's recorded voice filled our car: *Please leave a message. Charlie and Marilyn Fitzhubert will return your call as soon as possible.*

Wingsy and I exchanged glances. With his attention back on the motorway, I watched his profile as his forehead disappeared into his balding head while he thought the matter over. 'Don't you think it would be very weird,' he said, 'if the pregnant ex-girlfriend of the bloke who caused the train crash ended up marrying someone who was also on the train at the time?'

I tapped my notebook on the dashboard. 'Add to that, Wings, that she was pregnant by the man who set the whole thing up.'

'We need to find out exactly what Marilyn's part in all this is.'

47

We discussed whether we should turn around and head home, as our journey was looking a little pointless. But we agreed that, if nothing else, we could put a note through the door and hope they called back that night.

When we arrived at the address provided for Charles Fitzhubert, distinguished former footballer and next of kin for Tommy Ross, disgraced former player, we found he lived in an impressive house set back from the main road. As we drove up the leafy driveway, I thought how perfect a setting it was: far enough away from the noise of the traffic, but close enough to the road to stop the inhabitants feeling isolated. The size of the house and its grounds were similar to Tommy's, but this one was very much a home that was pulsing with life. The front garden was neat and tended, the windows sparkled, and the Jaguar parked outside the front door still had its windows open. Someone had only very recently arrived home.

Wingsy parked near to the Jaguar – far too near for my liking. In silence, we walked to the front door. I glanced down at the doormat telling me I was 'welcome'. That annoyed me for some reason. I was probably looking for an excuse not to like Charles Fitzhubert. He had a wife, a happy home, a successful footballing career to look back on. Tommy had none of that, and I couldn't help but wonder how easy it would have been for the two of them to have swapped places all those years ago, had one of them turned right instead of left – away from Leonard Rumbly.

Charles Fitzhubert opened the door and I tried not to hate him on sight. Wingsy introduced us, and I nodded at Fitzhubert as Wingsy told him my name. He barely glanced at me as he invited my colleague in. I followed in their wake and decided to leave Wingsy to do the talking; I knew I wouldn't win Fitzhubert over with my knowledge of football trivia.

He led us along the hallway towards the open door of a lounge, waving us in and gesturing towards a sofa facing the doorway. An incredibly beautiful woman sat on a matching sofa opposite. She looked in her late fifties but, if she was once Marilyn Springate, she must have been closer to her mid-seventies. Despite her youth being many decades behind her, however, she was the centre of attention in the room. That was no mean feat either: it was crammed full of so many tacky items, it was difficult to take it all in. She had a poise few could carry off without appearing haughty, which was also quite an achievement, since she was sitting beside an indoor water feature.

Raising his voice slightly over the sound of trickling water, Wingsy, having glanced around the room, said with no hint of sarcasm, 'Nice room. I'm DC John Wing and this is my colleague DC Nina Foster. I know that you're Charles Fitzhubert. May I ask your name?'

Before the woman had a chance to speak, Fitzhubert answered, 'This is my wife, Marilyn.'

Wingsy continued, 'We've come straight here from Worthing hospital.' My friend paused at this point – long enough to grab their attention but not enough to let them dwell and worry about what was to come next. 'Your friend Tommy Ross was taken in by ambulance earlier today.'

Both Wingsy and I had been looking at Fitzhubert. He had a look of mild surprise on his face at this announcement but seemed neither worried nor indifferent. I registered this in a split-second before my attention was ripped away by a gasp from Marilyn. Her poise had abandoned her. When I turned to look at her again, there was a definite curve in her back that hadn't been there moments earlier. A gentle crease brushed her forehead. That pleased me as, up until that point, I hadn't been entirely convinced that her features were Botox-free. What didn't please me was the expression of concern now showing on it.

Fitzhubert sat next to his wife and made a clumsy grab for her hand. His encased hers. I thought I'd try to get him to acknowledge me. 'Tommy named you as his next of kin, to be notified in case of emergency,' I said. 'Are you related?' I already knew the answer to that, but I wanted an explanation for why, after all these years of no contact, plus Tommy's chequered past, Fitzhubert would be named on his emergency contact forms.

'No, we aren't related,' he said, 'but we're old friends.' As I held his gaze, I saw from the corner of my eye the movement of his fingers as he squeezed his wife's hand. She flinched. They were making me very uncomfortable. Something was very wrong here.

'When did you last see him?' I asked.

'At his wife's funeral,' said Fitzhubert, 'and that was the first time in years. Before that, I couldn't tell you. I don't really understand why he's put me as his next of kin, to tell you the truth. I suppose that the sad old bastard didn't have anyone else.' He gave a hollow laugh. No one else joined in.

'What's he in the hospital for?' Marilyn asked, voice peppered with concern. 'It must be serious or you wouldn't be here.'

'Yes, it is,' I said. 'We had gone to Tommy's house in Sussex to speak to him about something and we found that he'd collapsed. We were already aware he's not been well for some time. He has cirrhosis of the liver. The hospital will have more details.'

I felt as if I would be giving away Tommy's secrets by telling these two anything else, even though Fitzhubert would find out more from the hospital; it felt like a betrayal on my part to give more than was necessary. What I'd travelled over one hundred miles for was their reaction to the train crash. I wanted to see the look on their faces after all this time. They didn't strike me as all that keen to get out of the door to visit their old friend on his sick bed. Medical details could wait.

'Officer,' said Marilyn, leaning forward a fraction, 'you're not from Sussex police, so why were you in Tommy's house?'

'We're from Riverstone police station,' I said. They both leaned back slightly as if something bad was coming. 'We're making enquiries into the 1964 Wickerstead Valley train crash.'

Mention of our home town didn't usually bring such a transformation in people's attitudes. Charles Fitzhubert had gone very pale, and Marilyn had begun to cry.

48

Eventually, Fitzhubert realised that his wife was weeping quietly next to him. He looked annoyed, but then made a show of producing a hanky from somewhere in his pockets.

'I was on the train, you see,' said Marilyn, biting her bottom lip. She held the handkerchief up to the side of her face nearest to her husband. It seemed as if she wanted to shield her words so that he couldn't overhear. A totally pointless gesture, but it added to my mounting concern that all was not as it would seem in their happy home.

It was time to put our cards on the table. I glanced at Wingsy and he gave me the tiniest of nods, the kind that only really good friends or very close colleagues might see and correctly interpret. I began.

'We know you were on the train, Marilyn, and you too, Charles. We have the original police file from 1964, complete with officers' notes and statements. We're rechecking everything. Absolutely everything from the original file.'

I was labouring the point because I could see how uncomfortable it was making Fitzhubert. He grabbed the handkerchief back from his wife and dabbed at his forehead with it. With that gesture I was able to see past the capped teeth and dark head of hair. It was either a remarkable wig or he'd gone prematurely mahogany. If he continued to sweat at the same rate, I might find out which. My mind dragged in a memory of Tommy Ross sitting on his own threadbare armchair, sweating in such a manner. It was funny how sorry I felt for him and how much loathing I was feeling for Fitzhubert. I couldn't work out why that should be.

Wingsy continued by adding, 'What's brought us here slightly earlier than our list of enquiries intended is Tommy's emergency admission to the hospital and our subsequent discovery that you're named as his next of kin.' He paused, and, resting his elbows on his knees, held his palms out towards the pair of them. 'Now would be the best time to talk to you both and get an account of what really happened on the train. Charles, how about I speak to you in another room? Nina and Marilyn, you stay here so we can all speak without interrupting one another.'

I liked that plan a lot and it would have been exactly what I'd have suggested, especially as Marilyn looked relieved at the thought of her husband leaving us to it. Charles, however, stood up suddenly and said, 'We should get to the hospital to see Tommy, if he's in as bad a way as you say he is.'

Marilyn looked up at her husband. 'You go, then, Charlie. I'm going to stay here and speak to the officers.' She held her chin high as she addressed him and met his gaze. After a second or two, Charles's face relaxed for the first time since he'd opened the door to us. He placed his hand on his wife's shoulder with the briefest of touches and nodded at her, as if he was accepting his fate.

Marilyn and I remained on our respective sofas while Wingsy and Charles Fitzhubert took themselves off to the kitchen. Hearing them get settled in another part of the house, I opened my notebook and looked Marilyn in the eye. I waited for her to speak.

'I was Marilyn Springate then. That was my maiden name. I had my whole future ahead of me: modelling career, good-looking boyfriend, Malcolm, and not a care in the world. You know what it's like, Nina.'

Actually, I had no idea what it was like to have a modelling career, or nothing to worry my waking thoughts, but I did have a good-looking boyfriend. One out of three wasn't bad. I smiled at the thought of Bill and then realised that I shouldn't be comparing my Bill to Malcolm Bring.

I dropped the smile and said, 'Tell me about Malcolm.'

'I'd been going out with him for about twelve months at the time of the train crash. All was going well, up to a point. He liked to gamble. It seemed nothing to worry about to begin with. He'd have a flutter on the horses, win some, lose some. He was earning good money from his lorry, travelling all over, picking up fruit and vegetables and taking them to market. I had some money coming in from my modelling and we managed to put a bit aside to save up and get married. We were planning on starting a family as soon as we could. The problem was that the gambling started to become a problem, and a problem that he hid from me. Malcolm had an addictive personality. He couldn't leave anything alone. He worked such long hours but then would gamble all the income away. I didn't become aware of that until he'd spent all of our savings too.'

Marilyn held out her left hand in front of her as she told me this. She used her right hand to turn the diamond ring next to her wedding band. I knew little about the price of diamonds, never having been in a position to purchase any, but if I were a gambler myself I'd have put a large stake on the price of her jewellery far outweighing any debt Malcolm had ever accrued.

When she'd finished staring sadly at her own good fortune in life, Marilyn continued telling me how she'd ended up where she currently was.

'When I found out that he'd spent all of our money, every penny we'd put away, plus he'd borrowed against his lorry and owed money to bookies, I was so angry with him. So, so angry.' Her voice caught slightly on the words, but she did a very good job of maintaining her dignity. 'It led to an enormous argument, the result of which made me think that I could do something to rectify the situation. I was so naïve.'

Once more, Marilyn paused. I didn't doubt that she'd finish the story, but sensed that she needed a push to do it.

'What did you do?' I asked.

'I did a very foolish thing. I went to see the person Malcolm owed all of our money and future to. I went to see Leonard Rumbly. That was where our troubles really began.'

49

I waited for Marilyn to tell me something I didn't know. I was waiting for her to tell me how she succumbed to Leonard Rumbly's charms and found herself pregnant. I already knew all that, but I thought it only polite to let her say it; it was her story, after all.

She smoothed her skirt a couple of times and cleared her throat before giving me a sad smile.

'I was desperate to marry Malcolm. I was still so very annoyed at all he'd put me through with the lying and gambling, but it's a disease at the end of the day. I justified what I did next by comparing it to cancer or any other debilitating illness Malc could have been suffering from. I went to see Rumbly to appeal to his better nature. I didn't know then that he didn't have one. You might never have met real evil in human form, Nina, but I have, and I met it that day. Being young and foolish, I thought that, if I showed him how desperate we really were, he would help us. Egotistically, I also thought he might take to me because, many years ago, I was an attractive woman. Vanity was partly to blame. Please understand, though, I only wanted to buy some time so that we could start again and salvage our relationship. It took a lot of guts for me to travel to Deptford and go to Leonard's warehouse. He had an office at the back. It was fairly smart, with a carpet, a desk, a sofa and a safe.'

Once more, Marilyn broke eye contact with me. She'd wavered at the word 'sofa', as if it had unpleasant memories for her, but bitten her lip after the word 'safe'. I wanted to know more about the sofa and the safe but we were both distracted by the sound of chairs scraping on the floor in the kitchen next door. To focus her once more, I said, 'Sofa and safe?', leaving it there.

'Gave too much away there, didn't I?' she said. 'The safe was behind the sofa and on my first visit to see Leonard it was open. It was piled high with banknotes. It was the year that £10 notes were reintroduced after the war. Few people would ever have seen so much cash. If you can imagine today seeing a safe bursting with brand new £200 notes, if such a thing existed... Over all these years I've liked to kid myself that it wasn't greed, but I saw an end to my and Malcolm's plight. Maybe it was greed that made me act the way I did, but I like to dress it up as love.' Once more she twisted the enormous diamond ring around her finger.

'I got very irritated with Leonard very quickly. I could see he was attracted to me but I thought I could make him see how we could all come to an arrangement to settle the matter. I wasn't going to be fobbed off, but I didn't want to rush things either. He was toying with me. He was an up-and-coming criminal making his mark on the underworld. He had connections and I was desperate enough to go along with him. He suggested that I come back another time when he had a free afternoon. Well, I did as he asked, and we went out to dinner a few times, that sort of thing. I didn't tell Malcolm any of this, of course. He was too busy lying low because he owed so many people money. He was working all over the southeast and parts of East Anglia too.' She paused at this point and said, 'I don't know much about the law, but I suppose that after all this time I can still be arrested for theft?'

I hadn't seen this one coming. 'Theft?' I asked. 'Of what?'

A look of slight annoyance crossed her face and once again a crease in her forehead showed. I'd given her the impression that I wasn't paying attention to her. Nothing could be further from the truth, but, if I wasn't very much mistaken, she was about to confess to stealing from Leonard Rumbly. Sex I had been prepared for, so to speak – theft, I was not.

'I took his money – Leonard Rumbly's. I took his money from the safe. After that first time I was there, he kept the safe closed to begin with. After we'd been on a few dates, though, he started leaving it open. I suppose that he began to trust me. Or that's what I thought anyway. After the event – and when I say "event" I mean my dalliance with grand larceny – when I reflected on what had happened, I could see that he set me up. I was so starry-eyed and full of innocence, certainly compared with women today; I had a foolish notion to trust people. You do learn the hard way, don't you? What you think of as life's ideals come back to you with a vengeance. I know what you're thinking.'

Marilyn actually had no idea what I was thinking. I was thinking, oh bloody hell, this was such a nightmare. For once, though, my thoughts couldn't have been written all over my face, as she then said, 'That's right, you're thinking, "How did Malcolm then find out about this?"'

I nodded as wisely as I could manage, all the while wishing that the sound of trickling water from the fountain wasn't blocking out any noise from Wingsy and Charles in the kitchen. I'd welcome the distraction. The enquiry was now heading in a whole new direction.

50

As if in answer to my wishes, the door opened to reveal Charles Fitzhubert, followed closely by Wingsy, who widened his eyes and gave a slight shake of his head. This had the hallmark of a detective constable who had been told the most fantastic piece of information he'd heard in a long time. At least we would both be startled together.

'I'm sorry, Marilyn,' said Charles before he was fully in the room, 'I had to tell the officer. There seemed little point in lying, and it's not as if Liam doesn't know.'

He sat beside his wife and took her hand. I watched as they grasped one another's fingers again, but this time in a comfortable movement, though their eyes focused strictly on their hands. They were avoiding eye contact now, and I had no idea why. Or who Liam was.

Wingsy sat beside me and began to tell me what Charles had been explaining to him in the kitchen. 'Marilyn was pregnant at the time of the train crash.' He paused, allowing the others in the room to glance up. 'She didn't have a chance to tell Malcolm this news before the derailment.'

Marilyn gave a small smile – one she clearly didn't mean. 'I was going to tell him in person but someone else told him. I always had my suspicions it was Martin Withey, Leonard's right-hand man at the time. He was always hanging around and trying to stir up trouble. He had a girlfriend around that time too, Dorothy something. She went off to live in Bristol, I think. I'd confided in her that I was pregnant. I can only think she told Withey, and not only did he tell my fiancé the news that I was expecting, he no doubt told him the father was Leonard. Withey hated Malcolm and never seemed fond of me, so, if he did tell Malcolm I was having an affair, he probably also told him I was going to be on the train. After nearly fifty years, I can still remember how I felt when I found out Malcolm was the cause of it all. I was lying in hospital and he came to see me…'

Marilyn made a noise that sounded like the start of a sob but I was guessing that over the decades between the train wreck and today she'd tried unsuccessfully to distance herself from the memories. Trouble was, they wouldn't always let us go. When we thought that they'd held on to us for long enough and wouldn't notice we'd given them the slip, we realised that they'd never gone away after all; they were standing right behind us all along. It might sometimes only take the tiniest of triggers to hurtle Marilyn back to her former mentally battered self, but today she had two police officers in her living room. A very large trigger by anyone's standards.

Emotions once more in check, she continued. 'We weren't having an affair. We went out to dinner a few times, but that was only my attempt to get Malc some breathing space for the money he – well, I suppose by that time it was money that *we* owed. He'd pulled me into the mess of his gambling debt and I was doing the only thing I could think of to get us out. I made it worse. I caused Malc to think that I'd been sleeping with Rumbly but instead I was stealing from him. The ironic part is that, if I hadn't stolen from Rumbly, things might have worked out very differently.'

These words made me feel a little uncomfortable. Her husband was sitting next to her on the sofa and must have thought the same as me: did she regret her current life and the one she missed out on with Malcolm Bring?

It seemed to me that, as a distraction from the awkward moment we were all feeling, Charles said, 'Liam is our son. Well, strictly speaking he's Marilyn's son. I brought him up as my own and, while he knows that I'm not his biological father, as far as he's concerned I'm his dad. He does know his actual father is Malcolm, but as far as we're aware he did very little to trace him when he had the opportunity.'

I was having trouble trying to work out why Marilyn had been pregnant with Malcolm's child but had married Charles Fitzhubert instead. I steeled myself to ask a personal question of her. As a detective constable I had to know. As a very nosy person, I wanted to know.

'So Malcolm knew you were pregnant?' I asked.

She nodded and tucked her hair behind her ears. 'Yes, he did. The trouble was, he thought that the father of my child was Leonard Rumbly. It was difficult enough to come to terms with my fiancé thinking I was cheating on him, with Rumbly of all people, but his last words to me will always be the worst thing I will ever have to deal with.' I watched her take a deep breath and press the bridge of her nose with her index finger. Up until now, Marilyn had remained almost motionless. I was seeing a woman struggle to form the words after so many years. Charles must have had an idea of what was coming as he sat stock still, idolising her from his seat. Yes, I was warming to him.

'Malcolm came to see me in the hospital, stood by my bed and leaned down to my ear. I thought he was going to kiss the side of my face. It was about the only part of me that wasn't bruised. He said to me, "I was supposed to hold the train up and delay it but I knocked it off its tracks. I wanted you and your bastard baby to die."'

Marilyn looked from me to Wingsy and drove her point home.

'Malcolm told me he tried to kill me and the baby. It wasn't an accident – he deliberately caused the train to crash. He felt so much hatred, he wanted me dead.'

51

My reaction to this news was mixed: Malcolm Bring was clearly more of an abhorrent individual than I had previously thought. In comparison, his son, Joe, was looking like a remarkable man. OK, he'd been locked up for more burglaries than I could recall, but, with a father prepared to kill and injure hundreds to get even with a woman who had only tried to help him, he had little in the way of role models. Bring senior had been angry enough to kill, and I couldn't begin to understand how Marilyn had felt all these years holding on to the memory of how much he had hated her. It didn't seem like the right time to bring it up, but no doubt she also felt that the seven deaths were her fault in some way. I thought that would keep for now.

Other than hatred for Malcolm Bring and admiration for Marilyn, my main emotion was one of cautious hope. We had a witness. Bring had told someone he'd caused the derailment on purpose. The only problem was, prosecution was far too late for Malcolm Bring, and Marilyn was telling us that this was all down to him. All we had so far was three people telling us that Leonard Rumbly had told Bring to hold the train up. He had never told him how to do it. I was getting a sinking feeling about how we took this further. I was desperate to know exactly what Rumbly and Malcolm Bring's conversation had been about when the plan was made to stop the train. I tried to think back many years to my CID courses, where an impossible amount of law and its practical application was taught us in only a few weeks, to determine whether we had enough to prosecute Rumbly for conspiracy to murder with what we had. I was so tired that I wasn't even able to work out if all the parties in a conspiracy had to be alive. That could cause a problem. The Crown Prosecution Service had standards, and that included only taking people to court who were still living. We had little, evidentially, to show that Rumbly had any knowledge that Bring had actually been going to kill people, but if we could somehow show Rumbly knew Bring would arrange for a five-ton truck to be on the line, we had him. This at least was a start.

'Marilyn,' I said, pitching myself as far forward as I could without falling at her feet, 'I realise that it was a long time ago, but would you be prepared to make a witness statement about the crash? Most importantly, about what Malcolm said to you afterwards.'

I regarded her with a look that I hoped would appeal to her sense of decency. She, in turn, looked at her husband.

'It has to be your decision,' he replied. 'You know that I'll stand by whatever you do. I always have and I always will.'

'Will I have to go to court?' Marilyn asked me.

'There is every chance.'

She blew a long breath through her barely parted lips. Then added a firm nod in my direction.

I got ready for a long night of note-taking as Marilyn began to tell me her story in more detail. To begin with, I let her talk and I made notes, scribbling furiously to keep up with her. I covered somewhere in the region of twenty pages of A4 in my notebook, marking in the margin where I needed to ask her questions. I didn't want to interrupt her any more than was strictly necessary. She looked far off into the distance on a number of occasions but mostly she told her tale with little emotion, other than the odd rueful smile. Wingsy and Charles had disappeared back into the kitchen and had at long last put the kettle on. Food I was able to go without, under protest, but not tea.

Charles brought in the tea. He stayed and poured it in silence, allowing his wife to talk. Even when he offered me my drink, he held the sugar bowl out rather than speak and interrupt his wife's narrative. When I shook my head at his offering, he replaced the bowl and left the room without uttering one word. So he wasn't quite the idiot I'd thought on our arrival. I was even beginning to find the sound of the water fairly soothing. But then, I was tired, and the lack of food had lowered my resistance.

When Marilyn had finished at last, I went over my notes and asked some questions to either fill in gaps in her account or to make certain I had completely understood her. I then began the laborious task of transferring the notes into a statement. It was going to take time and it was very late. The thought flicked through my brain that I could return the following day with her statement typed, ready for her to read and sign. I weighed up whether this was a good idea or not. It was unlikely she'd collapse and be rushed to hospital by ambulance like Tommy, but I didn't want to risk that by morning something else would have got in the way.

The statement taken, I asked one last question about Joe Bring's half-brother.

'What does Liam do for a job, Marilyn?'

Her reluctance to show her feelings vanished. Her face lit up as she said, 'He owns his own business. It's doing very well. He's recently expanded and taken on new premises. He's in security – burglar alarms, that kind of thing.'

I left it there.

As we packed up our paperwork, Marilyn told us that they would be visiting Tommy Ross first thing. We said our goodbyes and set off back to Riverstone. Wingsy offered to drive and I was happy to let him; I was shattered. I thought that the best thing was for me to get home and get some sleep. Before I succumbed to exhaustion, though, I wanted to discuss how the last few hours had gone. Wingsy hadn't heard everything Marilyn had told me, and I certainly had no idea what he'd discussed with Charles Fitzhubert in the kitchen.

'What do you think, Wings, about Malcolm Bring being told by Martin Withey that Marilyn was pregnant?'

I saw his shoulders shrug up and down in the dark of the car and he replied, 'My money's on Charles Fitzhubert telling him.'

'Really?' I said. 'What exactly would he have to gain from it all?'

'Well, Marilyn, of course. It seemed that, as well as the dinners she mentioned with Rumbly, she also went to a couple of functions and got herself noticed. I also explained to Charles before we began to write,' said Wingsy, 'that the declaration at the top of the statement clearly points out that lying in his statement may well end up with him getting arrested. It seemed to cause him a few memory problems when it came to anything regarding Rumbly's and Marilyn's "casual dating".'

'Do you think she had any reason to lie to me about there being no sexual relationship between her and Rumbly?' I asked. 'She seemed genuine, and she did admit to stealing from him. She could get charged with theft, but she'll never face a conviction for sleeping with him.'

'I don't know, but I think we need to speak to Harry and Ian Hammond about what we do next. They're going to have to decide if we arrest Leonard Rumbly yet or wait. The priority is going to be the shooting of Patrick Hudson, not a Cold Case investigation fifty years old, especially with so little at the moment against Rumbly for it. There's an overlap between the two, but a recent murder will always win.'

I understood very clearly what he was trying to tell me. We were going to have to try very hard to convince the DI that the arrest of Leonard Rumbly was worthy of immediate pursuit.

52

We drove back to Riverstone, tired yet elated by what we'd learnt. We stopped on the way to grab a sandwich that neither of us enjoyed, but we needed food, a break, and some space to call our other halves. Bill didn't sound too worried that I was going to be late but did remind me that I'd only been back at work a short while and wasn't supposed to be charging all over the country and working sixteen-hour days. No one seemed to have done very much to discourage me.

Eventually, we made it back to the yard, cleared the rubbish out of the car and carried the paperwork up to the Cold Case office. I logged on to the computer to the noise of Wingsy grumbling about Jim having taken his pens and his mousemat and what he was going to say to him in the morning. I was only half listening, as I wanted to check my emails and send one to Harry warning him that I might be in later than my duty time the next day. I knew he wouldn't mind me coming in an hour late, as long as I let him know.

The sound of Wingsy muttering about his stolen stationery was getting to me, as I was trying to read one of my emails and couldn't concentrate. When I could take no more, I said, 'Wind your neck in about your bloody highlighter. Go and get another one from the stationery cupboard.'

When Wingsy came back with armfuls of notepads and pens, I said, 'Let's call it a day, and when we get in tomorrow we can run everything we've got so far past Harry.'

'Good idea,' said Wingsy.

We shut up the office for the evening and signed out in the diary, letting the control room know we'd gone off duty, to prevent any phone calls in the middle of the night checking where we were.

As I pulled up on the driveway of Bill's house, I could see that he was still awake. The flicker of the television screen illuminated the living room and momentarily silhouetted my boyfriend as he sat in his armchair. I liked this. I really liked coming home to him at the end of the day. I sat in my car, leaning forward against the steering wheel, quietly savouring the moment and the stillness of the neighbourhood at one o'clock in the morning. Then I accidentally pressed the horn and saw Bill jump out of his seat to peer out of the window. I hurried from the car to the front door, deliberately avoiding looking at the neighbours' twitching curtains.

Bill saw my car through the window and disappeared from view on his way towards the front door. He let me in and I stood for a moment or two at the bottom of the stairs, glad to be home. I'd spent my day in A&E and two vastly different homes. It had been, as a detective constable's days often were, weird and unpredictable. Now I was back in familiar, cosy surroundings and I couldn't be happier about it.

'You look pleased to be home. Or is it the thought of wine?' said Bill, pausing to kiss me before disappearing towards the kitchen. It was a warm and lingering kiss, making me feel even better about walking through the door than I could have hoped.

'Bit of both really, but I'll pass on the wine tonight. Think I'll put the kettle on.' I had followed Bill into the kitchen and saw him pause with the wine bottle in his hand, concern creasing his face. 'I've got an early start tomorrow and think a cuppa's a better idea at the moment.' Actually, this wasn't true, but I couldn't get out of my mind the image of Tommy's ashen face as he lay on his lonely bed, fighting to breathe. I supposed so much alcohol was bound to take a toll after such a long time. I thought that I'd expand my life expectancy by one more day through my abstinence.

While I filled the kettle and Bill got the cups from the cupboard, he asked me how my day had been. I began to tell him about Tommy Ross and why we'd gone back to his house, although I left out the part about the chicken doner. We took our tea into the semi-darkness of the living room, settled back, and I asked Bill about his own day.

I watched him take a slurp of his hot drink, before he replied, 'Stopped a car. It turned out to be stolen and I spent most of the morning booking the prisoner into custody and completing the paperwork.' He then told me about his afternoon spent searching a house following a stabbing in the victim's front garden. Take out the part about CSIs searching premises and bloodstained clothing, and this was a normal domestic scene. I had never felt so comfortable in a relationship with someone.

I sipped at the rest of my drink, not even minding that it didn't contain anything stronger than caffeine, and allowed myself to enjoy being home.

My reverie was interrupted by Bill setting his cup on the table.

'There was something I wanted to speak to you about, actually,' he said.

'And not work-related?'

He shook his head. That was a shame. I could handle that.

'I've been thinking… Neither of us has lots of money to spare, and you never know what unexpected expenses are around the corner.'

'You want me to move out?'

'No, no, of course I don't. I'm thinking about your parents and the money you give them.'

I put my own cup down and went in the direction of the kitchen. I still wasn't in search of wine; I just wanted to get out of the room and avoid cross words.

Bill followed me. 'Nina, we need to talk about this.'

I had reached the sink so I turned and faced him. I crossed my arms and waited.

He took a deep breath and said, 'How about we offer them a compromise? We'll give them a fixed amount every month but less than you already give them – '

I opened my mouth to say something but Bill carried on talking.

'Your sister – '

My mouth was very much closed now. Lips pursed.

'She's a part of your family. And I know so little of her and…' He picked up my hand and took a deep breath. 'And when you're ready, if you want to, how about you tell me some more about her?'

'I'd like that,' I said. 'I'd really like that.'

53

Following a restless night, I got ready for work feeling as if I'd hardly slept at all. Bill was on a rest day so I kissed the top of his head and left him snoring away in bed.

The email I had sent Harry told him to call me if he needed me in urgently, otherwise I would be in a bit later. I knew he'd understand that the last few days had taken it out of me. I had expected to return to work and within a couple of days everything would be back to normal. That didn't feel as though it was happening. I didn't want to make too much fuss about how I was struggling, though, for fear they'd send me somewhere really dull. Admittedly my last murder investigation hadn't gone as smoothly as it should have done, but, despite all the personal problems it had brought with it, it had also produced one of the best rushes I'd ever known – the buzz, the thrill, the excitement of trying to catch a killer. I couldn't imagine taking another person's life or standing by and doing nothing to save one, but playing a part in a team that existed for the sole purpose of detecting murders and putting those responsible in prison was second to nothing.

Still feeling torn between wanting to go back home to bed and feeling myself settling into the Cold Case investigation, I walked into the office.

Jim Sullivan and Jemma Russell both looked up, but only Jemma acknowledged me. 'Morning, Nin. Harry and

Wings are in the conference room. Said when you get here, can you go up and join them?'

'Cheers, Jem,' I said, leaving my bag and jacket behind but grabbing my notebook. I set off up the stairs and was pleased that the one flight was a little less of a struggle than it had been a couple of days earlier.

I walked into the conference room, to find Wingsy and Harry sitting next to each other, heads bent together, engrossed in conversation. A messy spread of papers littered a large portion of the table. I could tell from several feet away that it was the file of the 1964 Wickerstead Valley train crash. It was looking distinctly as though the investigation was now being upgraded to a priority. The reason for that had to be the new evidence Wingsy and I had uncovered. I felt the tiredness ebb away and once again I was ready to throw myself back into the job in front of me.

Wingsy looked up and winked at me. Harry pulled out the chair next to me and pushed a cup of tea in my direction. I took the plastic lid off, opened my notebook and joined in. I expected some stick from Harry about not being able to get myself out of bed in the mornings but he didn't say a thing. I had forgotten that not only was he a formidable detective, he also knew when one of his members of staff needed to be cut a little slack. I knew he wouldn't make a habit of it, but I liked to think that part of the reason I was sent to Cold Case was because Harry would keep an eye on me.

'Wingsy was filling me in on the details of last night with the Fitzhuberts,' he said, Marilyn's statement in front of him. 'Seems like you two had a very eventful day yesterday.'

'You could say that,' I replied. 'I know that we're supposed to be looking at the 1964 incident, but it's bleeding into other areas.' I held my right hand up and counting on my fingers, said, 'Firstly, we have Leonard Rumbly's suspected involvement in that. Secondly, we have his family's connections to the heroin overdoses, and thirdly... well, that's about it.'

Harry was staring at me. I felt stupid with my hand up, so I put it down.

He glanced at the closed door and said, 'There's intelligence coming in. Janice Freeman wants to talk to us this afternoon. She's coming here. We have this room all day. We need to be in a position to present to her everything we've got so far about the Rumblys, particularly Leonard.'

'What's she got to do with our investigation?' I asked. 'Isn't she the SIO on Patrick Hudson's shooting? Her team's nothing to do with this.'

'Niall Rumbly was sharing a cell with Patrick before he was released from prison, remember?' said Wingsy.

'Yes, but he wasn't involved in the shooting, though. He was still locked up at the time,' I said.

'The evidence against Richard Hudson was always a bit on the thin side,' said Harry, taking a sip from his own tea. 'He was swabbed for gunshot residue – that was negative. He was the one who called the police, and the warrant on his home address didn't turn up anything untoward. He certainly didn't have a gun or ammunition. Janice Freeman's team have been very busy carrying out other enquiries and it would seem that the phone work and ANPR have turned up some very interesting stuff.' He paused. 'The black Polo that you and Wingsy saw outside the gold shop on the Noël Coward estate was in the area where Patrick was shot at the relevant time. When the three of them got lifted for handling stolen goods, their phones were downloaded and one of them had made several calls either side of the shooting.' He paused once more. 'And the number called was Andy Rumbly's landline.'

54

By the time Harry had finished speaking, I was open-mouthed. Wingsy didn't look as surprised as me, so he might well already have received the news. Apart from loving this update, I was secretly pleased it was Andy and not Leonard Rumbly's landline the calls had been made to. I knew only too well that they might regret their decision to let me near the shooting once it came to light that Leonard Rumbly's grandson was sharing a cell with Hudson, our shooting victim. Had we known at the time that we could link someone at the scene of the shooting straight to Andy Rumbly's home address, we might have taken a different approach, and Clint Stirling and Janice Freeman probably wouldn't have asked me to become involved in the first place. Still, now I was involved and with three more to arrest, I was banking on the shortage of staff to keep me well and truly in the thick of it.

Harry looked at his watch.

'We have about three hours to get whatever we have into a clear and concise format for the DCI. I'm not handing them the train crash, Nina. That's yours. We're going to have to work out a way of separating them. I know now that our job won't be dealt with before a current murder investigation but that's the way it goes. When she gets here, we'll talk about the logistics and when we nick Rumbly senior.'

Before we got to work on the hours of paperwork before us, I made a phone call to the hospital to check on Tommy Ross. His condition had changed little overnight but he had had two visitors that morning. The nurse I spoke to didn't know their names but told me that, even though it was outside visiting hours, they had been allowed to see him as they were named as his next of kin.

Perhaps it was the tight timescale I had before DCI Freeman arrived, wanting to know what we had on Leonard Rumbly, but I found it was the first time since my return to work that I wasn't constantly distracted. My concentration had improved and I felt as though we were getting somewhere. Wingsy and I worked in comfortable silence, only interrupting each other's thoughts to check facts or ask if the other wanted a cup of tea. At last, we were as content as we could be with our information, and waited for the SIO's arrival.

Harry rejoined us with Freeman and the four of us sat around the table in the conference room, talking through the options for Leonard Rumbly's arrest and how it would go ahead. Freeman began by explaining what enquiries had been carried out already.

'The DC here on the nick who dealt with the three from outside the gold shop for handling stolen goods downloaded their phones and realised that one of them, Philip Peters, had made a number of calls either side of the time of Patrick Hudson's shooting. He contacted the Major Incident Room and passed the information on. In the meantime, we'd already carried out ANPR enquiries around the scene of the shooting. The black Polo had come up, but it was on false plates so we couldn't locate it or the driver. There were a few other vehicles around at the time so it was one of many and not a particular priority. That was until you put it together with the driver of the Polo making a number of calls at the time of the murder. Oh, and there's this.' She pulled an ANPR photograph from her notebook and pushed it across the table to the three of us.

Even though it was taken at night and would usually show very little, we could see that the front passenger was wearing a high-visibility vest.

'Our next step,' she said, tapping the edge of the picture with her fingertips, 'is to arrest the three from the Polo for murder and see if we can at least find gunshot residue on their clothing or in the car.'

DCI Freeman's words sounded very positive, and there was enough to arrest on suspicion of Patrick Hudson's murder, but if you scratched beneath the surface of having the car in the area at the relevant time of the shooting, if the arrests and warrants to search their premises and vehicles turned up little, we didn't have much else. The glimmer of hope I had was a connection somewhere between Philip Peters and Leonard Rumbly. There had also been a link between the now-dead Patrick Hudson and Niall Rumbly. My personal feelings were that Patrick Hudson was no great loss to the world, but, that said, few people, me included, wanted to live in a society where people were gunned down next to Screwfix, even if those people were wife-beating criminals. Despite wanting to see someone charged and imprisoned for killing another, though, I couldn't help the feeling of impatience to get the murder of Hudson dealt with so that I could get on with the business of arresting Leonard Rumbly.

In the meantime, we had to assist with three warrants and arrests. Janice Freeman talked us through the list of resources she had and highlighted those roles that still needed assigning. She opened her SIO's policy file and, glancing up from time to time, said, 'My team has been briefed to plan for two days' time. I've liaised with firearms to be on standby for the three warrants. I have a DC assigned the job of getting three warrants sworn out at the Magistrates' Court and I've a list here of the staff to simultaneously enter and search the three target addresses. On top of that, of course, interview teams need to be made available. This is where we're going to need some assistance from you.'

I noticed that, as the DCI said this, she made a point of looking at Harry and Wingsy, avoiding my direction. Perhaps I was over-thinking it.

Janice Freeman continued, 'I've a CSI assigned to each premises, an exhibits officer to take possession of every item seized, a case officer in the form of Mark Russell to put the paperwork together, plus a detective sergeant to sort out any enquiries that needed allocating, and then one of my detective inspectors to deal with any issues from custody matters to a Warrant of Further Detention back at the Magistrates' Court if the need arises. I'm hoping that the enquiry team can be written off for as long as possible to free them up, so I'm praying that another job doesn't come in over the next few days. If it does, we are well and truly in trouble. I'm offering working rest days but hardly anyone wants the extra hours. Oh, and also, if we need to take anything to the lab on an urgent lab run, I've a civilian investigator on standby so she can, if needed, run exhibits and DNA to the lab and back for analysis or default to taking statements. There are three set aside for seizing CCTV and downloading mobile phones when they're seized. I only have two to take care of any fast-track actions coming out of the suspects' accounts in the interviews.'

As I listened to her, I remembered how much went into a murder investigation. It was such a massive task.

Unfortunately, the message I was getting was that I should stay out of the entire process.

'But,' Freeman added, breaking into my thoughts, 'if we have nothing else, they're still on bail for handling stolen goods from their last arrest. It's not much, but we've got enough to charge them with that. I think you'll agree, though, that murder would be so much better.'

55

Admittedly I had enough work of my own to get on with, but I wasn't happy about not being tasked with any part of the investigation. Try as I might, the following day I could not persuade Harry to let me get a look-in. I knew I was wasting my time, and only annoying him. He had been given instructions to keep me out of the arrests and subsequent interviews. Wingsy, however, had been sent to Headquarters to work alongside the arrest and interview teams. Cold Case was also part of the Serious Crime Directorate but, owing to lack of space, Cold Case remained on Riverstone police station while Major Crime, who were dealing with the murder suspects, worked from HQ. I'd kept out of the staffing struggles and was grateful that I was part of anything at all after being off sick for months. I hoped that being a part of Cold Case might mean I would be seen in a favourable light if vacancies became available on Major Crime. I needed to make myself enough of a nuisance that they would want me back, without being too much of a nuisance that they would turn me down.

Right now, what I needed to do was the best job I could manage.

I rang Wingsy. He sounded distant.

'How's it going, Wings?'

'Yeah, good. Going to be a long day tomorrow.'

'Don't forget that I'm here and I can come in early if you need me. You know – first-hand knowledge and all that.'

There was a pause. 'We're bringing our prisoner to Riverstone when he's in custody, so I'll see you tomorrow, but best make sure you keep out of the way. Got to go. I've loads to do. Bye, duchess.'

I stared at the receiver, before placing it back on its cradle.

When the paperwork that I was supposed to be reading couldn't hold my attention for another hour, I went to find Michaela Irving. She was in her empty office, looking through one of many blue files piled on her desk. Her team wasn't overstaffed at the best of times but I had rarely seen it so empty. She looked up and smiled as I walked in.

'Hi, Kayla,' I said, sitting at the desk opposite her. I wanted to pick her brain further and ask her what else she knew about the current investigation into the drugs deaths, but, as it was mixed in with the Rumblys and the three arrested for handling stolen goods, I had to be cautious about anything I told her. I wasn't sure how low-key the early-morning warrants were being kept.

As it turned out, I need not have worried.

'You on the five am start for Philip Peters and his associates in the morning, Nin?' she asked.

'The secret job that's on a need-to-know basis? No, I'm about the only one not involved.'

'Do you want to be?'

'Not sure, to tell you the truth.' I paused and found myself scratching my head, as if I was trying to labour the point that I'd thought about this long and hard. 'It is Saturday tomorrow, so I know that the staffing levels are low. Not being asked to help out when they're desperate is a bit of a kick in the teeth, but I have loads to do on

Rumbly senior and the train crash, not to mention all the other personal stuff that's mounting up. On the other hand, a bit of overtime wouldn't go amiss.'

'How many are they calling in to work on a rest day?'

'Enough to keep the superintendent's blood pressure sky-high.'

'Why don't they leave it till Monday?'

'In case someone else gets blown away over the weekend. There'd be hell to pay if that happened. And besides, I don't think there'll be any more on duty on Monday. Anyway, Kayla, I was going to ask you if there was any progress on Errol Chandler's drug overdose?'

'Yes, but you won't like it.' She rummaged through the rickety stack of files and removed one. As she pushed it towards me, I read the words 'CHANDLER, ERROL' and 'OVERDOSE' written in large capitals alongside his name.

'Why won't I like it?' I asked, settling back in my seat for whatever was coming next.

'Because there's little chance this is going anywhere, but it's too early to officially write it off.'

'What about the Rumblys supplying the drugs? What about Sidney Manning being given Naloxone by someone? What does Sidney remember?'

Kayla straightened the file in front of her before answering me. 'First off, all we have is a recorded message of a dying man, off his head on drugs, giving us the name of the Rumbly family. Secondly, Manning says he can't remember very much – only that he didn't inject his mate with anything at all – very convenient. There's a good chance his memory is hazy. Drug addicts aren't renowned for their total recall. We can't prove that Manning injected Chandler, or name anyone else who did, come to that. Put yourself in Manning's position: it could easily have been his dead body the paramedics were called to. If you want my opinion, for what it's worth, I think that someone turned up with a new batch of heroin to test, Chandler and Manning were the guinea pigs and it went wrong.'

'I understand what you're saying, but the Naloxone bottle had no prints on it at all – no identifying marks even though it was prescription-only. Who the hell did it belong to?'

'That's the problem, Nin – we don't know and we can't prove anything. I need to put you right on a couple of things, though.' She pulled out a colour photograph from the file and pushed it across to me. It was of an open pack labelled 'Naloxone Hydrochloride 1mg/ml solution for injection'. The pack was about eight inches long, with a label on one end with the expiry date, batch and manufacturing numbers. The identifying marks had been scratched out.

'As you can see,' she said, 'it's not a bottle. The pack contains a two ml prefilled syringe and two needles. None of this bears one single fingerprint. I've had a look at break-ins at pharmacies and doctor's surgeries throughout the division in the weeks leading up to Chandler's death. There's only one, but nationally it's more of a problem. In Scotland, addicts don't even need a prescription for Naloxone. Without any way of identifying the origins of the Naloxone, we're going nowhere with this.'

'It's hardly likely to have found its way down from the Highlands to get itself injected into some poor bugger in the southeast of England, though, is it? Was it on its holidays?'

I got the impression that Michaela didn't find my sarcasm all that helpful on top of her workload. 'Also, it would then still have a batch number,' she said. 'We don't even have that.'

'Yes, but the point is, why did someone save Sidney Manning, and go to the trouble of making sure the Naloxone was untraceable, but leave Errol Chandler to die or inject him with enough heroin to stop him seeing another day?'

'Well,' she said, 'my guess would be because he freely gave up the Rumbly name, and those dropping off the gear did what they needed to.'

'I get what you're saying,' I said. I sat bolt upright. 'These people watched Chandler die because of the phone call he made.'

Kayla answered me with a slow nod of her head, eyes boring into mine.

'So what we need to do is find out who delivers drugs for the Rumblys and we've got our murderer.'

56

Possibly the last words Errol Chandler ever uttered were to speak the name of the Rumbly family. I jumped to the conclusion that Leonard Rumbly was behind it all, although I recognised it as no more than a guess, and knew he would never admit to it under any circumstances. Perhaps I only wanted it to be him because of the picture I was building of the man and his criminality.

When I felt that I'd taken up enough of Michaela's time, I asked her if I could photocopy a couple of parts of the file for future reference. Back at my own desk, I spread the sheets out in front of me and prepared to highlight anything I thought might be relevant or that jumped out at me. I failed to find one single significant piece of evidence. I was beginning to see why Kayla had said it was going nowhere.

I spent the rest of the afternoon looking through the paperwork and trying to formulate some sort of plan to arrest Leonard Rumbly. My strategy was starting to look less sketchy but I still had a long way to go before I was convinced that the CPS would authorise charging him. I realised I had lost track of time when I was jolted into the present by my phone ringing on the desk next to me. The screen display showed it was Stan.

Initially I made a grab for the phone, pleased that my old friend was calling me. As I put my hand out, though,

I remembered what my mum had said about Stan wanting me to live with him. I needed to talk to the man who had looked out for me and my sister when we were recovering from our childhood ordeal, but still I hesitated.

I stared at my mobile, hand stretched out towards it. I was still deciding whether to answer it or not when it stopped ringing. I wanted to speak to Stan but the argument with my parents over dinner had tainted things: it was the first time that anyone had openly said to me that I could so easily now be enduring my sister's life, while she enjoyed mine. I had always known it but, if it wasn't said out loud, it remained in my head, where it stayed as a dirty little secret.

I took a deep breath and, without giving myself too much time to back out, I pressed his number on the screen.

'Hello, Nina,' he said.

'Hi, Stan. I'm in the office and couldn't get my phone out of my bag quick enough,' I lied.

'Thought I'd catch up and see how you were. You didn't answer my text on Wednesday about Sunday lunch. How are you fixed?'

I hesitated again. I couldn't avoid him forever.

'This Sunday would be great,' I answered with more enthusiasm in my voice than I felt.

'Splendid. Will Bill be joining us?'

I knew it was Bill's day off but I didn't know if I wanted him there. He had heard my mum's side of it, but I wasn't sure if it wouldn't be better if I spoke to Stan and dealt with my own feelings in private. 'Can I let you know?' I answered. 'I'm not sure if he's seeing his own folks this weekend.'

'OK, then. I'll see you at two o'clock on Sunday. I'll let you go; you sound a little distracted there at work.'

I was distracted, but probably not for the reasons he imagined.

57

When I got home, Bill was still out. He'd told me something about playing golf and having a couple of drinks with his friend afterwards. I didn't think he'd be that late, but I couldn't remember where he said he was going for a drink or who he was going with. I vaguely recalled him muttering something about a mate from work called Seth. It was an unusual name and I thought I would have heard of Seth before now, but I got to work planning our weekend. I thought it should start with loading some washing into the machine, or I'd have to go out and buy new clothes that I couldn't afford. I scoured the house for unmentionables to put on a forty-degree wash. Happy that I had stuffed the washer to its limits, I set about taking the dry clothes out of the airing cupboard and putting them back in their homes. Enjoying the distraction of domesticity, I allowed myself the happy thought that this was what my life could consist of for some time to come. Gathering several pairs of Bill's socks in my hand, I walked to the chest of drawers to replenish the stock.

On the many occasions I'd opened this particular drawer, it had been crammed with socks. We'd both been so busy lately that clean attire was at crisis point, so the contents had dwindled somewhat.

The drawer was empty. Empty apart from a small blue jewellery box. The type of box that would hold a ring.

I found myself, for the second time in a couple of hours, holding out my hand towards an object, hesitant as to whether I should pick it up or not. I tried to fight the urge to go back downstairs, leaving well alone. I wasn't supposed to be snooping around my boyfriend's home. He had asked me to move in with him, albeit temporarily. I had a very clear memory of how he'd shyly asked me, when I was released from the hospital, whether I wanted to move in for a week or two, or he could, he'd said, stay in my spare bedroom if I wanted to be in my own home. He'd been careful not to be too pushy. Despite the very good (but legal) drugs I was on at the time, I knew it had taken a lot for him to ask me, and it had made him feel uncomfortable. So from that to an engagement ring? That was all it could be, surely?

Sitting on the edge of the bed, I made up my mind that if I could face Stan in two days' time and ask him if, decades ago, he had wanted me to live with him and his wife when I was a child, I could face opening a small leather box.

It wasn't an engagement ring. It was a wedding ring.

I stared at it, shut the box and then opened it again, hoping it had changed into something else. Of course it hadn't. It was still a gold wedding band. From the size, it was a man's. I assumed it would fit Bill's ring finger. I was trying to convince myself so hard that this wasn't really Bill's gold wedding band, I even tried to convince myself that this somehow could be Walter McRay's wife's stolen wedding ring. I knew that was insane. And I knew this was turning into a very bad week.

I put the box back and went downstairs. I thought about having a glass of wine but, apart from it only being six-thirty in the evening, my mind was filled with the last time I had seen Tommy Ross. I thought about his yellow skin and sunken eyes. Then I remembered that I hadn't called the hospital to check how he was. I had too much to think about and I was coming undone.

At the back of the kitchen cupboard, I found some herbal tea. Something calming with camomile and rhubarb. It tasted like TCP but I was determined to avoid the wine.

I sat on the sofa in the approaching gloom of the evening light and waited for Bill to come home.

58

By the time he did, I was in a foul mood, but at least I was sober. I heard his cheery greeting from the front door as he abandoned his golf clubs and jacket.

'Why isn't the light on?' he said as he opened the door from the hallway. He stood still as he looked at my face. 'What's happened?' he said.

'I put the washing away,' I replied.

'Blimey, by the looks of you I thought someone had died.'

'I found your wedding ring.'

'Ah.'

I waited. At least he wasn't denying it.

Bill sat in the armchair opposite me. He ran his hands through his hair and said, 'It was meant to be a surprise.' I think I was sporting a look of horror as he rushed to add, 'Not a surprise that I've been married before, but that we could take it to the gold shop. I always meant to tell you I was married, but our relationship never got off to a particularly normal start. We had one date and then you ended up in hospital. I'm crazy about you, Nina, you know that. This weekend was the time I was going to tell you. I'd put the ring away and was only about to explain things to you because you've settled back into work and you're so much better. Ask me questions, any questions you like, and I'll answer them all.'

'Are you still married?'

'No – bloody hell, no. We got married when we were both twenty-one and it lasted less than three years. She's remarried and has three kids. I haven't seen her in years.'

'Why did you suddenly get the ring out after all this time?'

'Because I know how much it got to you that a total stranger had his dead wife's wedding band taken, and the stolen stuff being flogged at the gold shop gave me an idea. I don't want the ring. I wasn't even sure where I'd put it. I got it out to sell it. Having you living here with me has been great. I thought that we could take it to a gold shop, flog it and go for a beer on the proceeds. While we were there, we could ask if they've had any other rings in lately.'

I felt bad for doubting Bill, but who could have blamed me? I didn't really know that much about him at the end of the day. I certainly didn't know that he'd been married. I had mixed feelings: I felt that I didn't deserve happiness and someone to care for me, but also perhaps that I shouldn't rely on the relationship going anywhere with news like this being kept from me. Anything good that ever happened to me was always tainted in some way.

I smiled at Bill and told him what I thought he wanted to hear: I explained how much it meant that he had put me first, and then we spent the rest of the evening talking about his short-lived marriage and planning the rest of the weekend. We did all of our talking cuddled up on the sofa, a rapidly dwindling bottle of wine in front of us.

Saturday passed by in a blur: Bill and I had the usual weekend and 'days off' stuff to catch up on, and I felt more at home in his house. Then Sunday arrived and I did a terrible thing. Actually, two terrible things.

I cancelled on Stan. It was cowardly, I knew that, especially as I got Bill to call him and tell him I wasn't feeling well. This was something I had never done before and hoped I would never do again. I tried to rationalise it to myself by saying that I had only recently returned to work, I had taken on a massive workload, and I had a visit to my sister on the horizon – always one of the hardest things I had to face on a regular basis. I knew all along that I was avoiding Stan too.

The other terrible thing was that I went into work. I had seen on the news that the police had arrested four people in connection with the murder of Patrick Hudson in the early hours of Saturday morning. The arrests had been planned for three, not four. I was well aware that information often came into an enquiry late, leading to a further arrest – sometimes circumstances couldn't be foreseen and there were more people than anticipated on the premises – but a decision to arrest for murder was never taken lightly. I told Bill I was nipping out to the shop for painkillers, but I drove to the police station.

Parking on Sundays wasn't usually a problem so I drove my BMW through the gate to the back yard and drew up as close to the door as I could manage. I let myself in with my pass and then was uncertain where I should go. I wasn't supposed to be here on my day off, and, while it wasn't something I would get into trouble for, I couldn't justify wandering around Custody. That was certain to draw unnecessary attention to my presence, especially in connection with an enquiry I'd been told to stay away from. But it was easier for me to be at work than at Stan's, and staying at home was definitely not going to distract me from my thoughts.

I found myself walking along the corridor to the stairs leading to Cold Case.

I could hear Wingsy's voice as I arrived outside the office. It sounded as though he was talking to Clint Stirling, although the other voice wasn't as clear. I pushed the door open and saw Wingsy with his back to me, Clint sitting opposite him, and Joanna Styles, senior crime scene investigator, typing away at the desk I had been using for the last couple of weeks. Clint and Jo looked up as Wingsy turned in his chair towards me.

'Morning,' I said, unsure now what I was doing here at all. 'I left my phone charger here on Friday. My phone's gone flat so thought I'd drop in and get it.'

No one looked convinced but, in fairness, they didn't look that interested either.

'I heard there's four in custody now,' I said.

The thing about police officers was that it was usually easy to get them to talk about a job they were working on, unless it was something covert. Even then, it was worth a try.

'Yeah,' said Wingsy. 'We executed the warrant at Philip Peters' house and hiding in the loft was a bloke called Kieran Murray. He was arrested because, on top of hiding and not being too pleased to see us, he also had a set of car keys on him for the VW Polo that they've been driving around in.'

'Did you manage to recover the car too?' I asked, showing slightly more interest than I'd meant to.

Clint looked up from his paperwork. 'I'm working out the cost of sending off all the samples and the floor mats from the car now. There's about five of those we're sending from the vehicle. Each of those exhibits plus gunshot residue kits from each of our four in custody is...' He glanced across at Jo to help him out.

She allowed a frown to crinkle her brow before looking skywards and said, 'Allow about £500 per item. It's probably a bit more, but the lab will give a breakdown. We'll call it five grand for good measure.'

'So I hope you're not sniffing around for a working rest day, Foster,' said Wingsy. 'There's no money left to pay you.'

'And Jo,' said Clint, 'Kieran Murray's DNA went up to the lab too. Out of the four, he was the only one whose sample wasn't already on the national database. That's going up first thing in the morning. The Warrant of Further Detention was sorted today so we've got all four of them here until Tuesday at midday. Loads to do before then.' Clint went back to what he was doing, Jo had never really stopped her work, and Wingsy remained twisted in his chair to stare at me.

He got up and gestured that I follow him outside. Out of earshot of anyone else, my friend asked me, 'Why are you really here?'

'I wanted to know how things were going and I couldn't settle at home.' I glanced down and tapped the skirting board with my foot. 'I feel bad about Annie, I want to know if the Rumblys are connected to Patrick's death, and I'm avoiding Stan.'

Wingsy ran his hands through his thinning hair. 'Have you thought about counselling?'

'Have you thought about hair extensions?'

'Stop being stupid, Nina. I'm trying to help you. You can't do anything about Annie at the moment, you know that. What I can tell you – ' he dropped his voice at this point and led me further away from the offices ' – is that two of the four spoke in interview and said that they were all out together on the night of the shooting. One answered "no comment" to all questions and the bloke that I interviewed, Philip Peters, gave a prepared statement through his solicitor – the usual bollocks – "I wasn't there

242

and it was nothing to do with me and why would I shoot Patrick Hudson?" Not worth the paper it's written on, but the two who did speak said they were in the Polo on the night of the shooting.'

I got the point he was making. 'So if there were four of them in the Polo, they weren't likely to have squeezed Richard Hudson into the car too.'

'Exactly,' said Wingsy. 'We need DNA or GSR particles to come back and this not only strengthens this job, but helps both Richard and Annie. So far, the evidence on Richard is that he was very close to the scene when his father was killed. I know that you're still worried he may be rearrested at some point or charged when he comes back on bail, but someone else's DNA may prevent that ever happening.'

'What exactly are we looking for DNA on? Was the gun ever found?'

Wingsy glanced up the corridor as a uniform officer came to the top of the stairs. He and Wingsy exchanged hellos and, once the patrol officer was out of earshot, Wingsy said, 'No, but one thing that was a keep-back from all but the investigation team was that the CSI found a mobile phone within the cordon at the scene. It was unregistered and was previously used to make several calls to telephone numbers attributed to three of those currently in custody. It's also been sent off for fingerprinting and DNA. There's the likelihood that we can show it as belonging to Kieran Murray. That's why his DNA is being taken to the lab first thing.'

'That's looking positive then for charging Murray, if no one else,' I said, more to myself than Wingsy. 'But none of this has brought the arrest of Rumbly any closer.'

'We think it was the blokes in the Polo who might have been there when Errol Chandler overdosed and Sidney

Manning was injected with Naloxone. They work for Rumbly. All we need is for one of them to talk.'

This at least gave me hope that I'd get to see Rumbly held to account for something he'd done. Maybe his past was catching up with him at last.

'Why don't you go and see Stan and sort out whatever the problem is there?' said Wingsy. 'I know you, and that's bothering you more than anything else.'

'What makes you so sure I'm not just really keen and wanting to keep on top of the investigation?'

'Because, in all the years I've known you, you only ever set foot in a nick on your day off if the bar was open. We don't have a bar any more, so go and see Stan.'

Wingsy was right. Especially the part about the bar. I glanced at my watch. 'He'll be having his dinner by now. I'll ring him.' I smiled at my decision.

'You can't call him,' said Wingsy.

'Why not?'

'Because you left your charger in the office and your phone's gone flat. Remember?'

59

Before I left the building, I texted Bill to let him know that I was on my way to see Stan and that I was feeling much better.

He replied with one word: *Good*. He'd known I was avoiding my oldest friend, but he didn't know the real reason why. I hadn't wanted to admit even to myself that I could have had a better life with Stan than with my own parents, so I wasn't up for confessing to my boyfriend any time soon. I needed to deal with this so I could concentrate on work, and I needed to plan a visit to see Sara soon too.

I got to Stan's, and steeled myself for what I was going to say to him. He had always been the first person I turned to, but that was because he had never been the problem. Things were very out of kilter and I was finding it a difficult topic to tackle. One thing I did know was that I couldn't keep hiding from him. I'd already buried enough dark thoughts over the years; more would not help. I stood inside the porch, handbag gripped in one hand, the other on the doorbell before I changed my mind.

Stan opened the door and surprise was written all over his face, instantly replaced by another emotion. 'You look absolutely terrible. I didn't think you were coming. Come inside.' He stood back to give me room.

That would have been the moment to say something to him, but I wasn't sure if my voice was up to it. I kept my head down and headed into the hallway. Usually I would have stopped by now and got a hug, asked how Stan was, but I felt the urge to keep moving and avoid the issue. I was good at that.

When I reached the kitchen, I'd run out of house. 'You've had dinner,' I said, as if Stan needed to be told he'd eaten a meal.

'What's wrong?'

'I spoke to my mum...'

I stood uselessly in Stan's kitchen, next to his sink where the roasting tin had been put to soak. When he didn't speak, I felt compelled to. It was me, after all, who had turned up on his doorstep.

'She told me something. Something I didn't like. Don't like.'

Stan sat down at the kitchen table, and I moved to the seat opposite him. 'She told me that, when I was a child, you wanted me to live with you and Angela. Is it true?'

Stan sighed and reached for the bottle of red wine between us on the table. He half-filled his own glass and pointed at the dresser beside me where the remaining crystal wine glasses waited their turn. Not one to argue in such a situation, I reached over and took down the nearest one. As he poured, we both watched the cherry-red liquid fill the glass.

'Your mum – well, both of your parents, but particularly your mum – was exhausted after we found you and your sister. Sara needed constant looking after, and in those days your parents didn't have a car to get to the hospital. It was a real strain on her, and me and Angela didn't have any children yet – Samantha hadn't been born. We discussed it and thought that it might be of some advantage to everyone if you came and lived with us for a while. It was only ever going to be for a while. A month, perhaps two.'

He paused and took a sip of his drink. 'I think your mum might have made you think it was to be a permanent arrangement. It never was, and it never would have been allowed to be, because of my job. She hated the idea and so we never mentioned it again.'

I picked up my wine and gulped some down while I thought of my question. 'How many times did you discuss it with my mum and dad?'

'Once,' said Stan, 'only once. She said no and that was the end of it.'

I felt even worse being told it would only have been temporary. My mum had tried to make me think that there was something underhand going on, and all the while it had been one conversation nearly four decades ago. It had brought to the surface feelings of regret for a happier life I had been denied. A life without each and every day making me feel responsible for another's misery. I suspected that my face was reddening with embarrassment.

'Are you OK, Nina? You look as though you're burning up.'

I put my hand to my cheek and felt that it was a little on the warm side. Nevertheless, I took another swig of my wine, concentrating on its velvety texture rather than remembering how I had cowered behind her. My eight-year-old sister had shielded me and received the blows meant for me. The times when I allowed myself to wallow in this misery were few and far between, but, when they came, a huge hole of black appeared, trying to consume me. Once or twice, it almost managed it.

'Have you eaten today?' he asked.

Miserably I shook my head. I felt wretched. I barely noticed Stan get up but was aware of cutlery rattling behind me, accompanied by the sound of a microwave. I was about to protest that he really shouldn't worry and not to go to the bother of getting me something to eat, but then I realised I didn't have the energy to argue.

A scrounged Sunday lunch with all the trimmings would usually perk me up, but in my present mood I hardly ate a thing. The only reason for the improvement in my mood was talking things over with Stan and clearing the air. Not that he'd been aware there was a problem until I showed up on his door and pushed some roast potatoes around my plate. I did, however, help him out by drinking a large glass of his wine.

We put the world to rights once more, and I realised I should have talked things over with Stan much earlier rather than stewing on them for days. My mum had every right to overreact to situations, but I shouldn't have allowed myself to get wound up about anything she said. I felt much more at ease as I said goodbye to Stan.

We stood by his front door and he hugged me. 'Next time, Nina, tell me what the problem is, OK?'

I nodded, my face brushing his cashmere jumper. The thing was, I would never tell him what would now occupy my waking thoughts: I wished I had gone to stay with him and Angela and that I'd lived the last thirty-eight years as Stan's daughter.

60

When I returned to work the next morning, refreshed from a good night's sleep, I allowed my mind to fill with all the other problems I had to face, wondering which should get my attention first. Annie's ex-husband had been murdered, her son arrested along with another four people, Leonard Rumbly needed arresting, Joe Bring wanted me to get his son into boot camp in exchange for information, and people seemed to be dying all over the county from drug overdoses.

Bumping into a very flustered Michaela made my mind up earlier than I'd anticipated. She charged out of the door into the yard, colliding with me, and shouted, 'Fuck, sorry, darling. I'm off to HQ. All three drug deaths are being looked at today by Major Crime.'

This was good news.

'What's made them change their mind?' I asked.

'The toxicology came back on Lea Hollingsworth. She had enough heroin in her blood to kill her but there are no other signs that she was an addict or even a user. Add to that the fact that she had head injuries, and someone somewhere has realised that not only is this now a murder investigation, rather than an accidental overdose, but it's probably linked to the other two.'

I had a hundred more questions for Kayla but she had keys in her hand and was backing away from me towards the last unmarked job car in the yard, so I kept it brief. I called after her, 'Can you let me know more when you get back? I'm really keen to know details and if there's any overlap between suspects on both our jobs.'

I didn't hear her reply, as a marked car pulled out of one of the bays with its blue lights flashing and engine gunning, on its way to a call somewhere. I waved at Kayla and let myself into the building.

After making my way to the Cold Case office, saying hello and dropping my bag off, I told Harry that I was going to speak to the drug liaison officer. Lee Schofield had been the division's DLO for three years and there wasn't much he didn't know about controlled drugs. He had been on national Home Office courses up and down the country, and as a drug valuation officer, drug testing officer and drug evidence expert he assisted the Crown Court with knowledge or information about any drugs matters relevant to a trial. He knew just about everything there was to know, such as why a kilo of heroin was worth £25,000 when in reality its price was £3,000 if purchased in Pakistan or Afghanistan.

I knew that Lee always got in very early on a Monday morning to get ahead of the nine am meeting and arm himself with the facts and figures for drug-related crime over the weekend. The last time I had seen him was one Friday night about nine pm in Riverstone town centre. I'd fallen out of a bar with a couple of friends and he had been on duty at the door of the bar, swabbing those in the queue for drugs. He had told me that the weekend operations always resulted in a fair few people being arrested for possession of cocaine or another illegal substance. This was surely further reason for drugs never to be legalised. If you were daft enough to stand voluntarily in a queue and wait for a police officer to swab you for drugs, with a police sniffer dog nosing at your pockets, there was little hope for you.

This thought brought me to Lee's office. He was sitting at his desk, tapping away on the keyboard. He looked up as I got to the door.

'Hi, Nin,' he said, getting up to give me a quick peck on the cheek. 'Heard you were back. You alright?'

'Yeah, I'm OK, ta. Getting back into things. Do you have five minutes to talk to me about the recent drug ODs?'

'For you, course. I'll put the kettle on.' Lee set about making us both tea. He even offered me a doughnut. The stereotypes were true. I declined, mostly because they didn't look particularly appetising and had Friday's date on the box.

While he waited for the kettle to boil, he pushed three box files my way. One was marked 'Daryl Hopkins', another 'Errol Chandler' and the third 'Lea Hollingsworth'.

'Everything you need to know is in there,' he said, removing the teabags from the mugs. 'They're copies of all three files. I haven't had a chance to go through them in detail yet but, as you probably know, as DLO I get passed information on all drug-related deaths in the division and then have to pass it on to the drug and alcohol inspector – Susie Bradley. She in turn goes to meetings to look at how we dealt with them and what we could have done better, and shares the information with other agencies. It's all about reducing deaths due to any drugs at the end of the day. But this lot are a different story.'

He sat down opposite me. We both took a tentative sip from our steaming drinks.

Lee glanced at the stack of files. 'On all three of the deaths, the scene was sealed after police were called, a CSI attended, took scene photos – copies are in the files

– and then the CSIs went to the PMs so that the body samples were sent to the lab as soon as possible. Even though Daryl's death, the first one, wasn't thought to be suspicious at the time, the initial post mortem results were reviewed by another pathologist, who requested further tests. Toxicology results showed that the heroin in his bloodstream was within the fatal range, but there seemed to be no long-term drug use or dependence. Daryl wasn't known to police other than for shoplifting when he was a kid and, even though his parents said he used to smoke the odd joint, tests didn't even show up cannabis use. I don't think it would have gone much further, though, had it not been for the death of Errol Chandler.'

As Lee took Errol's file from the middle of the pile, I said, 'Yeah, I know a bit about this from Kayla and I was at Lea's PM.'

'I'm going to have to leave you to it soon, Nina. I have to be at the morning meeting. You're welcome to stay here and look through the files. I have to ask, though – what does this have to do with Cold Case?'

'I'm working on a historic train crash from the Sixties. The person we think was behind it all is Leonard Rumbly. His son and grandson probably had something to do with these drugs deaths, and I think he was involved in them too.' I placed my hand on the top of Lea's file. 'It's very doubtful if we'll ever get Rumbly senior charged with murder after fifty years because we need more evidence, but he deserves to go to prison. Even if it's for supplying the heroin rather than for murder. It won't be the result I hoped for, but it's better than nothing.'

'Well, good luck with it. I'll be back in an hour or so if there's anything else you want to ask.'

Lee locked his computer and set off in the direction of the conference room, taking his tea with him. I took the opportunity to look through the three files, complete with scene photos. I laid the pictures of the three victims side by side. To see all three young corpses, their exposed arms coloured purple, foam around their mouths, Daryl's nose bloody from where his face smashed into the corner of the table he was found beside… it was a montage of despair.

Someone, somewhere was responsible for the deaths of three young people. And I was desperate to know how their murders would lead me to the incarceration of Leonard Rumbly.

61

I took myself back to my own office, intending to speak to Harry about it. I couldn't deny being keen to leave the morbid photos behind, but I knew that I'd eventually return to view them again, and throw in the post mortem pictures for good measure. Somehow the photos were worse than actually being there. But they were useful for establishing the cause of death.

Harry was swearing at Jim when I got to the door. I wasn't sure what had caused his tirade but I wasn't all that interested. I waited until he'd finished ranting and then asked if I could have a word with him in the canteen.

He didn't look as though he had time for me today. 'I'll buy you one of those cheese and bacon twists,' I offered.

'Come on, then, Nin. And make sure you go out and get that bloody statement while I'm gone, Jim.' He turned his attention back to me and asked, 'Latte too?'

'When did getting your sergeant's attention become so expensive?'

I took my purse from my handbag and followed a clearly hungry and thirsty Harry out of the office. As we reached the top of the staircase, Harry held the door open for me and said, 'I heard you were in here over the weekend. What were you trying to find out?'

I hesitated only briefly before I said, 'I came in to get my phone charger.'

'Don't talk such bollocks,' he said as he followed me through the door. 'I wasn't born yesterday. I've only ever known you set foot in a nick on a rest day when you've been sat at the bar with wine on the go.'

'Yes, yes, I know, and we don't have a bar any more. I'll level with you: I wanted to find out what happened to the three who were arrested for the shooting – even more so when I heard there were four in custody. Curiosity won at the end of the day but I didn't want to put anyone on the spot by ringing them. Annie's my friend, but I don't want to get anyone here into trouble.'

By now we'd got to the counter, and Harry was choosing his breakfast and the most expensive beverage he could find. There was a lull in our conversation until we sat down at the quietest empty table, and I was £7 lighter.

'I wanted to catch up with you anyway,' said Harry, greasy pastry snack held to his lips. 'I've got to do a return-to-work assessment with you – see how you're getting on, that kind of thing.'

He took a bite and I took my chance to talk without him interrupting. At least, I hoped he wouldn't or he'd spray me with filo.

'I'm fine. Bit tired, but it's the train crash and the drugs deaths I really need to talk about.' He nodded as he chewed. I carried on. 'Well, I spoke to Lee Schofield this morning about the three deaths and I briefly saw Kayla as she rushed off to HQ for a meeting with Major Crime. It doesn't take a genius to know that these are being linked.'

He swallowed the mouthful of food and went for his coffee to wash it down. I knew I only had his attention for a short amount of time so I talked faster. 'They're linked – they have to be. This is the Rumblys. I know that the Intel unit would have been tasking source-handlers to speak to their contacts and find out about the drug supply and where it came from. I haven't got as far as the toxicology reports – that's even if they're all back yet, and I'm aware how long these things can take. Do we know if it was the amount of heroin that killed them, or its purity?'

Harry shrugged, folding the rest of his breakfast in two and shoving it into his mouth. He said something that sounded like, 'Not back yet.'

'What's not back yet? The toxicology?'

He nodded and then said, a little more clearly, 'Not all the results are back. Another pathologist reviewed them and asked for further tests. Three drug overdoses raised a lot of concerns. The balloon went up with the girl's death – what's her name?'

'Lea. Lea Hollingsworth.'

'Yeah, her. She had absolutely no link to drugs or drug supply; her medical history didn't show any signs of drugs or dependence, and I take it from the PM that her organs all looked intact?'

I broke eye contact and glanced in the direction of the two civilian property officers walking past our table, taking a break from booking in overnight seizures of drugs, keys, shoplifted shopping and all manner of other items. They both waved and took a seat with their own ridiculously priced teas. I smiled at them, something I didn't feel like doing, before I answered Harry. 'I'm no expert on the workings of the human body, but her liver, kidneys and so on looked very healthy to me.' I thought of Lea's body stretched out for examination in the PM. She was years younger than me but I realised how close I had come the previous year to being on just such a mortuary table. I hoped they would have sent an out-of-county SIO to watch my post mortem. There was no dignity in death, despite the professional attitude everyone adopted. I shuddered at the thought of a DCI I knew watching my corpse being cut open. Harry brushed the flakes from his mouth with his thumb and forefinger.

'Don't go dwelling on it.'

'On what?'

'Lea's death and the post mortem. We'll sort it. We'll get Rumbly. Every dog has its day, and the Rumblys' is soon. What's got to you, anyway?'

'It's not fair, that's what,' I said. 'People like Rumbly make their money from gambling, drugs, exploiting others. They sell drugs to people who can't afford them so they steal, burgle, take from the elderly and vulnerable, leaving their lives in misery. These fucking people get me down.'

Harry crushed the paper cup he was holding and said, 'Well, think yourself lucky. I've had ten more years of this endless bollocks than you have. Think how sodding miserable it's making me. Now stop moaning; I've been told to update you about what you'll be doing next.'

'Really,' I said. 'What am I to be doing?'

'Kayla's been sent to HQ because of the drug deaths.'

'I know that,' I said, 'I've just told you that.'

'But what you don't know is that we're being given the go-ahead to bring Rumbly in for the train crash. With what you've got from Joe Bring, Tommy Ross and Marilyn Fitzhubert, the decision was made to make the arrest and see what other evidence we get.' He paused and glanced at the nearby occupied tables, moved a few inches closer to me across the table and added, 'See what else we get from the searches.'

'OK, I'm aware of what you're saying. But what's my task?'

'You're to be working with Mark Russell. And the bit you're really going to like is that you're arresting and interviewing none other than Leonard Rumbly.'

My detective sergeant was right: I really did like that.

62

At five am on strike day, I got out of bed and crept around the house, trying to get ready for work without waking Bill. I wasn't used to being so careful, or quiet. Several times I dropped something or had to sneak back into our bedroom. I should have slept in the spare room but the ever-thoughtful Bill had told me he didn't mind and that, even if I did wake him up, he would easily get back to sleep. I'd have liked to say I had been that courteous on the few occasions in the last couple of months when he'd woken me up. But no, I had tutted and moaned, turned over and over and eventually told him to 'turn the poxy light off'. Still he let me live here. There wasn't a day that went by when I didn't realise how lucky I was.

I got ready for work excited at the thought of being about to enter Leonard Rumbly's home and arrest him, and finally ask him about the train crash. As I attempted to calm my hair down by attacking it with the straighteners, I made my mind up that as soon as Leonard Rumbly had been arrested and I'd finished interviewing him, I was going to confront Bill. I couldn't go on like this. I didn't want his sympathy. I had to be here for a better reason than that.

The singed smell coming from my hair jolted me back to where I was standing in the hallway, trying to make the lead from the straighteners stretch across to the bathroom mirror. British safety standards would never allow me in a bathroom with live electrical items but I still thought it was worth a try. I could only see the reflection of the left-hand side of my hair, so I had a guess at the other side. It was five-thirty in the morning. Who was likely to care?

I grabbed a Danish pastry on my way through the kitchen to where I'd left my handbag, keys and security pass, and went to work.

Despite the early hour, the entire police station was lit up when I got there. Several lads and lasses in uniform were already at work in the back yard, filling their vans, checking the equipment, winding each other up. Some were getting ready to go off duty and some just starting. I waved half-heartedly at one or two, still a bit drowsy but feeling the excitement start to build. I was very much looking forward to meeting the man I'd heard so much about. With any luck, I wouldn't be disappointed with whatever the next couple of hours brought my way.

Janice Freeman kept the briefing short. Following a quick, 'Morning, all, and thanks for getting up a bit earlier than usual,' she gave us concise instructions about that morning's warrants and arrests. She scanned the room and said, 'Mark and Nina, you're to go with Sergeant George Keane to Leonard Rumbly's address.' I looked around the room at the uniform officers and nodded at George. He replied with a wink at me and a wave of the search warrant at the DCI.

'Arrest him for conspiracy to commit murder – the exact wording I want you to use is on the briefing sheet,' she continued. 'As agreed, we're going for a knock on the door, rather than forcing entry. Whatever we may all think of our suspect, he is, at the end of the day, in his seventies, has only historic warning signs of violence, and the only links we have with the shooting of Patrick Hudson are via his son, Andy, through the telephone calls to his landline from someone at the scene. We've had recent information that Andy hasn't visited his father for some time. We think there may have been some sort of a falling out between them over the grandson, Niall. Andy Rumbly is at his own home address as we speak.'

I was watching Freeman intently. As she said the word 'information', her eyes flicked in the direction of the plain clothes intelligence officer sitting at the side of the room. The DCI didn't allow herself to look at him but I got the impression that the Rumbly family had been under surveillance for some time. No one was going to tell me the truth about it, as it was always on a need-to-know basis, but all officers knew it went on.

'The rest of those here are going out to arrest Andy Rumbly for possession with intent to supply class A drugs,' continued Freeman. 'You've all had the briefing sheets sent to you by email so you're aware of what you're doing. Never know, we may still be able to link him to our drug overdoses yet.'

A murmur went around the room and someone muttered, 'Believe it when I see it.'

'Any questions?' asked DCI Freeman, scanning the room.

'What about Niall Rumbly, ma'am?' said Wingsy.

'Good point, John,' she replied, 'but, as he's in prison and has been throughout this, we'll deal with him another day, after we've dealt with the rest of his family.'

At six-thirty, we piled out of the conference room. Stab-proof vest on, I left the building with Mark Russell and we chatted as we walked to the car. I had worked with him for a short spell the previous year but didn't know him very well. As with most police officers, when you were thrown together to carry out an enquiry, small talk was rarely a problem. We had something in common to dissect, as well as the usual moaning and complaining about the job in general.

Mark drove behind the marked police van to Leonard Rumbly's address. It was neither the time nor the place to dwell on family, boyfriend or financial problems, so I focused on what I had to do. I'd been so keen to finally arrest Rumbly, I couldn't afford to let my concentration slip.

Within twenty minutes we'd pulled up opposite Leonard Rumbly's address across from the police van which was blocking his driveway. The uniform team within it had already started to approach the front door, so Mark and I jumped out of the car and joined the advance party. When everyone was in position at the front and back of the house, I knocked at the door.

A minute or two passed before we heard movement from inside. We had the legal power to force the door open but Freeman had told us to avoid that if possible. It was cheaper and involved a lot less paperwork if we could get inside without taking the door off its hinges. As we were arresting Rumbly for something that had happened so long ago, it would be more difficult to justify it, too.

The door opened. An open-mouthed, dishevelled, pyjama-clad man stood before two detectives and five uniform officers.

'Leonard Rumbly?' I asked.

'Yes.'

By now, George Keane had taken the warrant from his jacket and was showing it to Rumbly. I took this chance to run an eye over him. He was shorter than I'd pictured him, but then I had to take his bare feet into account. He was also stouter than I'd imagined. Some of my preconceptions could have been down to the old photograph I'd seen of him with his arm around Tommy Ross. That was a long time ago, but Rumbly didn't look as though he'd aged much better than Tommy. I wasn't getting the impression it was down to alcohol in his case, but the decades hadn't been particularly kind to Rumbly either. Of course, most people probably wouldn't look their best at such an hour, having been woken by a crowd of police outside their home, banging to get in.

The person I was looking at seemed to be taking the presence of so many officers on his doorstep in his stride. I felt genuine relief at this, because I didn't want him to collapse. An old man being taken ill when the police arrived at his house was bound to propel the whole incident on to the local news and into the paper. And then we would all end up being interviewed by our force's Professional Standards Department – not something I fancied. Not to mention that I was looking forward to asking him about the Wickerstead Valley train crash.

Leonard Rumbly stood back to let us into his home. It was an impressive house, probably thanks to a life of crime.

'Anyone else here, Mr Rumbly?' I asked.

'No. I live alone. What's this about?'

'It's about the Wickerstead Valley train crash in 1964. I'm arresting you on suspicion of conspiracy to commit murder.' As I cautioned him and told him why it was necessary that he be arrested, he continued to stare straight at me. He didn't blink, look away or seem concerned in any way. It wasn't his first arrest and he probably thought that, since so much time had passed between the crash and police knocking on his door, he could still get away with causing the death of so many people. It was true that we didn't have much evidence, but he didn't need to know that. Certainly not at this stage.

Mark took Rumbly upstairs to get dressed as the search team came in. George spoke to the officer with the video camera whose job it was to film every room and part of the house that we entered and searched, as well as anything we seized as evidence. By the time my prisoner reappeared at the bottom of the stairs, he was wearing a shirt, trousers and a bemused look.

'I need my medication,' he said. 'It's for my heart. You don't want me collapsing on you.'

'Where is it? We can get it for you,' said Mark.

'I'd rather get it myself. I don't trust you foot soldiers to get the right tablets.'

I caught Mark's eye over Rumbly's shoulder as he shook his head and looked to the ceiling.

Rumbly made to go past me towards the back of the house, in the direction of the kitchen. I couldn't let him out of my sight now. In the very unlikely event that he made a run for it, I would have some serious explaining to do as to why I was unable to catch a seventy-six-year-old man. What I couldn't chance was that he might try to injure himself or one of us. He was my prisoner and my responsibility now, and allowing him into the kitchen – the place with the knives – was an unnecessary risk to take.

George appeared in the kitchen doorway, possibly having the same thought as me. Instead of heading where I thought he was going, though, Rumbly turned left before he got to the kitchen. I could hear two officers already in the room he entered, but I followed him nevertheless. He stopped inside the door, scanned the room and let out a sigh. Even though I saw him sweep the whole room once, he turned three times in the direction of a small, low table underneath the window. Initially I thought he was looking at a large desk which held only an old-fashioned blotter and a telephone, but when I followed his line of vision I saw that he was eyeing the table beyond that.

The wooden table-top held only a vase of flowers, but beneath, on its base, a couple of inches from the floor, were a couple of piles of stacked papers.

Unless I was very much mistaken, there was something in the paperwork that Leonard Rumbly didn't want us to see.

63

Mark and I got Rumbly into the car without any issues. He drove while I sent a text message to the search team sergeant to let him know about the papers Rumbly had been casting an eye over. There was no chance that his team would miss them, but I knew how important it was to pass my concerns on. Then I thought about making small talk with our man in custody. I was well aware of the topics I had to steer clear of, such as, what part did you play in a train journey ending in carnage? Even so, I really didn't feel like rapport-building with him.

Eventually, I said, 'When we get to the custody desk, the sergeant will go through your rights with you. One thing you'll be asked is if you want a solicitor. The choice is yours, but if – '

'I don't need a solicitor. I've got nothing to say to any of you.'

I'd tested the ground with a neutral but important subject, and got a very clear indication of how he was going to be handling himself. He was unlikely to give us any trouble, but he wasn't going to be any more accommodating than he had to be.

We pulled into the yard at Riverstone police station a short time later, and led him to the custody area. After he'd been booked in by a sergeant, his DNA and fingerprints taken, and he'd been searched once more and seen by the nurse, we took him to the only available interview room.

It was the smallest of the three, holding a table fixed to the floor, three heavy wooden seats, and the recording equipment. The air was always stale and the only things on offer were teas and coffees in polystyrene cups. Even the hot chocolate that so many of the prisoners were fond of had been cut back in the budget slashes.

Mark went to make Rumbly a coffee and enter on his custody record that he'd been given a hot drink. Everything had to be logged in case he later claimed that he had been kept without food and drink. It was a procedure we had to go through for every detainee, but my guard was very much up on this occasion. When Mark left us alone, I propped the interview room door open.

'Saw you on the news last year,' he muttered.

I paused with the DVDs for the interview in my hand. I fought to remain impassive but I had a sense of what was coming next.

The civilian detention officer who was behind the custody desk was directly in my eyeline. She could also see my prisoner. The only problem was, she couldn't hear him, and we hadn't yet started recording.

'I thought I recognised you earlier at my house, but I saw the way the others danced around you, trying not to upset you, and then I realised that you were the one that got stabbed last year.'

I felt my face twitch. I wanted to look away. I wished for Mark to return and put a stop to this. I heard his footsteps coming along the corridor but then my heart lurched when it was followed by the sound of another officer stopping him and asking how married life was treating him. Crumbling in front of Leonard Rumbly was not an option, but I didn't want to leave him alone either.

He'd met me only a couple of hours earlier and he'd already found one of my weaknesses. I had hesitated for far too long to now deny the story of my stabbing, which had been broadcast for a number of days, in what had probably been a very slow news week. A factory closure in Charlton had eventually taken its place.

'You would only have been one more dead copper at the end of the day.'

My grip tightened on the DVDs, flexing their cheap plastic casing. I thought about ramming the corners into his face but the only purpose that would serve would be to get me arrested, suspended and probably sent to prison. It would be my word against his that he'd said something to inflame my anger so much and to provoke me.

Whatever he thought of me, or all police officers, I knew I had to approach the whole thing impartially. And that involved interviewing him and evidence-gathering. Not smashing him in the face with the recording equipment.

Mark finished his conversation with his old acquaintance and appeared back in the room. He placed the unappetising beverage within Rumbly's reach.

'What did I miss?' he asked, looking at me and the prisoner in turn. Neither of us said a word.

64

The interview began. I did my best to keep my voice even and all traces of emotion from it. I had a couple of minutes to think about whether I was going to mention Rumbly's comments to me once the discs started to record. I only had a short time to make my mind up: just long enough to unwrap the discs and for the machine to whirr into life.

Introductions made, caution given and explained and the other interview formalities all completed, I said, 'And before the DVDs were recording, we didn't ask you any questions about the offence or why you've been arrested?'

'No, officer. It was all above board.'

'In fact, you mentioned that you thought you'd recognised me from the news last year?'

A smile played around his mouth. If I wasn't very much mistaken, his eyes twinkled. It was game on for Leonard Rumbly. This was very much how he took his pleasure in life – by toying with people. I could only imagine how Marilyn Springate had felt all those years ago when she'd gone to him for help. I was in control of the interview, despite the way he'd behaved towards me, whereas she had been clueless about what she was getting herself into. I liked to think I was more of a match for him, but that remained to be seen.

'Yes, indeed, officer,' was all he said, after a brief pause.

'I've explained that you've been arrested on suspicion of conspiracy to commit murder.' I had the list in front of me, but I had no need to look at it. 'Martha White, Gerald Downing, Susan Drayton, Leslie Lawrence, Kenneth Andrews, Sylvia Peterson and Mathew Cole. They all died in the train crash. Do those names mean anything to you? They should.'

I'd hoped that hearing their names and making them real might at least lessen his resolve. I was wrong. He crossed his legs and sat back in his hard wooden seat before clearing his throat and saying, 'The only thing I do have to say to you is, why would I arrange for the train to crash if I was actually on it? I was sitting beside Marilyn Springate. And I walked away without a scratch. Ask her.'

How had I missed this crucial bit of information, and why had no one mentioned it to me? This threw me completely, and I battled to appear composed before asking, 'What were you doing on the train?'

'No comment.'

'Why were you travelling with Marilyn Springate?'

'No comment.'

I was crestfallen, but I hid it from Rumbly as best I could and fought on. For the remainder of the interview, in spite of my repeated attempts to get him to talk to me, nothing worked. Even questions about his family that caused his face to drop elicited a reply of, 'No comment.' Mark then asked him dozens of questions and again, to each of them, he replied, 'No comment.' We went on like that for an hour and a half before pausing for a break.

Mark put Rumbly back in his cell with another cup of tea. It hardly counted as torture, but the drinks really were like warm pondwater. Sometimes you had to make the most of a bad situation and enjoy the little victories. We went up to the CID office for a proper brew and to speak to Janice Freeman about what he'd said so far.

When we found her, she was in the interview monitoring room, neutral expression on her face.

'You get that, ma'am?' I asked, taking a seat opposite her.

'Even though Rumbly's not talking to you, he doesn't seem to be giving you too much trouble.' I saw her glance up over my shoulder to where Mark was standing in the doorway. 'Do me a favour, could you?' she asked him, 'Find Clint and ask him to go to Custody. I need him to check the custody record for something. He's not answering his phone.'

This seemed a little odd to me, firstly as we'd just come from Custody and she could have sent us back there – but also, her phone was beside her, on silent mode. I could see the screen illuminating and the name 'Clint Stirling' flashing as he tried to call her.

Once Mark was out of earshot, she leaned in closer to me across the desk and said, 'I came up here to monitor the interview. I heard what Rumbly said to you when you were alone.'

I stared at the DCI. What he'd said to me hadn't been a threat and evidentially was completely irrelevant. So, he didn't like the police? Most people we arrested didn't want to be our friends. But this had seemed personal. He knew that; that was why he had said it. He wanted to be spiteful and knock me off track. It didn't make any difference. Either we had the evidence to charge him, or we didn't.

Janice's voice focused me once more. 'We've been in touch with the Crown Prosecution Service already but so far we're probably going to have to bail Rumbly unless the interviews throw any light on anything else.' She paused and pursed her lips at me. 'I don't like this man any more than you do. Trust me, we're not putting all of our eggs in one basket when it comes to the interview process.'

I heard a noise behind me and saw her look up. 'Speak of the devil,' she said. 'Nina, if you could give us a few minutes.'

I got up out of my chair to leave the room. I came face to face with the plain clothes officer I'd seen in the briefing.

Things were looking up.

65

Rarely was the interviewing process rapid: something as serious as interviewing a murder suspect might take hours, if not days. It was clear from the start that we were not going to be able to keep Rumbly in custody for much longer than the initial twenty-four hours, and even that had to be justified at several stages throughout the timescale. Rumbly declined a solicitor at every opportunity afforded to him and remained impassive whenever he was spoken to. He even came across as courteous – that was, if you didn't know what he was capable of.

During our breaks, Mark and I went to see Janice Freeman or Clint Stirling to ask if the team of six officers searching his house since seven that morning had uncovered anything useful. I knew I was being impatient as we would be told as soon as anything of importance came to light, but it didn't stop me asking.

As I stood in the CID office doorway, Clint looked at me for the third time and shook his head as if to dismiss me. I was about to leave him to it when his phone rang. I watched Clint's face brighten as he listened for a short time before he said, 'That's very interesting.'

Mark and I took a step towards him.

'Did he really?' said Clint, eyeing us both. 'Nina and Mark are both standing in front of me. They're going to be pleased to hear that. I'll let them know.'

'Come on, then, sir,' said Mark. 'What's happened?'

'You're going to like this.' Clint paused. I wasn't beyond telling a detective inspector to bloody well get on with it. My impatience often knew no bounds.

'And?' I said, after what seemed like enough time for him to say something.

'We've found a quantity of class A drugs at Andy Rumbly's home. They were buried in the garden.'

'Heroin?' I asked, taking another step forward.

'Looks like it. Needs testing, but what you're really going to like is that, when it was put to him in interview, he claimed it wasn't his.'

'I don't want to be rude to you, sir, a man of rank and all that, but why should that please me? Unless…'

Clint gave me a smile and raised an eyebrow, coaxing my next words out of me.

'Unless,' I said, 'he's claiming that the drugs belong to his dad.'

'That's exactly what he said. The details are on an email you should have by now. You and Mark can get back down to the interview room and ask your suspect if he wants to tell you why his son is claiming the drugs are nothing to do with him but were buried in his garden by his old man.'

'I might just do that, sir.' I moved back towards the door where Mark was standing.

'It would seem,' said Clint, 'that all is not harmonious in the Rumbly family: Andy is blaming his father for Niall's spell in prison.'

I turned and stared at Clint, no doubt a look of stupidity on my face.

'Niall's in prison for assaulting a doorman. The doorman was rude to Leonard. He told him he was too old to go into the club, so Niall went back and gave him a hiding, and all to impress his grandad. It would seem that Andy wants better for his son than he had himself – now that he has a nice home paid for by drugs and burglary, of course.'

'Of course,' I echoed. 'Poxy people never fail to astound me.'

'Let's go and ask him about all this,' said Mark rubbing his hands together. I'm going to enjoy this one.'

'Not as much as me, not as much as me.'

Ten minutes later, back in the interview room, I sat beside the recording equipment and Rumbly sat opposite me, looking as though he didn't have a care in the world. With the introduction and legal obligations out of the way again, I paused for breath and savoured the moment as I said, 'Leonard Rumbly, I'm arresting you on suspicion of possession of a class A drug, namely heroin.'

I watched him closely as I cautioned him: a barely perceptible tightness appeared around his eyes. Nothing else gave him away. His body language kept his secret, as well as his expression, but there was something I couldn't define. Perhaps I was merely hoping he was guilty. If we couldn't prove he had been behind the deaths of seven innocent people in 1964, a drugs charge was better than nothing.

He kept perfectly still until I'd finished and then leaned forward and said, 'There were no drugs in my house. You've planted them there.'

'The drugs weren't in your house. They don't have to be on your property for you to be in possession of them. Let me explain to you where they were and the circumstances.'

For the first time since I'd clapped eyes on Rumbly, I was enjoying myself. I felt as though I had the upper hand. Even though I had my doubts whether his own son would eventually give evidence against him, it was the best we had so far. Whatever the rest of the team were doing, I hoped they were building a better case than we had.

'We arrested your son, Andy, this morning.'

I paused and it worked. Rumbly blanched.

'We didn't find all that much at his place but he was very helpful… If it weren't for him, we might not have found the heroin buried in his garden. In a metal box. A metal box that belonged to you. We – '

'How do you know it belonged to me?' It wasn't just Rumbly senior's tone but the fidgeting and finger-flexing that gave him away. Now he was worried.

'I'm coming to that. We know it's your box because Andy's told us it's yours.'

I was greeted with an open-mouthed stare across the cheap wooden table. Rumbly eased himself back in the seat and dropped his hands beside him. He broke his gaze away from me and sought out the answer in the distance. I thought I heard him say, 'He didn't.'

'Sorry, Leonard. What did you say then?'

But his guard was back up. 'Anyone could have buried a box in Andy's garden.'

'OK, Leonard.' I smiled, but not out of kindness – because I felt smug. 'Here's a colour photograph of you holding the metal box.' I took an A4 still from my notebook and pushed it across the desk. I looked at him and not the picture – I'd already seen it.

Curiosity won and he peered at the photo. 'Proves nothing. It's me with a box. So what?'

'It doesn't stop there. Here are some more, showing you putting the box in the hole.' I showed him another four stills, reading out the exhibit references, although no one in the room was listening at this point. I watched his face studying the photos, trying to work out how they'd come to be taken and who had done it. I knew he'd get there eventually.

'I remember now,' he said, 'my great-grandson's hamster died and Andy asked me to bury it. That was months ago. Anyone could have dug up the box I buried and put heroin in it. There is no logical reason for me burying heroin in my son's back garden. You know that and I know that. Someone's stitching me up. Even someone as dim-witted as you can see that. They must have dug the box back up again.'

Even if it hadn't been a necessary part of the interview procedure, I took so much delight in saying, 'These stills were taken by your son, Andy. He gave them to police officers today. He also gave us dated video footage of you digging the hole and burying the box, so there's not much chance of anyone else having buried it. And whose fingerprints will we find on the drugs' wrappings? Anything you want to say about the box or its contents now?'

Rumbly had gone very grey and had started to slip down the chair. He put his hand to his chest and said, 'I don't feel very well.'

Within seconds he had fallen to the floor. I left Mark with him, while I ran to the Custody desk to call for an ambulance.

66

Truth? The only reason I wanted Leonard Rumbly to live was because I didn't want to be associated with his death. It meant a lot of paperwork and an investigation. I couldn't face being suspended after spending so long at home on sick leave. And I wanted him to go to prison.

Grateful that a custody nurse was also on the station, I stood in the interview room a few feet away from Rumbly prone on the floor, willing him to live. I couldn't see his face just the back of the nurse's blue uniform as he attended to our prisoner.

I'd also left the DVDs running. If he did die, it was better to have it recorded. I was nothing if not practical in a crisis. I also knew that my actions and demeanour might end up being scrutinised by the Professional Standards Department, and possibly even at an inquest or by a court. I pulled my concerned look on to my face, not giving a jot for his welfare, only my reputation.

The paramedics arrived within a couple of minutes. It was time I gave them room and left them to do their job.

Mark and I went back upstairs, not speaking one word about what had just happened. We reached the office where earlier we had spoken to Janice Freeman. She was still sitting where we'd left her but she'd now been joined by Clint. 'That was some interview technique, Nina,' Clint said, laughing.

'Funny, Clint, funny.' This earned me a look from the DCI. 'I didn't do anything – he collapsed.'

'Probably nothing to worry about,' said Janice. 'I've seen heart attacks and that looked very mild, if it was even genuine. We'll know when he gets to hospital. And that's a point: he's still under arrest, so which one of you is going with him?'

'Not really appropriate, is it, ma'am, one of us going? What if he makes allegations?' Mark said. He was thinking on his feet, and clearly didn't want to spend hours at the hospital either.

'Um, good point,' she said. I started to relax. It didn't last long. 'You both go. It'll be both of your words against his. There's no one else and we've already depleted the uniform officers on the arrests and warrants for this. Call me when you've got an update.'

That was that, then. We were dismissed to the hospital with Rumbly. We went back down to Custody where he was about to be stretchered to the ambulance. I made a stop to get the DVDs from the machine and then went to join Mark in the car for a stint beside Rumbly's sick bed.

'He's still under arrest,' said Mark from the driver's seat, when I opened the car door.

'Oh, good,' I sighed, 'a ride in an ambulance. Exactly what my day was missing.'

I climbed in behind the paramedics and watched Leonard Rumbly's ashen face and shallow breaths all the way to the Accident and Emergency department.

67

Several hours later, when I thought the day would never end, our relief arrived to take over for the night. I never expected to feel pleased to see Jim Sullivan but I even managed a smile at him when he arrived with Jemma. She and Mark said a quick hello and goodbye in private out of our earshot, while I told Jim what little I knew about Rumbly's condition.

'You're like the kiss of death at the moment, aren't you, Nina?' he said.

'And you're a dickhead. He hasn't really woken up, but that's mostly due to the medication they've given him here. There's not really much of an update for you, except he's stable and should be awake later on tonight, or first thing in the morning.'

'When Jemma and I left, the brief from Freeman was to bail him whenever he wakes up and is coherent enough to know what's going on. He's an old man and we haven't got enough to charge him at the moment for the train crash.'

I led Jim away from Rumbly's bedside in case he could hear, despite the nurse's reassurance that, even if he was able to hear what was going on, he wouldn't remember it when he woke up.

Keeping my voice very low for the sake of the other patients in the ward, I asked Jim, 'Anything else turn up so far?'

He shook his head. 'Still early days – don't give up. I know you've put a lot of work into this one. We'll get there.'

I thought perhaps I'd misjudged my colleague – that was, until he added, 'Try not to put anyone else in the back of an ambulance today. You'll get a reputation.'

Too tired to spar any longer, I gave Mark a wave and told him I'd meet him in the car park. He gave Jemma a kiss goodbye and followed me out of the ward.

Once we were in the car, I gave myself a few minutes to calm down before I tried to talk. Mark seemed to realise I wasn't really in the mood to chat, as he made no attempt to speak to me either. He might simply have been thinking about his wife, whom he wasn't likely to see for another day or so. Whatever the reason, I was glad of the quiet.

'Some day,' I said when the hospital was well behind us.

'You could say that.'

'Early morning warrant, followed by arrest and heart attack.'

'At least he's going to be OK,' said Mark. 'Well enough to answer a few more questions at a later date. I'd like to see how he's going to get out of the drugs, even if the stuff we have on the train crash is a little shaky.'

'We can find more out in the morning, at the briefing. In the meantime, I'm glad to be out of the hospital. I seem to spend far too much of my time in there lately.'

'Sorry, I should have asked if you're OK,' said Mark, glancing away from the road to look at my profile. I didn't want to turn towards him. It was getting dark so I hoped he couldn't read my expression, and I wanted it to stay that way. It wasn't something I wanted to talk about, especially with Mark. I didn't know him that well and, despite being sure he was only asking out of politeness or perhaps even genuine concern, I wanted to pretend it hadn't happened. I couldn't do that if I talked about it. I would have to address it and not cover it up with jokes or drinking to excess and carrying lumps of chicken home in my handbag.

'Yeah, I'm OK. So tell me where you and Jemma went on honeymoon.'

'We went to St Lucia. It was beautiful. We combined it with spending a couple of days with my mum.'

'Oh, is she from St Lucia?'

'No, she's from Margate. She moved out there a couple of years ago.'

'Sorry, Mark. I assumed. There's definitely a diversity course with my name on it.'

'You should get yourself off somewhere sunny. I mean somewhere like St Lucia rather than Margate. You could probably do with a break. Get Bill to spend some of his overtime on you.'

That gave me something to think about for the rest of the journey back to the police station. It was probably what our relationship was missing: something relaxing and enjoyable, like a holiday. Or simply fewer dead bodies and visits to the hospital.

68

I arrived at work the next day, tired but optimistic about how the previous twenty-four hours had gone. I made my way to the temporary Incident Room via the deserted Cold Case office. Stacked 'in' and 'out' trays were strewn all over the conference room where the investigation team had housed themselves. Exhibits were piled up in the corner and a mass of staff from Headquarters had arrived and taken up all available space. Several officers and civilian employees had found themselves computers in offices both sides of the corridor, and the entire floor had a hum about it that I hadn't been a part of since my stint on a murder investigation the previous year.

Feeling very much at home, I went over to the person dealing with the exhibits, who was desperately trying to put them into some sort of order. I recognised her as Karen Pickering and asked her if she could point me in the direction of the paperwork taken from Rumbly's house.

'I can do more than that,' she replied, opening a box file. 'I've already photocopied everything and put it in here. Just put it back on the desk when you're done.'

I left her rummaging through plastic and brown paper bags, holding what looked like several hundred items of personal belongings from Andy and Leonard Rumbly's homes. I left her to it and found myself a quiet corner to leaf through the paperwork my prisoner had seemed unable to stop himself from looking at.

An hour later, I gave up. I knew I was looking at the right stuff, but it was general household bills, leaflets that had fallen out of magazines, and mailshots. Disappointed, not to mention bored, I went off in search of Wingsy to brighten his day with an update on my own morning so far.

I tracked him down to the canteen.

'Morning,' I said, taking the seat opposite him.

'Alright?'

'You don't look very pleased to see me.'

'I was enjoying the peace and quiet.'

'How did you get on yesterday?' I asked, watching him remove the teabag from his mug.

'Pierre and I ended up interviewing Andy Rumbly.' He paused, squeezing the water from the bag suspended by its string. Just as he finished, he dropped it and the bag hit the drink again, splashing brown water up the front of his white shirt.

'I'm surprised Mel doesn't make you wear a bib.'

'What happened to your prisoner, then? I heard he ended up in hospital. I know you'd taken a dislike to him. I hope you didn't bring on his medical condition.'

'I'm not as stupid as I look.'

'Thank fuck for that.'

'Don't get annoyed with me just because you've started the day with tea down your shirt.'

I'd sought out my friend because I wanted him to come with me to Worthing to visit Tommy Ross. Wingsy and I had made frequent contact with Marilyn and Charles Fitzhubert for updates about Tommy Ross's welfare. The news was always the same: he was awake for short periods of time and was very weak when he was. The only thing

I did insist on was that the Fitzhuberts collect Tommy's door keys, which I had taken to the hospital, and rescue his cat. Tommy owed the cat, and our ineptitude, his life. It seemed to be the least I could do.

I didn't fancy the long drive by myself but I had some idea of what might greet me when I got there, and I certainly didn't relish the idea of the long, silent journey back with only my own thoughts for company. I wasn't sure whether he would agree to come with me, though, or whether Harry would allow it. Something seemed to be troubling Wingsy and, as work didn't often affect him, I guessed it was personal. It was unlikely that he would ever tell me, but I stayed in my seat on the off-chance that he wanted to talk.

'What are your plans today, then?' he asked after a few seconds of silence.

'I was thinking of visiting Tommy in hospital.'

Wingsy nodded, picked up his tea and before taking a sip said, 'Be easier if you phoned. Long way to go by yourself.'

That seemed to be as much as I was going to get from my friend today. I made to get up. As I hovered above my seat, though, he said, 'Unless you fancy some company?'

'I'll let Harry know. We can drop in and see Charles and Marilyn on the way back. Justify the journey and all that.' I hesitated. 'Wings, are you OK? You don't seem to be yourself today.'

'I've got a few things on my mind.'

'Can I help?'

'Not really, girl. But thanks.'

I left it there and strode off to find Harry to tell him our plans, but he already had his hands full. He was dealing with staffing issues and was mid-row with the DI over why we needed more officers in Cold Case. I signed out in the diary, making a note that there was a briefing at six o'clock that evening for everyone to get together with their updates on what had happened during the arrest and interview phases. I wasn't sure if we'd be back in time, but I'd already picked up most of what I needed to know from speaking to Mark Russell and others who had been working the last couple of days.

I knew that I was taking advantage of being a temporary member of staff on Cold Case. I had slipped under the radar by being unaccountable to anyone but Harry, and he had more important things to worry about. Normally with so much going on I wouldn't have been allowed to drive off to visit a sick witness in the Worthing hospital and drop in on a couple of other witnesses in Portsmouth on the way back. They all had to be seen again but I knew this wasn't really the time for it.

Apart from having him along for company, I was glad that Wingsy had agreed to come with me because I wanted to find out what was bugging him. Even though I was the first to admit what a nosy person I was, it was concern and not my prying nature that made me determined to get to the bottom of it. I had never known him have a serious problem in all the years we'd known each other. If he needed my help, I would do whatever was in my capacity to fix it.

69

As we drove out of the yard, I tried to engage Wingsy in conversation but I was met with one- or two-word answers. After a few minutes, I gave up. I was even getting on my own nerves, so I was grateful for the silence. The quiet only lasted a short time, until he switched the radio on and the car was filled with sounds of the local station playing a familiar song. I thought back to when I'd last heard it and remembered it had been in the background in the mortuary when I went to Lea Hollingsworth's post mortem. And here we were, off to see a dying man. At least the sun had come out and Wingsy had offered to drive first. I was grateful for the small mercies in life. It was just as well, really, as the major ones were often a disappointment.

The song finished and was followed by adverts. I was only half-listening and caught something about Hallowe'en. As I was thinking that ghost and witch costumes were months away, Wingsy let out a long sigh.

'What's the matter with you?' I said.

'Bloody Hallowe'en,' he said, shaking his head. He gripped the steering wheel until his knuckles went white.

'Alright, mate. It's not for six months and it's only a couple of bags of Haribos. You can always pretend you're out and eat the sweets yourself. Don't take it personally.'

'No, it's not that. It's got me into more trouble.'

'I'm not following you.'

'Well, you know I got in the cack because of the email I sent to the chief constable from Jim's computer?' He paused at a roundabout and glanced across at me.

'Go on,' I said.

'I had to see Chief Inspector Spencer Halliday about it. I joined up with Spence and always thought he was a good old boy. I thought he could take a joke.'

'What did you do?'

He pointed a thumb to the back seat. 'Have a look in my file.'

As I leaned across to retrieve his file, Wingsy continued to talk. 'He told me that I should make up for what I'd done, and put me on a neighbourhood project. It included designing community posters. One of them was for Hallowe'en, so those who didn't want kids knocking on their door at night could display the poster and they wouldn't get pestered.'

'What did you do?' I said as I opened the file.

The answer to my question was right there in front of me. I held up the A4 piece of paper.

'Let me get this right, John. You were in trouble for messing about at work so, when asked by a chief inspector to design a poster for use in the community, you filled a page with an orange pumpkin with a cross through it and printed in bold, "Fuck off or I'll call the police". What's the matter with you? If you're going through a mid-life crisis, buy a sports car or have an affair. Don't throw your career away.'

'It's Mel,' he said. 'She had a miscarriage a week ago.'

This halted my tirade in its tracks. 'I'm so sorry. I didn't know.'

He waved away my words. 'It's hit her really hard. She keeps crying and the kids are getting scared. She keeps taking herself off to bed when I get home in the evening. It's not helped that she knew I didn't want any more kids. Three are expensive enough as it is.' He exhaled, puffing out his cheeks.

'Is there anything I can do?' I asked. 'Anything at all?' I knew it was unlikely that I could, and the offer was only the smallest of gestures.

'You can always come round and babysit some time.'

'Anything apart from babysit. I don't fancy that.'

'No.' He smiled wanly. 'But thanks anyway.'

We drove the rest of the way to Worthing in companionable silence. I thought about Mel and tried to imagine how wretched she was feeling but, having never been in her position, I didn't know what else to say. Instead, I concentrated on how Tommy Ross was going to be when we got to the hospital. Unlike Mel, his physical condition was not going to be getting much better any time soon.

70

Before we'd left, I had checked with the hospital that Tommy was still there and what department he was now in. That hadn't been easy, as they were cautious about giving out information, but what they had told me was that, shortly after the paramedics had rushed him to Accident and Emergency, he'd been transferred to an acute medical ward.

We drove around the car park a couple of times before I spotted a space, and then nipped off to get a ticket for two hours. I didn't think we'd be there that long, but if Tommy was up for talking I didn't want to rush away. I wondered if I was being too optimistic, though, as the nurse I spoke to on the phone hadn't even been willing to tell me if he was conscious or not. If meeting Tommy had done nothing else, it had forced me to take it easy with the wine.

Wingsy and I picked our way through the familiar gaggle of smokers at the main entrance and on towards Tommy's bedside. Once inside, Sister Denise Lyle led us to a relatives' room, where I explained that Tommy was a witness and Wingsy and I had found him collapsed on his bedroom floor.

'We've done as much as we can for him,' Sister Lyle explained. 'He was resuscitated with fluids, and given intravenous antibiotics and medication to prevent him having alcohol withdrawal symptoms.' She paused and smiled a small, sweet smile. No doubt she was used to giving bad news to friends and relatives about their loved ones, and probably well aware that, as detectives, our knowledge of medical procedures was almost nil. It had been a long couple of days and I was probably wearing my vacant expression. It often helped me out and was doing a very good job today.

'Mr Ross had an ultrasound scan taken of his liver and abdomen when he was brought in,' she continued. 'His condition is very far advanced. There isn't much we can do for him now, but we're making him as comfortable as we can.'

'Can I ask you a couple of things, please?' I said. I wasn't sure I was going to like her answer but I couldn't leave it unsaid. I fidgeted on my chair and unbuttoned my jacket. 'Would Tommy have recovered if he'd stopped drinking when he first became ill and then had some treatment?'

'It's difficult to say. It's likely that he would have improved slightly, but the damage was already done. In this kind of situation, most people carry on drinking, as they know there's little chance of a drastic improvement. We knew from his history that we were looking at end-of-life care.'

Denise Lyle paused, head tilted in my direction. She had kind eyes that had probably looked at hundreds of bewildered loved ones asking about their nearest and dearest's chances. She was probably being a little more honest with me than usual owing to our official capacity.

'And the other thing...' I said taking a deep breath. 'We'd been to see Tommy and he was – well, he was helping us with something.' I stole a glance in Wingsy's direction. He was looking at his feet. 'He stopped drinking, you see. The thing that he was helping us with meant a lot to him,

290

and he was determined to see a trial out and to lay some personal matters to rest. If we hadn't knocked on his door and asked for his help, propelling him towards sobriety, would he have stood a better chance if he'd received scheduled treatment via the hospital consultant?'

Sister Lyle closed her eyes, pursed her lips and shook her head. 'No. It's the kind of thing we get asked a lot,' she said, looking at me again. 'Liver cirrhosis brings with it multiple organ complications such as heart problems. Excessive alcohol will kill you. It's that simple. You've come all this way, so would you like to see Tommy now?'

The answer to that was no, not really. What I wanted to do was go home and put the kettle on. But we had after all driven a fair distance and, however uncomfortable I was with seeing him, it was the main purpose of the journey.

I steeled myself for an uncomfortable time and followed her to Tommy's bedside. I had had enough of hospitals to last me a lifetime.

71

Wingsy and I felt equally glum when we left the hospital. I even offered to buy us both something to eat, but he wasn't to be cheered up that easily.

'You only said that you'll pay because you're going to claim it back on expenses anyway,' he said from the passenger seat.

'There's no pleasing you, is there? Of course I'm going to claim it back, but it's the thought that counts. I hoped lunch would cheer you up, plus keep the tea stains on your shirt company.'

We continued to bicker about stopping for food until we got to Marilyn and Charles Fitzhubert's house. Earlier I'd left a message on their answerphone saying that we'd drop in as we were passing by, but so far I'd received no reply. I'd got used to unreturned messages from the public and professionals over the years, though, so I didn't read too much into it any more. Even when I pulled up outside their house and noticed the lack of a car outside, Wingsy and I still got our paperwork from the back seat and headed to the front door, optimistic that someone would be home.

Marilyn opened the door, telephone in hand. 'Hello,' she said. 'I just listened to your message. Please come in. I'm glad we didn't miss each other.' She stood back to allow us into her home. 'Charles had to go out,' she added as I passed her in the hallway. 'Go into the kitchen. I was about to make myself a coffee.'

The three of us sat around the counter in the centre of the room, waiting for the kettle to boil. It didn't escape my notice that, despite the pod coffee maker, coffee grinder and cafetière, she chose the kettle and instant granules.

Marilyn said, 'I wanted to tell you something, Nina. Since we spoke the day Tommy went into hospital, I've been to see him a couple of times. He wasn't very coherent most of the time but he did talk about Shona's accident once or twice. It was all quite garbled but he muttered something about it being his fault and being weak. I don't know what he was really talking about, if I'm honest, but he did mention Leonard Rumbly and how he should have done something about Leonard when he could.'

I waited for her to go on, but Marilyn got off her kitchen stool and walked to the fridge, heels clipping on the ceramic tiled floor. As she came back over to us, steaming mugs in hand, I waited until she put them down before I got straight to the point. 'Why didn't you tell us that Leonard Rumbly had the seat next to you on the Chilhampton Express when it crashed?'

The colour didn't so much drain from her face as fall off. An almost transparent Marilyn answered, 'No one was ever supposed to know we had planned to spend a couple of days away together. I couldn't get out of it, I really couldn't. Leonard bought my train ticket and I told Malcolm I was visiting my aunt at the seaside. I was only going along with it because I wanted to tell Leonard I was in love with Malcolm and I was pregnant with his child.' She fought back tears at this point and I saw her pause, regain control of her emotions before she said, 'Malcolm knew I was going to be on the train, you see. He waved me off that morning to the station. He knew all along, and even after all these years I'm still lying over this sorry incident.'

I tried to feel sorry for her. On first meeting Marilyn, she had seemed upset and tearful at the very mention of the train crash. It was all beginning to fall into place now: she had failed to control her life all those years ago and the consequences of it were still plaguing her.

I got the feeling there was more Marilyn wasn't telling me, but I wasn't sure I was going to get to the bottom of it this way. I tried a different approach.

'Do you have any idea why Tommy named Charles as next of kin?'

She sat back in her seat. 'Tommy and his wife Shona were my son Liam's godparents. Tommy and Charles knew each other from football, of course. Tommy hadn't seen Liam for years but I know that he always kept tabs on him and was as proud of him as if he was his own flesh and blood.'

She paused to pick up her cup, and watched me take a sip of my own coffee.

'Go on,' I said, coaxing her to tell me more than she really wanted to.

She sighed and looked up to the ceiling. 'Tommy and I got to know each other after the crash. We were in hospital at the same time and we got talking. I can't remember now whether we bumped into each other in a corridor or canteen, or the nurses got us together, or what it was. Anyway, we got chatting about the crash and I was in such a state. Physically I was on the mend, but Malcolm had hurt me very much by what he'd said, not to mention having a baby on the way, no father for it and no family around me. Tommy and Shona took me in. They were newly married and took pity on me.'

I sat listening to Marilyn, picturing a very scared and lonely young woman in an age when unmarried mothers faced a very different scenario from the one they might expect today. Little wonder that she'd latched on to Tommy, a man in whom I'd seen only kindness and sadness.

'Well, Tommy and Shona spoilt me rotten,' said Marilyn with a sad smile. 'I felt at ease with them in their home. I was too proud to crawl back to Malcolm but too stupid to stay away from Leonard.'

Saying his name brought on a tightening in her neck and facial muscles. It was gone with such speed I might have imagined it, had I not met the man and found he made my own flesh crawl.

Composure regained, she continued her tale. 'Four months pregnant, I went to visit Leonard. I knew that I couldn't stay at the Rosses' forever, despite their kindness, and…' I noticed that Marilyn seemed to be breathing heavily. She closed her eyes and pinched the top of her nose. 'When I got to Leonard's office, I could hear noises coming from inside. Several people were shouting. I could make out that they were all men and it was getting violent. I didn't want to know what it was about because I had enough on my plate. I turned to leave but not before I heard Leonard's voice say something like, "Stupid bitch is better off dead." I thought he was talking about me.' She gave another bitter laugh. 'That's how important I still thought I was, even after everything else. But next thing I heard was a voice saying, 'How do we get rid of the body? We should chuck her in the river. Why the fuck have you kept this here, Len? Get rid of it with the body; it's covered in blood. Half of her head is caved in." Lord knows what I'd got involved in.'

Marilyn had sat unmoving, eyes still closed. They fluttered open but she couldn't look at me. She looked towards her kitchen window but I doubted she was focusing on the yellow patio roses swaying just outside it. She was looking into an office at the back of a warehouse in Deptford fifty years ago.

'I ran,' she said at last. 'I ran. I was straight out of there and found myself on Deptford High Street. The first bus I saw was a number 53 and I knew it ran to the centre of town. I wasn't sure where I was going but I pulled myself together by the time we reached the Old Kent Road. I got off at the Bricklayer's Arms and found myself on Tower Bridge Road. I rang Shona and told her where I was. I was in such a state, crying and sobbing, Shona could hardly make me out. The Sixties were a time for heavy black eyeliner and mascara, so you can imagine how much attention I attracted. Tommy wasn't in, but Shona said she'd try to track him down and I was to stay put. I'd rung her from a phone box and I waited in a café on the corner of Rothsay Street. I can remember it very clearly. It was called Rossi's and owned by an Italian family. I got some strange looks, no doubt because I was in such a mess, but the owner was very kind and kept asking me if he could help or call anyone for me. I got a cup of tea, and I'd hardly touched it when I saw Tommy's car pull up outside the Pagoda Pub. I've never been so glad to see someone, I can tell you.'

Watching Marilyn's face, I could see how pained she was. Leaving my personal feelings aside, I had a nagging doubt about something. I'd learned to seek out the worst in people; it prevented me from being had over more often than was strictly necessary.

Tommy Ross had my empathy for his shattered, lonely life. Marilyn had made me feel sympathy towards her because of her earlier life. But right now I could only feel suspicious.

'How long was it between you calling Shona and Tommy turning up?' I said, banishing any hint of accusation from my tone.

Marilyn's pretty face looked up. 'It's difficult to say. The café was fairly empty, I got served, sat down and before I knew it Tommy was there.' She frowned. The lines on her forehead were more prominent in the daylight than they had been a few days earlier in the gloom of their living room. 'I suppose he wasn't all that long at all, now you mention it.'

'Did you ever ask Tommy where he'd been when Shona managed to track him down?' I asked, letting suspicion in.

'Not at the time, I didn't,' she replied, 'not the state I was in. We drove back to their flat in Belgravia and I went to bed. Tommy kept trying to ask me what I'd heard and who had been there. I told him what I just told you. I was frightened of Leonard and begged Tommy not to say anything to him.'

I tried again. 'Marilyn, this is important. The tea you were drinking in the café. Was it that you didn't try to drink it, or was it that you didn't have time to drink it?'

'I'm not sure I follow you,' she said. 'What's so important about a cup of tea from fifty years ago?'

'What I'm trying to work out is how long it took Tommy to get to you.'

'Let me think,' she said. 'Tommy said something to me later about being on his way to Manze's pie and mash shop. Footballers' diets then weren't anything like they are today. Manze's was his favourite, and only around the corner from where he picked me up.'

I looked back down at the cooling coffee in front of me. I glanced down to hide my eyes. I wasn't happy with Marilyn's explanation, as Shona wouldn't have been able to get hold of Tommy if he had been on his way to get pie and mash, in an age long before mobile phones. She would have had to know where he was.

Wingsy leaned forward, looking straight at Marilyn's ashen face. 'I think, that day, it was Tommy you overheard with Leonard Rumbly and someone else discussing a murder they'd committed and how they were going to get rid of her body. Then Tommy picked you up from the café and drove you home.'

72

Marilyn didn't seem to take the news as badly as I would have expected. She remained very still for several seconds, before she said, 'It's something I've not allowed myself to dwell on. My only thoughts back then were for my unborn child. Tommy and Shona introduced me to Charles a month or so later and, much to my astonishment, he proposed. I refused to let anything unpleasant occupy my thoughts, so I moved on and didn't look back. It might seem harsh, but things were finally looking up and – well, it's not as though I heard them planning a murder. From what they said, the girl was already dead. So I didn't tell anyone.'

Marilyn seemed to decide this was the moment that the cups needed washing up. She gathered our cups and saucers and turned her back on us at the sink. Her back was rigid as she clinked her good china together. I guessed we were moments away from being asked to leave.

'Who was the other person in the office with Tommy and Rumbly?' I asked the back of her head.

She looked to the side and said over her shoulder, 'I've told you, I didn't recognise the voice.'

'You may not have at the time, but do you now know who it was?'

'My husband will be home soon,' she said, as she turned to face us, wiping her hands on a towel. 'I have things to do before I go back to the hospital to see Tommy later.'

Neither I nor Wingsy resisted her request; we started to gather our stuff together. I made a point of leaving her a business card printed with my name, mobile and office number, information I knew she already had.

'We'll be in touch soon, Marilyn, about a statement,' I said as I got down from the kitchen stool and picked up my bag. 'Do you have any idea who the woman was they were talking about?'

She wouldn't look me in the eye and took to fiddling with the pendant on her necklace.

I couldn't resist a parting shot at her: she knew more than she was letting on but I needed to be armed with more information before I pushed her.

'For what it's worth, Marilyn,' I said as I hoisted my bag on to my shoulder, 'I think it could easily have been you next. It may only have been your unborn baby that saved you.' I paused to let that sink in and then added, 'In the meantime, you know where we are.'

My comments were met with a glare, but our hostess followed us to the front door, held it open and thanked us for coming. She even added, 'Safe journey, officers,' although I wasn't sure she meant it.

We got back into the car and started our journey back to the large pile of paperwork waiting for us in the Cold Case office. 'What do you reckon about Charles being the other person in the room that day?' I said as we reached the main road.

Wingsy shrugged and said, 'It could be him but, even if she was desperate, would Marilyn have married a man she knew was involved in covering up a murder?'

'I don't know, but the more I speak to her and find out about her, the more I think she's got by on her looks and leeched off people.'

My friend turned across to look at me and said, 'I thought you'd taken to her?'

'I had, but, when you look at everything, firstly she's dating Malcolm Bring who was a bit of a loser even back then; then she confronts Rumbly about the gambling debts but goes on several dates with him – not to mention steals from him. And then, pregnant, she moves in with Tommy and Shona who are only just married, then she gets introduced to a wealthy, good-looking footballer who plays for England, but won't consider the possibility that her now very rich husband may have done something wrong.'

'Perhaps she'll call you,' said Wingsy.

'I bet she won't,' I said. 'In fact, I bet you lunch that I'll have to call – ' My phone started to ring. The caller display on the hands-free showed the name *Marilyn F.*

'Don't look so bloody smug, Baldy. We didn't shake on it.' I hit the Answer button.

A slightly shaking voice said, 'Hello, Nina. Minutes after you left, the hospital called. Tommy had a stroke. He died an hour ago.'

73

Tommy's death was hardly a surprise, but it still shook me. It did, of course, mean that, if he had been involved in the murder of a woman in 1964, or in covering it up, he'd got away with it. Leonard Rumbly wasn't likely to want to help us with her identification or the investigation into her death, either. We had no idea who she was, but it wouldn't stop us trying. I liked a sense of justice and people being held to account for what they'd done, even though we had little to go on. Missing women from 1964 or unidentified bodies fished from the Thames fifty years ago would be a start, so that was where we would begin, as soon as we were back at the station.

Despite everything that was unfolding, Tommy still had my sympathy, although now I wondered what else he might have been involved in. Rumbly, however, still had my loathing. I would have preferred it to have been Rumbly, with his lifetime of criminal activity, who had died alone in a hospital bed, feeling he had nothing worth living for, but life wasn't always that fair.

We got back to Riverstone police station feeling worn out by a morning of emotions, rather than hard work. I'd given in and bought Wingsy's lunch, although I argued that not only had we not actually made a deal, Marilyn had telephoned for something completely different. Largely because he'd sulked, I had splashed out on a tea and sandwich for him in the service stop, and now he was moaning that he had indigestion.

'Stop going on about it,' I said as we went back through the office door. 'Anyone would think I made you eat it.'

The sight of Harry staring straight at us as we came through the door stopped me in my tracks. Wingsy halted beside me too.

'I've been with the CPS today,' he said. 'They're saying we definitely don't have enough on Leonard Rumbly as far as the train crash goes. It's too long ago, only a couple of people saying he was behind the conspiracy to delay it by any means, and now, to top it all, we find out that he was on the sodding thing.'

'I thought they might at least give it a go,' I said, sitting down opposite Harry, feeling misery taking hold. 'They knew we were going out to arrest him. There's something else?'

'The drugs we dug up from his garden.' Harry loosened his tie. 'They said that the photos and video we have showed him burying the box, but the contents aren't seen in the pictures. CPS are saying that the information came from his son and his son has a lot to gain from putting his own father in prison. There's all sorts coming to light about Leonard and Andy falling out about one thing and another – probably drugs – but, whatever the reason, there's a good chance anything Andy is telling us is to be taken with a pinch of salt.'

'Hang on,' said Wingsy. 'Did the drugs' wrappings have Leonard Rumbly's fingerprints on them?'

'They've just come back, and yes,' answered Harry. 'But no one else's. No one else's at all. Pretty unusual, wouldn't you say? What are the chances of a man who's escaped the law for so long getting caught for something so trivial, not to mention careless?'

This was now a very bad day.

'We really can't charge him with anything at all?' Wingsy asked.

Harry laughed humourlessly. 'CPS suggested he might accept a caution for possession.'

'Well, there is something else,' I said, sitting down beside Harry. 'We've been speaking to Marilyn and there is a chance that Rumbly senior was involved in a murder in the 1960s. What with you being the DS for Cold Case and all, you're definitely the best person for me and Wings to start with.'

Harry listened as Wingsy and I went through Marilyn's account of the conversation she'd overheard many years before. He flicked through my notebook so he could read for himself my scribblings as she'd spoken to us.

'We start off in force,' he began as he leafed through the pages, scratching his stubble with his cheap, police-issued pen. 'We search on any missing persons, unsolved murders, that kind of thing. We're only assuming that the body ended up in the Thames because of the conversation that Marilyn overheard: they were in London near the Thames, that's all. Even so, we'll liaise with the Met's Cold Case that covers that location, speak to Case Review – both theirs and ours – check old newspapers and see what SCAS turns up.'

I must have pulled my 'what are you talking about?' face, as he glanced up and added, 'Serious Case Analysis Section.'

'Are we going to find out who she is, Harry?'

'When do we ever give up?' He winked at me before looking at his watch and saying, 'You two get yourselves off home too, but in the morning there's something I need you to sort out. Rumbly's at home on the mend and he's now got a solicitor. She's been on the phone and he wants his passport and a couple of other things back. Can one of you sort it out?'

'First thing,' said Wingsy. 'We can go together and wake him up. He's an old man, but it's probably safer if we both go.'

'That's a good idea,' I said, putting my jacket back on. 'Old man with a heart problem or not, I feel like shoving his passport somewhere. I'll probably be in a better mood by tomorrow.'

I said my goodnights and made for home. It had been a difficult day but another was about to follow, starting with a visit to Leonard Rumbly.

74

The office was empty when I got to work at eight o'clock the next morning. I checked the diary and saw that Jemma and Micky had already gone out, Jim was on leave but Harry and Wingsy were nowhere to be found. As I was pondering calling one of them, Harry came through the door, swearing and moaning about an overnight kidnap he'd been called out for at three in the morning. I let him get it out of his system as he rummaged through his desk, found the notebook he'd been looking for and left.

Alone once more, I called Wingsy's mobile. He answered on the first ring.

'Hi, duchess,' he said, 'I was about to call you.'

'Everything OK?'

On the other end of the line, I heard a door click shut. 'Don't want the kids to hear,' he said. 'Mel's not too well. I'm going to have to sort out a lift to school for the kids and then I'll be in.'

'You sure you don't need anything?'

'No, no. Wait for me. I've sorted the stuff out for Rumbly. It's locked in my drawer. I'll be in in about twenty minutes and we can go over there then.'

I set about busying myself and trying to take my mind off the last few days. Nothing seemed to be working to distract me. In the end, I went over to Wingsy's desk to see what he was planning on returning to Rumbly. He had locked the stuff in his desk, but I knew that he always kept the key under his coffee cup when he wasn't on duty. I unlocked the drawer and was bent over, mid-rifle, when Kayla appeared in the doorway.

'Yous look guilty,' she said as I looked up.

'I'm going through Wingsy's desk,' I told her.

'Need a hand?'

'No, I've got this. Were you looking for me?'

'Yes, I thought I'd drop by and say hello,' she said. 'I've been in since six. I've got so much to do. I wanted to let you know that we've had some more developments from the Lea Hollingsworth murder. I've just got an update on the head injuries. You know that they were caused by something long and possibly tapered at one end, like a baseball bat?'

I nodded. I remembered the pathologist saying at the post mortem that she had head injuries.

Kayla continued, 'There was a tiny fragment embedded in the back of her skull, and it turned out to be wood. It was being dealt with as a murder anyway because of the other drugs deaths, but this has really pushed the button.' She yawned and stretched out her arms. 'No prizes for what I'll be spending the next six months doing. Well, I'll leave you to it.'

I watched her walk back out of the office and into the corridor.

I busied myself until I heard Wingsy bang through the office door, swearing and muttering under his breath.

I wasn't sure how to approach the subject of his wife, so I went with, 'Still OK to take this stuff back to Rumbly today?'

He glanced at the items in front of me on the desk, raised his eyebrows at me and said, 'You managed to find them in my locked drawer, then.'

'Latte? Or do you want to talk?'

'Latte, please. And a sausage roll.'

Even I realised it wasn't a good time to tell him that Mel wouldn't like him eating that, so I got my purse and spent my last fiver.

75

Finding myself back at Leonard Rumbly's house so soon was not something I was particularly pleased about. I knew who he was, how he'd made his money and the dirty, low tactics he'd think nothing of sinking to. However, as we pulled up outside in the muddy unmarked police Ford, I had to hand it to him: he had a very fancy house. On my other visit to his home I had only glanced at it from an officer safety point of view. Today, I was able to take my time. The three-storey Georgian vicarage stood within its own gardens and orchard. I liked orchards, apart from in the month of September when they were full of wasps. Perhaps they'd all attack him and sting him when the time was right and bring on another heart attack. A woman had to live in hope.

Wingsy hadn't said a word to me on the journey over, so I gave him some peace. As soon as we finished at Rumbly's house, I'd have one last try talking to him. I watched him get his notebook from the back seat and saw how he kept his eyes and the corners of his mouth towards the ground.

Grabbing my own notebook and bag from behind the driver's seat, I locked the car and made my way along the gravel drive. Glancing up at the sash windows, I thought how pretty they looked and how easy they were to gain entry through if you were intent on burglary.

Despite never having broken into a property in my life, I expected I could manage it well enough. It was something often shown on daytime television, in case you were a criminal on a career break and didn't fancy in-the-field research.

By the time, we'd reached the front door, Leonard Rumbly was waiting on the doorstep for us.

'Mr Rumbly,' I began. 'You're dressed. We thought we'd make an early start. You wanted some of your property back.' All the time I was thinking how much I hated this individual. He'd made his living and livelihood by ruining other people's lives. He'd taken full advantage of those with a weakness and exploited them. The world would always have despicable bastards like him in it, but few of them would be standing before me looking so smug, taunting me, knowing that there was nothing I could do to bring about his downfall.

As he smiled at me, I wanted desperately to punch him into the middle of next week. Two things stopped me: I was a police officer, and he was a septuagenarian. Even so, the first outweighed the second.

I took a deep breath and remembered the simple task we'd come here for.

'Hello, officers,' he said. 'Please, come in. I was making tea.' He fully opened the door to allow us inside. As I stepped over the threshold, he said, 'What can I get for you both?'

'Some further information on the 1964 train crash would do for starters,' I said glaring straight into his gaze for a second. 'You can follow it up with what you know about drug overdoses in the local area. I'm guessing that you don't know what I'm talking about?'

'Officer, officer – ' he chuckled as he leaned across behind Wingsy to shut the front door ' – not only do I not have a clue what you're talking about, but I think you're forgetting that I'm not a well man.'

Now I was really angry. Evil took many forms, and here it was in an M&S cardigan.

We stood in the hall waiting for him to lead the way. He shuffled in his carpet slippers past us towards the kitchen. I'd bought my great-uncle Eric similar slippers for three consecutive Christmases because he kept losing them. I then figured out that he'd been throwing them away because he hated them so much. That, of course, made me think of Walter McRay's wife's lost wedding ring, burglary, and how people robbed and stole to get their hands on drugs provided by the likes of this git.

Rumbly's breathing was laboured as he made his way along the bright and airy hall towards the kitchen.

He sat in the chair furthest from the dim light. Without being asked, I took a seat opposite him. Wingsy drew up a chair next to me. Rumbly's creepy smile broke halfway and became a wince. I watched him bring one gnarled knuckle up to his chest. Don't try that one again, you old codger, I thought. It might have got you out of the last tricky situation but it isn't going to wash with me now.

Fake chest pains under control, Rumbly locked eyes with me.

'So, Miss Foster,' he said. 'What brings you and your colleague to my house on this beautiful morning?'

'I have some receipts for you to sign and some property to return.' I bent down to pick up the briefcase I had placed next to my chair. I rummaged through it and got out his passport and a couple of paper items DI Hammond had agreed he could have back.

Rumbly reached out his liver-spotted hand for the passport. I snatched it away. I gave him a look that seemed to make amusement flare around his cold eyes.

'If you can just sign the receipt? It's not that I don't trust you…' I paused and then added, 'Oh, no – actually, I don't trust you.'

I pushed the paper and a pen towards him.

'Officer, how kind. You've even put kisses where you want me to sign.'

I watched the top of his bald head as he bent forward to sign the paperwork. Our faces were feet apart. I could see every line and wrinkle on his face. He'd added a few to my own, too.

'It's very quiet here, Mr Rumbly,' I said, not moving an inch despite being repelled. 'You seem to be in your beautiful home all alone. Where is everyone? I suspect that your own grandson's doing time because of you. Your son is nowhere to be seen. What about your great-grandchildren? Are they allowed anywhere near you?'

As I spoke to him, as I mentioned each generation of his family, he moved his face back an inch at a time. It was quite a relief, as his breath smelt of death. I watched his snaky little tongue dart across dry, cracked lips.

'Where are your family, Leonard? Where are your friends? At the end of the day, you can buy people to do jobs for you, beat people up for you, even kill them, but you can't even buy someone to be here with you. You're a lonely old man.'

Rumbly's face had gone very pale. I seemed to have hit a nerve. I was feeling fairly pleased with myself. He put his hand up to his chest and grimaced.

'Here's your passport,' I said, throwing it on to the table and taking the receipt. 'And the other bills and identification we took from you. Happy it's all here?'

He nodded at me, still holding his chest. This time, he gave a sharp intake of breath.

'And you can cut that out. I'm not falling for that.'

I pushed my chair out, scraping its legs along the stone floor of the kitchen. For the first time since we'd left the office, Wingsy spoke. 'I don't think he's kidding. He doesn't look well.'

Standing there ready to leave, I watched Rumbly's face contort with pain. This time, I was inclined to agree with Wingsy: I was no longer sure he was pretending. My initial instinct was to help a fellow human being – rush around the table, call an ambulance. Then I remembered: he wasn't a human being. He was Leonard Rumbly. I stayed exactly where I was, next to a motionless Wingsy.

Despite the nastier side of my personality tempting me into walking away from a dying man, without realising I'd done it I had my phone out of my bag and in my hand to dial three nines. It had no signal. Rumbly was making the worst kinds of noises I've ever heard someone emit. The moaning noises coming from his throat were a sound I'd never heard before but, by instinct, I knew what I was listening to. I could hear Leonard Rumbly's dying breaths. If we didn't do something, and do it fast, he was going to die.

For a few seconds, we stood side by side watching him. 'We should do something,' said Wingsy, backing away. I wanted to back away too, shut the door and pretend I hadn't seen what was happening. Deny all knowledge when I was eventually hauled into the DCI's office and asked how Rumbly had been when I last saw him. In weeks from now, when his decomposing body was riddled with maggots.

Something stopped me. Something else jolted me out of it. At the time I wasn't sure what it was, but whenever I played the scene back in my mind I think it was my shock at Wingsy's attempt to distance himself. His action forced me to do the right thing. I owed my friend more than he could ever know – he stopped me from walking away from a dying man.

I ran around the table to Rumbly as he slid off his chair. His body was contorted with pain. Helpless to stop his clumsy impact with the floor, I got to him just as I saw the back of his skull smack against the red tiles. I knelt beside him. He gave a low groan like a wounded animal. His face was now a ruddy colour, similar to that of the tiles his head was on, jerking from side to side.

His eyes were open but his eyeballs had started their ascent towards his eyelids. They couldn't quite manage it. Some part of my brain reminded me that many years ago I had stood in a Magistrates' Court and proudly sworn an oath to the Queen. Preservation of life was my number one priority. Even a life as disgusting and parasitical as Rumbly's.

'Wingsy!' I shouted. 'Help me!'

He jolted, as if he too realised he couldn't stand by and do nothing. He knelt down beside Rumbly and held his hand out towards the groaning figure. He felt for a pulse.

Leaving him to it, I ran to the hallway, looking for a landline. I hesitated at the foot of the stairs. An old man who lived alone would probably have a phone in the bedroom, but the house was massive and I might miss it. I ran back towards the kitchen, aware of Wingsy saying something to Rumbly, but I didn't concentrate on the words.

I opened the door that I remembered led to the study. Panic subsiding, thinking more clearly, I was sure I had seen a phone on the desk the day we'd arrested him. I was right: an old-fashioned black telephone with gold trim sat on the leather top of the enormous oak desk in the centre of the room. I ran over to it and put my hand out to pick up the receiver, but my attention flew to something else beside it. Something that hadn't been here before when we searched.

Everything stopped.

When we'd come to arrest Rumbly, I'd watched him from the door of the study as he looked towards a stack of paperwork. But I'd been wrong about his concern. It had had nothing to do with papers.

I was staring at an old-fashioned wooden police truncheon. A truncheon that had been hit against a surface with so much force, the wood had cracked.

I heard a moan from the kitchen which jolted me back to reality. Rumbly was scum and deserved to die alone, in pain, on a cold, tiled kitchen floor. But I didn't get to be judge, jury and executioner. What if I was wrong and this wasn't, as I suspected, the weapon that had killed Lea?

My hand was still hovering above the telephone. I could go back into the kitchen, talk Wingsy into leaving with me, take the passport and paperwork back to the station and pretend Rumbly hadn't been in. We couldn't say we hadn't been here at all, because of the black box in the police car.

Then I did the right thing and called an ambulance.

76

O nce I had the emergency services on the phone, I shouted to Wingsy to run to the front door and prop it open. I took the phone to the kitchen but the lead was too short and made it impossible to hear what the operator was saying to me. Having only recently assisted with Tommy's CPR, though, Wingsy knew what he had to do, but he drew the line at mouth-to-mouth.

Relief flooded every part of me when I heard an ambulance approaching along the nearby streets before coming to a stop on the gravel outside. Two paramedics arrived and took over. Wingsy and I gave them a rapid explanation of what had happened, got out of their way and then I called Harry's mobile.

From the kitchen door, I watched them working on him. It took a few seconds for it to register that his blood was seeping across the floor. Initially I thought it had come from his head where he'd hit it on the tiles, but I soon realised from its flow that it was from the veins in his arms. They'd injected him at speed with various drugs so his blood was spreading out over the terracotta flooring. I stood uselessly by while they took him to the front of the house, leaving the paper wrappings from their disposable equipment, and the clothing they'd cut from him, upon the bloodied tiles.

I'd declined their offer of going with them to the hospital, insisting that I wait for my supervisor. Wingsy had gone out through the front door when the ambulance crew arrived and seemed to be staying clear for the time being. I started to explain that it was our duty to make sure his house was secure and that, once I shut the door, we'd have to force entry. They weren't listening: my legal powers of search and entry were as interesting to them as Rumbly's vital signs were to me.

I wasn't sure how long I stood in the open doorway. I looked out on to the street, keeping an eye on Wingsy, as well as impatient for Harry to arrive. I didn't want to go into the empty house with its bloodied kitchen tiles. I also didn't want to go into the study again on my own. I needed a witness, and it was clear to me that Wingsy wasn't himself.

The sound of a cheap, high-mileage diesel car heading my way snapped me to attention. I watched Harry turn into the road and speed towards us. He was out of the car and coming towards me almost before the engine died.

'He's gone,' I said.

'What, you mean...?' said Harry.

'No, no,' I said. 'At least, I don't think so. Come inside. I have something to show you.'

'What's he doing?' Harry asked, pointing at Wingsy. 'Wingnut, stop moping around and get over here.' Wingsy ambled towards us.

I led them to the study and turned to face them. 'Lea Hollingsworth was hit on the head with something like a baseball bat.' I stepped away from the desk and watched them both as their eyes rested on the police truncheon. Harry's stubble-covered jaw tightened. Wingsy's eyes widened and his mouth dropped open. Normally I would tell him how simple he looked. It wasn't the right time.

'When we were here to arrest Rumbly, I saw him looking over in this direction,' I said. 'The truncheon

317

definitely wasn't here then or we'd have seized it. It must have been concealed in this desk somewhere. And take a look in the fireplace – it looks as though he was about to light a fire.'

'Do you reckon it could be?' said Harry in hushed tones I'd never heard him adopt before. 'What connects him to Lea Hollingsworth? Other than possibly her blood all over that.'

'I'm not sure, Harry, but when I was speaking to Joe Bring in prison he told me that her boyfriend owed money for drugs. I'm seeing a very unpleasant pattern emerge with people who upset Leonard Rumbly in some way.'

He stared at me. I could see him digest the magnitude of what I was saying: there could be more victims. Rumbly had been untouchable for so long, he thought he could act with impunity. That was about to change.

Then Harry had his phone out of his pocket and was striding to the front door to get a signal in the street. I heard him talking to DI Hammond as he got outside, telling the DI that he wanted a warrant as soon as possible, as well as a search team and an officer with a video camera to film the whole thing, including the fireplace. I heard the beginnings of a row over how we missed it the first time around and Harry hollering that it must have been hidden somewhere, and then the tone changed as Harry began to explain about our earlier requests for information on bodies found in 1964.

I turned my attention to Wingsy. 'What's the matter?' I asked. 'You look beside yourself.'

He glanced in the direction of Harry in the doorway, now launched into a conversation about warrants, scene preservation and getting an officer to the hospital as soon as possible. He ran a hand through what was left of his hair.

'We knew we were on a hiding to nothing with Rumbly before today.' He paused as if unsure whether to carry on. 'You know,' he said, 'the only thing that stopped me talking you into leaving him to die on the floor was the fear of getting caught.'

I couldn't look him in the eye.

Wingsy sighed. 'Yeah, I know, Nin. I'm ashamed of myself.'

I couldn't let him carry this on his own. I took a deep breath and, putting my hand on his arm, said, 'If you hadn't been with me, I think I would have done just that. You're no worse than me. We did the right thing, though, and that's what matters. If he lives and that truncheon has been used to kill Lea, he'll probably spend what time he has left in prison. Let's agree that we don't ever admit this again. Not to anyone.'

The last thing I wanted was another secret, but I knew it was safe with Wingsy.

'You two,' said Harry, having ended his call, 'when you've finished consoling each other, I've got some news. I may just make your day.'

We waited.

'While you two were getting your beauty sleep last night, some of us were working. The DI's had a call about a woman who went missing in 1964. She was last seen with her boyfriend, according to what's been uncovered.'

'And?' asked Wingsy.

'The boyfriend's name was Withey. Martin Withey. Mean anything to you?'

77

Back at the police station. Wingsy and I spent hours putting together our statements about what had happened. We were warned by everyone from Harry to the superintendent that we wouldn't be working on anything to do with Rumbly and we would be formally spoken to about what had happened in his house. It wasn't the first time he'd collapsed in my presence, so I was feeling particularly nervous.

Twice Bill called me to find out what time I was coming home, and twice I told him that I didn't know.

Just as I finished the last signature of my statement, the tannoy announced that I had a visitor at the front counter. Wondering why everyone wouldn't simply leave me alone, I grabbed my pen and notebook and went downstairs to find out who it was.

The front counter assistant was on the telephone when I poked my head around the door to the station's foyer. She gestured to a tall, good-looking man standing just inside the main entrance.

'Hello,' I said, 'I'm Nina Foster. Can I help you?'

He looked familiar, although I didn't think we'd met. I tried to place him but he was like another version of someone else. Other than his looks, I couldn't fail to notice that he was wearing an expensive blue suit with very shiny shoes.

'I'm Liam Fitzhubert,' he said. 'Marilyn's son. I think you know my half-brother Joe.'

Hiding my surprise, I said, 'Let's go into one of the interview rooms,' and pointed to the door to his left. We shook hands and sat facing each other at the desk strewn with blank statement sheets and crime prevention leaflets.

'I've been to see Joe,' he began. 'In prison.'

'I'm glad you added that last bit.' We both smiled at each other.

'He told me about you and that you'd been to see him a couple of times,' said Liam.

I wasn't going to discuss with a stranger what Joe had told me. I only had this man's word for it that he was Liam Fitzhubert, although the Bring likeness was most definitely there.

'Yes, I've visited him.'

Liam looked down at the table and thumbed the curly edge of a statement form. 'He also told me that he was going to give you some names – names of people who may help you prosecute Leonard Rumbly. Joe mentioned something about this man's criminal past and the stuff he's still involved in now.'

He took a deep breath and met my stare.

'No one likes a grass. I don't move in the same circles as Joe, but I know it won't make him any friends passing you a list of names. But he's told me who you need to speak to.' He paused and reached inside his jacket pocket. 'I have a list here. How about we say they came from me?'

He held the list towards me. It was within my grasp. I wanted to shake my head and tell him no, this was a murder enquiry. Instead I took the paper from his hand and unfolded it.

My eyes ran down the handwritten list. Five names. Joe had told me that he had five or six names to give me.

Some were probably dead, but this was more than we'd had moments earlier for the train crash.

'Thank you, Liam. Did Joe offer these names freely?'

He gave a small laugh, unnatural compared to the rest of him. 'I had to promise him that I'd take his son away for a week or two. Some sort of boot camp. He told me that Luke doesn't have any other relations, so I suppose I'm lucky to be able to spend time with him. I thought I might even be able to offer Joe some sort of work when he comes out of prison.'

I heard this comment with a mixture of surprise and concern. Liam was apparently a successful businessman, so I had been under the impression that he wasn't a fool when it came to who he employed. 'What sort of work?'

'Who better to test my security systems than a very successful burglar?'

I didn't have the heart to tell him.

78

Completing everything I needed to before I went home for the day took much longer than it should have done. Liam and I talked for a while and then I made sure I got a statement from him before he left the building. I knew that I was being overly fastidious in everything I did, but I wanted to hand over properly.

I was about to leave when I had another call from Bill.

'Hey, hon. You any closer to leaving work?'

'I'm about done. In fact I'm heading out of the door now.' I grabbed my jacket and bag, fiddling for my car keys as I trotted downstairs, phone held in place by my shoulder.

'You're definitely coming straight home, though?'

'Yes, I am. Where are my bloody keys? Oh, got them. It's been a very interesting day. I'll tell you all about it when I get home I'm so shattered, I've taken tomorrow off. We could do something together.'

'OK, then. See you in twenty minutes or so.'

Outside, it was getting dark. As I drove home, I thought how good it was at the end of the day to be able to talk to someone about my job, the strange things I often dealt with and, most importantly, to be understood. That made me smile. I wasn't sure what Bill would make of Liam Fitzhubert visiting his half-brother in prison and then coming to see me with evidence against Rumbly, or of the fact that, if we hadn't investigated a train crash from 1964 with only a shred of evidence, we wouldn't now be getting closer to charging Rumbly with Lea's death, plus another from 1964. This was all down to Marilyn, who had told us that the conversation she overheard in Deptford fifty years ago involved the concealment of a woman's body with head injuries.

Harry had been right: Leonard Rumbly was getting what was coming to him. Everyone had turned on him, and his empire would be no more.

I pulled up on the drive and saw movement behind the front room curtain. I got to the door, went inside and called out, 'I've had the strangest day. Wait until I tell you what's happened. The arrogance of Rumbly, chatting to me and Wings with the murder weapon in the next room and about to burn it. The man is unbelievable.'

I hung my jacket on the bottom of the banister, dropped my bag and kicked my shoes off. Bill wasn't in the kitchen so I headed to the living room.

He was standing in the middle of the room, arms by his sides, chewing the inside of his mouth.

'You're home,' he said. 'I've been thinking... You said you were going to visit your sister soon and I really want to come with you. Why don't we go tomorrow? Please, don't say no.'

I was stuck to the spot. This wasn't what I'd expected to come home to. I had pictured a night with my boyfriend, explaining all about a murder enquiry and my part in it, how Wingsy and I had saved a man's life, why Liam Fitzhubert had been to see his half-brother in prison, how I was going to be busier than ever on Cold Case. I hadn't imagined this when I'd walked through the door. I could see how on edge it was making Bill, and it hit home:

perhaps it was time I stopped being so defensive about everything, and tried to put it behind me.

Morning came round before I knew it. I was dreading taking Bill with me, letting him see the full extent of my misery. I still had to gear myself up to visit my sister every time, and I was aware that, as the journey to the clinic went on, I was saying less and less in reply to Bill's questions. Eventually, he gave up. I was used to driving over by myself and practising looking pleased to see Sara without really letting on how I was feeling.

Not today though.

Bill and I walked towards the home, across the pathway cut through the neat garden. I supposed that I always felt the same way, but now it was different. Despite the warm feelings I had about Bill's company, they couldn't completely chase away the chill I felt. I would always have bad memories to keep me company. I lived with the fact that, one day, prison would no longer hold the person responsible for those memories and he could come looking for us. At work I had thousands to watch my back, but, out here, I had got used to feeling lonely.

Not today, though. Today I wasn't alone.

Acknowledgements

Once again, I'm grateful to everyone at Myriad Editions for their never-ending enthusiasm, encouragement and expertise. Vicky Blunden's editing and Linda McQueen's copy-editing skills are truly amazing, although many others at Myriad, especially Candida Lacey, have helped me so much in getting to the final stage. Thank you all.

Thanks too to my agent, Cathryn Summerhayes at WME, for having so much faith in me.

There are many others to thank for their assistance with some of the details in the book. PC Adrian Parsons, drugs guru, for his knowledge of all things drug-related, and for steering me in the right direction on a couple of technical matters. As they say, any mistakes are definitely mine and not his. I'm also grateful to Caroline Noyes for her assistance with medical procedures and an understanding of liver cirrhosis and its treatment. Again, if I've misunderstood her explanations, that is all down to me. My thanks also to DS Andrea Richards from Kent Police's Cold Case Team and DC Tara Melton for wading through an early draft – it's much better now than when I subjected you to it, honest!

And to my husband, Graham, for also reading through many drafts, and to Elizabeth Haynes for taking the time, as ever, to help me out by reading through the book.

The fruit and vegetable theme in the book came about following a conversation with my dad over a couple of drinks, with him telling me how, before he joined the

Metropolitan Police, he would travel with my grandad from the Elephant and Castle to farms in Kent. They'd pick up perishable goods and take them to markets, including the Borough Market. (Joe Bring's description of the modern-day Borough is very like my grandad's, except my grandad never swore.) My dad then later bought a greengrocer's shop in Trundleys Road, Deptford, before joining the Met. All fruit and veg errors are my own, largely due to the conversation being over a fair number of pints.

One of the best things about my job in Kent Police, other than the satisfaction of a successful investigation, is the team I work with. Apart from their professionalism, their sense of humour has been a sanity-saver on occasions too many to recall. A few of those funny moments and anecdotes have made it in here. I would like to thank DS Andrew Chapman (cat story), DC Chris Coddington (pumpkin poster) and DC Rocky Moan (Sellotape and many others!) for supplying me with a few of them. This is book two in a series, so you never know...

If you enjoyed *Remember, Remember*,
why not read the bestselling first book in the
DC Nina Foster series, *Never Forget*.

For an exclusive extract, read on…

NEVER FORGET

LISA CUTTS

'Keeps you guessing until the final, thrilling sentence'
ELIZABETH HAYNES

1976

Later I would recognise the smell as blood. Much, much later. At the age of five, I had no idea what it was. The room was dark and I was scared. My sister wasn't moving but her face and clothes felt sticky. I suppose I was panicking, but at that age, with no frame of reference, I wasn't likely to know that.

Although I couldn't see anything, not even my own hand in front of my face, I could hear something. A loud cracking. It was followed by shouting and heavy footsteps, lots of pairs of feet, on the stairs.

Light was now coming from under the door. Shadows appearing within the sliver of brightness meant that someone was outside the room, waiting to come in.

'Nina, Sara, move away from the door.'

I didn't recognise the man's voice and couldn't decide whether his arrival meant good news or bad. I was on the far side of the room already; I couldn't have moved even if I'd wanted to. Another cracking noise and the door swung in, flooding the room with light.

I looked away from the open door, which was filled by the silhouette of a man. I couldn't make out his face but he was huge. Now the room was bright enough to see, I felt compelled to look round. She was my big sister and I couldn't help myself. I knew it wasn't going to be good. But the man was across the room before my eyes reached

Sara. He scooped me up and hugged me to him. 'Nina,' he said quietly, 'I'm a policeman. I'm Stan. I've come to take you home.'

He was acting strangely. Few grown-ups had ever picked me up – parents, grandparents, the usual; not strangers. Somehow I didn't mind. I could tell he was there for the right reasons. Never underestimate a child's instinct.

'Guv,' whispered a woman I hadn't noticed before, 'let me take her downstairs.'

'No,' came Stan's abrupt reply. 'I've got her.' He began backing out of the room. It seemed strange at the time but at some point, years later, it became blindingly obvious. He backed out because, if he had turned around, I would have turned around. He wasn't about to risk me seeing my sister's bloodied body lying there on the bare boards.

When I grew up I wanted to be a policewoman. Not to tear around the streets trying to right a wrong that had happened to me and my sister twenty years earlier, not to be a one-woman crusade against the forces of evil, but because, from the moment Stan McGuire had picked me up, I'd been safe. What other profession cared so much? Well, I could have become a doctor, but that took years and I wasn't bright enough. Besides, it wasn't a team of surgeons or nurses who tracked us, kicked the door down, had a 'quiet word' with our abductor, and made sure he went to prison for a very long time.

1

'Dozens of separate stab wounds and it appears that none of them would have killed her. It's possible she died because she drowned in her own blood... Come in, Nina. Welcome to Operation Guard.'

I hadn't even been aware that DCI Nottingham knew my name – but then, as I was the only one who hadn't made it to the briefing on time, I guessed he'd worked it out. The man wasn't a detective chief inspector for nothing.

About half an hour earlier, my detective sergeant, Sandra Beckensale, had called me into her office and, with her usual look of disdain, broken the news that I was to go and work with Serious Crime. 'You're to get yourself over to Divisional HQ as soon as you can. They want someone who can work long hours for the next couple of weeks and can be spared here. I told them that you're opinionated, loud, often aggressive, and that quite frankly I'd be glad to be shot of you.'

Cheers, you old hag, I thought to myself. Usually I would say it to her face too, but I wanted to avoid a row and get going. If she'd really said all that, it was a wonder they hadn't told her to send someone else.

'I did add, though...' she paused as if the next words were bile in her throat '...that you are a good worker, seem to get on with most people and can be relied upon to deal with anything competently, from mortgage fraud to our favourite shoplifter Joe. So you're to go, and I'll see you in a couple of weeks. Oh, and of course,' she added, rummaging through her handbag for a lighter to accompany the cigarette she was already holding, 'give us a call if you have any welfare issues.'

Not likely. The miserable cow didn't even look up as she said it. I went out into the main office and looked for my friend Laura. I wanted to tell her I wouldn't be around for a couple of weeks, and also to find out how she was fixed if it turned out that they needed any extra help. She wasn't at her desk by the window, so I scribbled her a note, grabbed my stuff and left for Divisional HQ.

On the way I thought about the defrosting dinner in my kitchen sink, the Pilates class I wasn't going to make it to and how I really hated getting to briefings late. It always made the boss focus on you, and that usually meant that a griefy job was more likely to come your way. I also thought about long-time criminal Joe Bring. Before my speedy departure had been arranged, I'd been assigned to interview Joe. He'd been arrested coming out of Tesco Express with three chickens down the front of his joggers. Tesco didn't want their chickens back. That had made me smile. It was the little things in this job that cheered me up. That, and of course walking down the steps of the Crown Court following a jury's guilty verdict. I'd been quite looking forward to asking Joe a few questions under caution. Although he smelt bad – as if he had poultry in his pants – he was actually quite a laugh. He never gave me a difficult time and usually didn't want a solicitor. There wasn't really much point when you'd been caught with food secreted in your underwear.

When I got to the conference room at Divisional HQ, it was already packed. There must have been sixty people there. Some I knew, but most I didn't. I'd never met DCI

Nottingham but I had heard of him – it was hard to not hear of people in a force the size of ours. We were a county force, bordering London, but with our own crimes and problems keeping us as busy as the capital.

The room contained a handful of uniform lads and lasses – I knew all of them as they, like me, were local – but there were a lot of older detectives in the room too. As a group, I reckoned that we had over a thousand years' policing between us. Pretty scary when you put it like that.

As I squeezed my way to a space at the back, I spotted John Wing, another detective from my nick. I was pleased he was here as we got on well. He also had a few years' more experience than me in CID and had worked on a number of murders. I stood next to him and whispered, 'Fill me in later, Wingsy?'

'No worries, Nin.'

The huge white projection screen in the room was showing a map of the area where the body had been discovered.

'For those who have just come in, this is where our victim, Amanda Bell, was found.' DCI Nottingham pointed to a large green area on the map and explained that it was the site of an old hospital, recently burnt down, and shortly to be turned into a new housing estate. 'The body was here, behind some bushes, fairly well hidden, and was found by a member of the public, Graham Redman, who was out walking his dog.' The DCI pointed to a corner in the northwestern part of the site close to the edge of the green area. 'Mr Redman has been spoken to by local officers and his statement taken. Absolutely no reason to suspect him of anything at this stage. We haven't had the post mortem yet, but early indications are that death was some time before Miss Bell was found. I'll let you know more when I return from the PM.

'She was found at 7.45 this morning and patrols were called straight away by our witness at the scene, using his mobile. Nearest patrol was on the dual carriageway the other side of the old hospital site and took three minutes to get there. Crime scene investigators have taken photos and I'll show you where the body was found and images of Miss Bell's body in just a minute. Right – Kim, I know that you've had an update from Harry Powell, the family liaison officer who's with the family now. What has Harry passed on to you about Miss Bell?'

The DCI was addressing a woman dressed in a white shirt and crisp black suit, about thirty-five years old, blonde, and unfamiliar to me. She was sitting by the door and sixty or so heads turned to look at her as she spoke, amid a rustle of paper as notebooks were opened and pens poised.

'Well, boss, her full name is Amanda Janine Bell, born 19th July 1978, last known address of 127 Upper Bond Street, Berrybourne. She had no recent boyfriend or partner and has one young son, an eight-year-old boy, Kyle Bell, who lives with his dad. While that's unusual, from what I can glean it all seems to be very amicable, but I'll find out more later from Harry when I speak to him again. Kyle is understandably very distressed. The ex, James or Jim Hamilton, is on hand to identify the body as we haven't been able to locate any other relative nearby – but we're working on it.'

I was distracted by Wingsy passing me a piece of paper. It was a list of names and phone numbers, with DCI Eric Nottingham at the top, then DI Simon Patterson, followed by the details of everyone in the room, except the latecomers like me. I added 'DC Nina Foster', my phone number and 'Borough Staff'. Above my name was that of DS Harry Powell, presumably added by someone other than Harry, since he was elsewhere coping with the grief of an eight-year-old who was never going to see his mum again. Not the job for me. I could cope with the dead just fine, but the grieving were too much for me. Harry and I went back several years, professionally. Sadly for me, he was another happily married man. He'd been my first DS, and a more decent bloke you'd be hard pushed to meet. I hoped that I'd catch up with him at some point during the investigation.

Kim, who I learned from the contact list was Detective Sergeant Kim Cotton, continued with a very brief history of Operation Guard's victim. Amanda Bell had few relatives, a couple of close friends, and had been arrested on four occasions: once as a teenager for shoplifting, once as an adult for shoplifting, once for drunk and disorderly and the final time, a month ago, for assault. As a result, establishing her identity had been simple. Her most recent arrest had been by PC Ollie Murphy, who had also been the nearby patrol on the dual carriageway that had been called to the body at 7.45am. He had thought he'd recognised her but, because of the blood and the position of the body, he hadn't been certain. He hadn't moved the body or turned it over to identify her, as minimum disturbance at the scene of an obvious death was always the correct procedure; anything else might destroy evidence.

I listened as Kim explained that Amanda was known to have worked as a prostitute in the area and had mainly used the money to buy alcohol. Drugs, unusually, did not seem to be her vice of choice. Despite the four arrests, Amanda's police record consisted only of one caution for shoplifting and a marker for being on police bail for the assault. It wasn't much of a criminal record in the scheme of things. We did however have her DNA, photograph and fingerprints.

'Thanks, Kim,' said Eric Nottingham when Kim finished reporting Harry Powell's insight so far into Amanda Bell's life. 'Harry is, of course, getting the ex-partner's movements to rule him in or out.' He said the last to Kim, receiving an efficient nod in return, before continuing, 'Here are the photos from the hospital site, or scene one as it now is.'

The area had a bank of trees running along its perimeter, separating it from the dual carriageway on one side and school playing fields on the other. Amanda had been found several metres from the trees, hidden among low bushes and shrubs. Without passing by close to the body, it would have been unlikely for anyone to stumble across her lonely grave. The photos taken from the most obvious approach path showed her lying among the thorns. If she had been alive when thrown into the scrub, I could imagine her wondering if there was anywhere lonelier on earth. What an awful way to go.

Next, Amanda's face filled the screen. The crime scene investigator had taken a close-up of the head and shoulders. Her expression wasn't scared, at peace or terrified. She just looked dead. As the photos scanned out from the facial close-up they showed the broken, dumped body of a prematurely middle-aged woman, dressed in a dirty, tattered skirt which was raised slightly, caught on the low-lying branches. The thin, thorny extensions held berries coloured bright red, in stark contrast to Amanda's exposed flesh, her white legs, streaked dark with a mixture of dried, smeared blood and mud.

She was lying on her left side but with her right leg extended, as if to stop her toppling forward on to her face. Her left arm was out in front of her and her right hand tucked underneath her. It was as if she'd been reaching for something, with maximum effort, but then it had all become too much.

My thoughts were interrupted by Nottingham's voice as he said, 'The dark marks you can see here on her legs are stab wounds. They cover her body. It's difficult to see from the way Miss Bell is lying, but her navy blue top is open at the back. It would appear it's been cut with a knife as there's a single, clean slit. The CSI had difficulty taking photos from behind the body, as you can see, because of this very dense and spiky scrubland.'

By the time he'd finished talking us through the evidence, Nottingham looked energised, well up for the task. Solving murders had that effect.

'We have loads to do. I've declared this a Category A murder, and that means pulling out all the stops. Right now we believe we're dealing with a stranger murder, a body in a public place, which may either be the kill site or the dump site. However, I'm not ruling anything out at the moment. There is no obvious motive and we're talking multiple injuries so the press are bound to pick up on that soon; the media release from our press office is being put together. I'll leave Kim to assign roles and tasks to you all. I've kept it short, as time is getting on and I want you out on the ground. We'll have another briefing in here at six. Either be here or call Kim with your updates and reasons why you won't be. Someone take the contact sheet and make copies for everyone, so we can keep in touch with you all. Thanks, everyone. It'll be a late one.'

We began filing out of the room towards fresher air, some people pausing to talk to those in charge, check details and submit paperwork.

'Wingsy, long time no see. How've you been?' I asked as I leant over to give him a kiss on the cheek.

'I'm good. Great to see you, Nin. How did you manage to get on this enquiry?'

'Right place, right time, I suppose. I was just off to interview Joe Bring when my DS told me to get to Divisional HQ to help out.'

'The great farmyard thief of the county. Nice one. See if we can work together, shall we? You can tell me all about that Portuguese bloke you were seeing.'

'He was Russian and also married. Oh, yeah, and a total wanker to boot.'

'You do pick 'em, Nin. Come on, let's have a word with Kim and see what she's got for us.'

Photocopying the contact list was my first job. I made seventy copies just in case, while Wingsy continued to wind me up.

'Well done, Detective Foster. Your first job in the murder investigation team and you appear not to have cocked it up. If only your love life was so easily solved.'

'Or this murder, you jug-eared halfwit.'

MORE FROM MYRIAD EDITIONS

MORE FROM MYRIAD EDITIONS

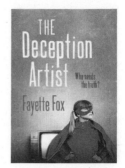

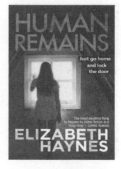

MORE FROM MYRIAD EDITIONS

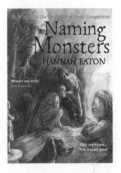

MORE FROM MYRIAD EDITIONS

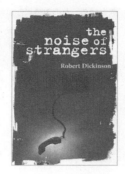

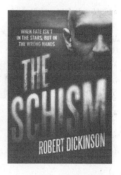

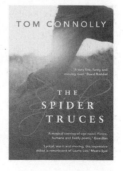